The Tree of Red Stars

The Tree of Red Stars

Tessa Bridal

MILKWEED EDITIONS

This is a work of fiction. Although it was inspired by real persons and events, the characters, incidents, and dialogue are products of the author's imagination and, except for appearances by some public figures, do not portray actual persons.

Published 1997 by Milkweed Editions
First paperback edition published 1998
Printed in the United States of America
Cover design by Beth Olson and Sarah Purdy
Cover painting by Fran Gregory
Inset cover photograph by Richard Schneider / The Image Bank
Interior design by Wendy Holdman

The text of this book is set in Centaur.
07 08 09 10 11   7 6 5

Milkweed Editions is a not-for-profit publisher. We gratefully thank the Cowles Media Foundation for underwriting the Milkweed Fiction Prize, and we acknowledge additional support from the Bush Foundation; Target Stores, Dayton's, and Mervyn's by the Dayton Hudson Foundation; Ecolab Foundation; General Mills Foundation; Honeywell Foundation; Jerome Foundation; The McKnight Foundation; Andrew W. Mellon Foundation; Kathy Stevens Dougherty and Michael E. Dougherty Fund of the Minneapolis Foundation; Minnesota State Arts Board through an appropriation by the Minnesota State Legislature; Challenge and Literature Programs of the National Endowment for the Arts: Lawrence and Elizabeth Ann O'Shaughnessy Charitable Income Trust in honor of Lawrence M. O'Shaughnessy; Piper Jaffray Companies, Inc.; Ritz Foundation on behalf of Mr. and Mrs. E. J. Phelps, Jr.; John and Beverly Rollwagen Fund of the Minneapolis Foundation; The St. Paul Companies, Inc.; Star Tribune/Cowles Media Foundation; Surdna Foundation; James R. Thorpe Foundation; U.S. West Foundation; Lila Wallace-Reader's Digest Literary Publishers Marketing Development Program, funded through a grant to the Council of Literary Magazines and Presses; and generous individuals.

Library of Congress Cataloging-in-Publication Data

Bridal, Tessa, 1947–
    The tree of red stars / Tessa Bridal. — 1st ed.
      p.   cm.
    ISBN 1-57131-013-4 (cl); 1-57131-023-1 (pb)
    1. Uruguay—History—1904–1973—Fiction. I. Title.
PS3552.R4542T7   1997
813'.54—dc21   96-40156
                                      CIP

This book is printed on acid-free paper.

To my mother, in loving memory

He who lives more lives than one,
more deaths than one must die.

OSCAR WILDE

*. . . Palabras desde las cenizas . . . para servir de puente entre los que se
quedaron y aquellos que se fueron y entonces volverán . . . les ayudaremos
a recordar lo que vieron. Y también lo que no vieron.*

MARIO BENEDETTI

The Tree of Red Stars

Prologue

He was a prisoner because of me, and I could not rest until he was free. My face was by now a familiar one at human rights' agencies in Paris and London, and Marco Aurelio Pereira's name well known to all the people who worked at them. It was 1980, and for seven years I had knocked on doors, filled out forms, circulated petitions, written articles, and lobbied any government official willing to listen. Seven years, during which one of Latin America's oldest and most stable democracies fell and was replaced by a military dictatorship.

The doors to my past appeared closed forever, and somewhere behind them, Marco lay in solitary confinement, not knowing that leaving him had been the most difficult decision I had ever faced. I kept my mind occupied weaving the memories that made it possible for me to get up every morning and continue my efforts on Marco's behalf. I crossed and recrossed the Channel between London and Paris, living apart from the life of both cities, supporting myself by doing private translations and secretarial work. My visas were renewed by allies, often strangers to me, who had never witnessed torture or suffered political arrest, but who were of that number described by Che Guevara in a speech I had once heard him give praising those who cannot rest easy while injustice is being done to anyone, anywhere in the world.

In spite of the support of these often anonymous friends,

Marco's cause seemed lost to me. This would be my final trip,
I decided, as I watched the dark waters of the English Channel
churning behind the ferry. I longed for my own river, that
changeable, friendly giant. The Río de la Plata was moody,
rough, gentle, and wild, and to me, always beautiful. The river
rejected unwanted offerings, harbored life, and took it. Marco,
our friend Emilia, and I always brought our sorrows and our
fears for an airing along its sandy shores. Something about the
river's changeable colors and the music of its movement against
sand and rocks soothed and comforted. I would have found it
easy to let the Río de la Plata take me. I was weary with loneliness and worn down by the fight for Marco's freedom. So tired,
I had not even opened the letter from Emilia that had arrived
that morning.

For the first few years, a surge of hope had accompanied the
receipt of such letters. Perhaps there would be news of Marco's
release or of our childhood friend Cora, who had been among
the disappeared for as long as Marco had been imprisoned.
Gradually, I put hope aside. Letters arrived with news of my
Aunt Aurora's battle with cancer, of neighbor's leaving the old
barrio, and finally, in Emilia's last letter, of her mother's death.
I did not have the strength to confront any more bad news, and
I had left Emilia's letter unopened all day as I trudged from
office to office trying to show my gratitude for the efforts made
on my behalf by the human rights' workers I had come to know
over the years. Mixed with my profound gratitude toward these
Europeans was envy of the fact that they could go home at
night to a glow of comfort and of safety, while I found sleep
elusive and felt driven to walk the streets of London and Paris
keeping the memories alive and the ghosts at bay. I think I was
afraid that if I slept for too long I might wake up having forgotten why I left Uruguay. I was finding it difficult to trust my

memory, to separate imagination from reality. It was my imagination, after all, that had kept me alive, and now it was no longer clear to me what I had imagined and what had truly happened. Often in our letters, Emilia and I promised ourselves that one day we would sit down together and relive it all.

I shivered as I pulled Emilia's letter from my pocket and smoothed the crumpled envelope. I considered dropping the letter into the water but knew I wanted to read it. I removed the single sheet of airmail paper the envelope contained.

As I read, my grip on the letter weakened, and a gust of wind nearly tore it out of my hands. I stumbled to a bench, protecting the flimsy paper that bore the news I had been waiting seven years to hear. My ears were ringing, and for a moment, I did not know if it was joy or a most savage grief invading me.

I knew only that I had to return to Uruguay, even if I was arrested the moment I stepped off the plane.

I do not remember packing or saying farewell or boarding the plane or how I spent the hours during the long journey south. I was first conscious of returning to Uruguay after I changed planes in Buenos Aires for the final, twenty-minute leg to Montevideo. The pattern of streams and small rivers below me was a reminder that somewhere along one of them my grandmother, my *Mamasita,* was waiting. I knew from her letters that she still raised and rode her *criollo* horses at the ranch she called Caupolicán, after the Araucanian chief who had fiercely defended the lands beyond the Andes from Spanish invaders. Often, during the years of exile, I had imagined myself returning to the grape arbor where I had last seen Marco and to the open *campo* where *Mamasita* had taught me to ride.

I heard hatches opening, and bags, overnight cases, coats, and baggage carts tumbled into the aisles. The impact of no longer being in Europe was suddenly brought home to me by the passengers' lack of regard for the pilot's requests not to move until the aircraft had landed. I had become accustomed to the orderly life of Europeans, and this determined disobedience to authority was a strong reminder of what I was returning to.

The view out of the window had changed.

I could see Montevideo's airport building in the distance, its terraces crowded with people waving, cheering, holding up hand-painted signs of welcome for those returning from vacations and business trips. I had no idea what kind of welcome to expect. My political actions had brought shame and hardship on my family. Friends had disappeared or died in prison. At my request, only Emilia knew of my arrival.

My hands closed around the black leather straps of my handbag. Soon, very soon, I would have to leave the safety of my seat and step into the vortex of the past.

A stewardess leaned over me to ask if I was all right. I managed a smile and a weak gesture toward my stomach. The stewardess brought a cup of water, and I swallowed it eagerly.

I could always turn around and return to the safety and anonymity of Europe, I told myself. I could forget the past and start a new life. I could shelter the good times in my heart and let go once and for all of the horror, the grief, and the guilt. As if to bring me back from this wishful thinking, the plane banked, and in the distance, the Río de la Plata winked at me.

One hundred twenty miles wide, the river resembled the Atlantic Ocean, with which it merged at its widest point. I had walked its shores, loved its changing colors, and been buffeted by its waves all my growing-up years. My family's ties with the river were strong. My grandfather had once owned a hotel on the beaches of Montevideo, and its foundations could still be seen in the sand. The government had bought the hotel from him at the turn of the century and demolished it. All building on the beach itself and within a wide radius of the promenade had been forbidden by a law designed to keep the riverfront untouched by development. I had always enjoyed looking at photos of the old hotel, with orchestras playing while couples danced under the moonlight on the wide terraces over the river.

"Old friend," I whispered, *"preciso coraje, amigo."*

The sun hit me with a familiar glare as I stepped out of the plane. The bus waiting to drive passengers to the airport building had a high step. Someone reached out to take my heavy overnight bag. I was offered a seat.

"Aquí, señora, siéntese."

I was home, with all its horror and glory.

My passport was merely glanced at, stamped in haste, and returned to me without a word. My suitcases rolled toward me on the carousel, and a porter appeared to bear them away. I followed him, and only then did I allow myself to look at the anxious, smiling faces beyond the glass doors.

Emilia was waiting, her dark hair touched with gray and pulled into a tight bun. Her anxious eyes opened wide as she saw me walking toward her.

It was all right to cry now. To leave the years of longing behind, to embrace and kiss and sob, obstructing the impatient traffic behind us.

"Has vuelto," Emilia said. "You have come back."

We drove along the coastal road, our view unimpeded, as the sands, the rocks, and the gulls stretched for miles before us. I put my head out of the window of Emilia's Volkswagen and breathed the cool air, sensing welcome in the Río de la Plata's pale blue waters.

We reached the Avenida Brasil and turned inland onto our

street. Standing on the sweet turf of my childhood, with the
shade of the large *tipa* protecting me, I could only stare as I held
Emilia's arm.

The street, too, had suffered. Trim hedges and orderly bushes
stood where a riot of jasmines, bougainvillea, and climbing
roses had once tumbled across the low walls separating one
house from another. The old stained glass that had reflected the
sun in shafts of colored light was gone from the front doors,
replaced by solid, unbreakable wood.

The white stucco front of Emilia's apartment building was
gray and chipped. The entrance door no longer stood open
to welcome visitors, and bars covered the ground-floor window on which I had knocked so often as a child. In those days,
Emilia would fling it wide, jumping easily out onto the pavement by my side. Sometimes, her mother, Lilita, would be there
to see us off, her elbows resting on the sill, the curtains billowing around her as disturbingly as her thoughts. Lilita, in whom
despair ran like the river's silver current and whose funeral I had
been unable to return to Uruguay to attend.

"I've bought it, you know," Emilia said, as we stood arm in
arm surveying the old building.

I nodded.

"I want to live here, where she died."

Emilia took several keys from her handbag and used one to
open the lobby door. As the key turned in the old lock, I half
expected to see Lilita appear on the other side, her hands in her
apron pockets, her feet shuffling along the floor on the two
soft cloths she kept by the door, ready to add brightness to the
highly polished wooden floor. On good days, she pushed the
cloths along in an effort to soften what she saw in the wood.
For wood, she had once told me, was always alive, and the
reflections of her floor resonated with old memories.

As Emilia led me into the apartment that had been my second home, I saw that nothing had changed.

The tiny living room was furnished as I remembered it, with a brown sofa and two chairs. The flannel polishing cloths were gone, but the floor still held its old shine. The dining-room table at which I had watched the family eat countless meals, stood bare. We walked past Lilita's room, with the two single beds, and entered Emilia's little room, where we took off our shoes and knelt, as we had done throughout our childhood, on the bed in the corner under the window.

We parted the lace curtain and looked down the street at the now empty house where I had grown up. In what had once been a thriving flower garden the old poinsettia tree stood like a gnarled and solitary guardian of the past.

One

From the time I was five years old, I had studied the *barrio* from the sheltering branches of the old poinsettia tree.

In summer, the pale green leaves cast refreshing shadows on my skin; in winter, the brilliant red flowers nodded in the wind, like a hundred small fires holding the cold at bay.

The *estrella federal* was my favorite place in the whole world, and I had never invited anyone to join me in it until the day I decided I wanted Emilia to be my best friend. The only thing I knew about her when she moved to the *barrio* was that her grandfather was Brazilian.

Emilia and I went to different elementary schools. Emilia walked two blocks to the nearest public school, dressed in the white, long-sleeved pinafore with a broad blue ribbon around the neck that all students wore. I was picked up by a school bus and sent several miles distant to a severe private establishment that guaranteed I would speak English fluently by the age of ten. One of my earliest memories was of being buttoned into the overall I would wear every day in kindergarten. The flowered fabric was the only acknowledgment that we kindergartners were different from the other children in their grim green tunics, ties, and white shirts. The teachers were just as strict, the discipline just as inflexible for five-year-olds as for the older students.

The money for the privilege of attending this school had been left by my English grandfather, who had decreed that all

his descendants would speak his language. I had refused. It was
a point of great embarrassment to my family, this reluctance
on my part to claim my heritage, and so I was taken three times
a week to a private tutor to ensure that my grandfather's wishes
were upheld.

It was August of 1954, and I was on my way to my English
lesson, holding tightly to my mother's hand as she swayed gracefully on her high heels toward the bus stop around the corner,
when I met Emilia.

A small Brazilian flag was flying at half-mast outside our
new neighbors' bedroom window, and I saw Emilia engaged in
helping her mother install a vase of flowers at the base of this
flag. As my mother and I walked by, several roses fell from
Emilia's hands onto the pavement below, and I stopped to pick
them up and hand them to her, standing on tiptoe to reach
Emilia's outstretched hand as our mothers exchanged greetings.

My mother inquired of Lilita whether the flag flew at half-
mast for President Vargas of Brazil, who had killed himself
the day before. It had not taken long for the news to reach us
in Uruguay, and both the evening and morning papers had
headlined the event on their front pages.

"I hear that President Vargas remarked that he was leaving
life to enter history," my mother said sympathetically.

"I refrain from spitting at the sound of his name only out
of respect for you, *señora* Ortega," Emilia's mother stated. "The
flag flies for his victims, among whom was my father's friend,
Olga Benario."

We were late for my English lesson, and I could tell from
the way my mother's hand tightened around mine that she had
no desire to hear any more. She murmured her regrets and tried
to glide away, but Lilita was not to be deterred. Something in
her sad and resolute manner seemed to permeate my mother's

concerns about punctuality, and she gave a small sigh and stopped to listen.

"Olga," Lilita said, "marched with the workers against the lords of sugar and coffee. Vargas had her arrested, put on a ship to Germany, and delivered into the hands of the Nazis. Olga was Jewish. She died in an extermination camp." She took the flowers from Emilia and arranged them by a tiny newspaper photograph of Olga pinned to the flag. Her hands shook slightly as she did so, and Emilia lay a gentle, steady hand on her mother's arm.

Young as I was, I recognized in this gesture a tenderness toward others that drew me to Emilia.

Next day, I invited her to join me in the poinsettia tree to study the *barrio* together, for people had begun to fascinate me, and had I been able to, I would have taken them apart to see not how, but why, they worked.

Emilia, as it turned out, was not at all curious about our fellow beings. If she could have had her way, I discovered, she would have sat them all around a laden table and attended to their comfort.

Emilia believed that the world would be a better place if only people shared good food, flowers, and soft cushions with one another. Imagine, she said, how different history might have been if Jesus had given his disciples a proper meal of *churrascos* and fried potatoes instead of bread and wine. I was being prepared for my first communion, and the idea of Jesus serving steak and fried potatoes at the Last Supper seemed sacrilegious. I asked Emilia if she was Catholic, and Emilia said she thought she was.

"Are you learning about the *ostia* and how to swallow it without biting it?" The nuns had told me that I would be committing no sin if the host touched my teeth, but I must not bite it.

Emilia knew nothing about this, which explained her desire to change the menu at the Last Supper, and her lack of understanding about the bread and wine.

"No, no," Emilia said, when I explained that Jesus, anticipating future masses, had understandably chosen to be embodied in bread and not in *churrascos.* "No, no," she repeated. "What I mean, Magdalena, is if he had fed them and taken care of them, then Judas might have been a happier man and not betrayed him. And if Jesus hadn't been killed then he could still be on Earth helping us to live more happily with one another."

I studied my new friend closely. It appeared that she possessed insights into human nature that I could learn from. I was about to ask Emilia if she wanted to go for a walk by the river when a horse-drawn cart turned the corner onto our street.

"It's Gabriela!" I said.

Emilia looked at the cart and nodded. "I will go and tell *mamá.*"

Each neighborhood had its own regular beggars, in whom I saw romantic characters who entered our *barrio* and then disappeared into the distant Cerro. The Cerro was Uruguay's tallest hill. In 1520, it had been spotted by a Portuguese sailor who called out *"Monte vide eu,"*—"I see a mountain." Two hundred years later, a city was built at its feet and named Montevideo. The walls surrounding the city had long since disappeared, as had the Indians the city's inhabitants wished to keep at a distance. The city now sprawled along the riverbanks, and the mountain was abandoned by all except the soldiers who guarded the fortress museum at the top of the Cerro and by the city's poorest residents, who lived on the hillside in houses made from the city's leftovers.

Gabriela was a redheaded young woman who arrived in our *barrio* every morning at the same hour driving a rather fine horse, unlike the tough and dusty animals pulling the carts of other beggars. She was no more than eighteen, tall and slender, with green eyes and features that in a different time and place would have made her a movie star. Her teeth needed work, but I had not yet noticed that. I was much more interested in the baby Gabriela carried on her hip.

Emilia returned, and Gabriela waved at us from my front gate as she rang the bell.

My mother came out herself to attend to Gabriela. She had followed Gabriela's pregnancy with interest and wanted to make sure that the baby was being well taken care of. She ushered them both into the house, and I heard her say that today Gabriela was going to learn how to give the baby a bath.

An idea took sudden shape in my mind. "Let's follow Gabriela home!" I said.

"Why?" Emilia asked, looking at me in surprise.

"I want to see her house."

Emilia frowned. "How would we get there?"

"While Gabriela is begging, we will hide in the cart."

"What if she finds us?"

"She will send us home on the bus. Come on!"

The door was closing behind my mother and Gabriela as Emilia and I ran to the cart and climbed in. Several burlap sacks lay piled in a corner, and we burrowed under them. The cart smelled of old shoes, and Emilia held her nose.

It took quite a long time for Gabriela to bathe the baby and complete her round of the neighborhood houses, from which she collected food, money, and any clothing no longer in use. She returned, telling the baby he smelled almost as good as the croissants *señora* Lilita had given them. We heard the cart creak as Gabriela climbed back in and clicked her tongue to the horse. We held hands tightly as the cart began to move.

The blocks went slowly by, with Gabriela stopping every now and then to go through piles of rubbish by the road. Once, with a cry of delight, she found a pair of shoes she told the baby would be just right for his aunt. She tossed them in the back, hitting Emilia on the head under her cover of burlap. More from surprise than pain, Emilia let out a small cry, and we held our breath. She had not been heard, and soon the cart was moving once more.

We followed the Río de la Plata for a short distance, and Gabriela talked to the baby about whether or not to let the horse swim that day. He enjoyed the water. But this had been an easy day, she said, and the horse was not sweating. Besides, the wind was rather cold, and he might get chilled. We turned away from the river, and gradually the streets became unfamiliar.

We no longer knew where we were, and I wondered if Emilia was as afraid as she had been only a few weeks before when I had scared her by swimming out to a small island while she stood on the beach, watching to see if I would drown. On our way home, she had held my hand almost as tightly as she was holding it now.

After what seemed like hours, we saw the Cerro in the distance. Shacks littered the hillside like a patchwork of dirty handkerchiefs woven from all the refuse of the city: cardboard walls, newspaper floors, roofs made of pieces of plastic and corrugated metal, an occasional wooden door, rags for curtains. Lines of washing, hung with tattered clothing, rippled in the afternoon breeze, and children ran barefoot in the grass.

This was where Montevideo's *bichicomes* lived. I had once asked my mother what *bichicome* meant, and she had explained that it was the Spanish variation of the word *beachcomber.*

Emilia whispered that we were very far from home, and I

nodded eagerly, my eyes roaming the streets as the cart climbed a
steep hill, bumped over deep ruts in the road, and made its way
across the hillside, pulling up outside a shack made of wooden
planks full of knotholes and a flat tin roof. Gabriela jumped
off the cart, put the baby down with his back to the wall, and
started to unload. Children gathered to see what she had
brought back, and one or two women joined them. It was not
long before the sacks under which we crouched were removed,
and Emilia and I discovered.

"*¡Madre de Diós!*" Gabriela cried. "What are you two doing
in there?"

Emilia and I both started to speak at once as we jumped off
the cart onto the ground at Gabriela's side.

"*¡Una a la vez! ¡No oigo nada!*" Gabriela cried. "One at a time.
Now, tell me what you are doing here."

"We wanted to visit your house," I said.

"She did," Emilia added. "I . . . I wasn't so sure we should."

Gabriela clasped her hands. "What if they think I've
taken you?"

"Who would think that?" I asked.

"The police!"

"We'll tell them you didn't."

"How will you get home?" Gabriela wanted to know.

"We'll take the bus."

"Your poor mothers! They'll be worried to death! And they
are so good to me!"

By now we had attracted quite a crowd. More children gathered, as well as several men. All agreed that the situation was
bad. One man offered to drive us back. He had not been out
that day, and his horse was fresh.

"We are really sorry," Emilia said.

"We didn't mean to cause so much trouble," I added.

Gabriela sighed. "Do you want something to eat before you go?"

"Oh, yes!" I cried.

"No, thank you," Emilia said, pulling on my sleeve. "We are both very full."

I looked at Emilia in astonishment. We had missed lunch, and our stomachs grumbled so loudly in the cart we were afraid Gabriela would hear them, yet here was Emilia refusing food. Then it dawned on me that what Gabriela was offering us were the croissants and apples our mothers had just given her. In all likelihood, it was all she had for the day.

I made up a story about having had a huge breakfast and eating *chocolatines*. As soon as the words left my mouth, several children gathered, their eyes eager, to see if I had any chocolates left to give them, and I felt embarrassed and sad at having to say no to them.

"Well," Gabriela sighed, "come in the house while we get a fresh horse. I don't want the soldiers to see you, and that hair of yours, Magdalena, is like a *farol.*" She glanced nervously up at the battlements overhead in the distance.

I had never thought of my light hair as a beacon before and wished I had worn my sun hat. "Why don't you want the soldiers to see us?" I asked.

"They might think I kidnapped you."

We stepped into the little hut through a rag door onto an earthen floor. In the center was a pit with a large pot over it on a metal grid. In one corner, an old mattress lay on a carpet of newspapers. Several patched blankets were folded on it. In another corner, a chair, held together with twine, was stacked high with neatly folded piles of old clothing. Several gardening tools rested against the walls. It had an air of cleanliness and

proud housekeeping even though there was nothing there but
earth and newspapers and rags.

Gabriela lay a gentle hand on my shoulder. "Look," she
said, pointing to the wall.

When I was in kindergarten, I had worked with clay and
made several little plates, which I had colored and painted.
I was very proud of them and hoped they would hang in my
house somewhere. I gave them to my mother, who admired
them and put them on her dresser. A few days later they were
gone. I asked what had happened to them, and my mother told
me they had been broken accidentally and she had had to throw
them away. A sadness had lingered with me around this event
until, hanging in a place of honor, the only ornament in the little hut, I saw the clay plates with their flowers and stick figures.
I turned away so that Gabriela would not see me cry.

"*Es una linda casita, Gabriela,*" Emilia said, and Gabriela
beamed at the compliment.

She pointed to another corner. "Those are the curtains your
mother gave me, Emilia. My sister says I should sell them, but
I am going to make a cover for my bed."

"The yellow will brighten the room," Emilia answered. "Is
there enough to make a cushion cover for the chair too?"

The two of them walked over to measure the curtains, leaving me to dry my eyes and watch for the man who was to take
us home.

At the last minute, Gabriela decided that she should go
too, to explain personally to *señora* Rita and *señora* Lilita that she
had not known we were in her cart.

It was almost dark by the time we got home, and the entire
neighborhood was in an uproar. The women were all gathered
around my mother and Lilita, who were weeping, and the men
were running in and out of the houses making telephone calls

to friends and relatives all over town. Pepe, the policeman in charge of our *barrio,* was taking notes with the blunt stub of a pencil in his tiny notebook. At sight of us sitting in the cart, everyone ran to greet us, and for several minutes no explanations were possible. We were hugged and kissed repeatedly by everyone present, and Pepe had to blow his nose several times on a borrowed handkerchief.

The neighborhood dogs caught the excitement and joined in the din by barking joyously and scaring the horse. The driver, whose hands were being shaken simultaneously by Pepe and by Emilia's father, had some trouble disengaging himself to see to his horse, who was threatening to bolt.

In all the excitement, Gabriela's baby was passed to Marco's mother, *señora* Marta, who absentmindedly took the child with her when she finally returned home with Marco and his brothers. Gabriela was forgotten, and I heard her calling the baby's name softly as she looked for him.

"Where is Gervasio, Gabriela?" I asked.

Gabriela's eyes filled with tears. "Gone! *¡Ha desaparecido!* Someone took him!" She looked so terrified that I put my arms around her for a moment before running to my mother.

"*¡Mamá!* Gervasio is missing!"

My mother threw her hands up in the air. "*¡No puede ser!*" she said. "It's not possible! We get you back and lose him!"

Pepe blew his whistle and everyone looked at him in surprise. "*¿Dónde está* Gervasio?" he asked in a stern voice.

Everyone looked around, shrugging their shoulders. Soon the noise level rose again as questions flew back and forth, and Pepe was forced to blow his whistle once more. Before he could speak, an embarrassed *señora* Marta hurried toward us.

"I am so sorry! So sorry!" she panted. "I am accustomed to having at least one baby in my arms, you see, and I wasn't thinking, in the joy of seeing the girls safely home, that I have no babies now, only big boys, but they are always hugging me, and I'm used to my arms being full and when someone gave Gervasio to me I didn't even think—" Her apology was cut short by Gabriela's cry of relief. She took the baby and rocked him back and forth, retreating to the cart before anyone could touch him again.

The neighbors dispersed, Pepe returned to the police station to file his report, and Emilia and I went home, to be bathed, fed, and made much of by those to whom we had caused nothing but distress that day.

Two

The following morning, Emilia and I were back in the poinsettia tree, just in time to see a moving van loaded with new furniture pull up outside a house recently vacated by an elderly widower who had moved to a small apartment. The van was followed by a stately black Ford from which a couple descended, ushering out a young girl of about our age. Seeing us watching her from the tree, she raised a neatly gloved hand and waved. There was something cautious about the wave that prevented us from running at once to introduce ourselves.

"Cora!" her mother called sternly and gestured for her to follow her parents inside. With one last look at the two of us perched in the tree, Cora disappeared.

From that moment, her house came to be as invitingly secret as she herself was.

Behind the brick wall, by the steps leading to a small portico covered with white jasmine, grew a tall, spreading shade tree, its thick green canopy casting a protective cover over the entire house. Every midsummer the *tipa* shed its myriads of tiny flowers, carpeting the street all around it in brilliant yellow and casting a golden glow onto the front of the house. Cora's front door, smaller than others on the block, contributed to my illusion that, like Alice, I could step through it into another world—a sheltered, private world, where no Mad Hatter dwelt and the only fear, I would learn, was of losing one's heart, not one's head.

Emilia and I could not resist this house. We played mischief galore on all the other houses in the neighborhood, but when we approached Cora's house, we did so on tiptoe, hearts beating fast and lips pressed tightly lest a sound should escape and drift like the unwelcome river mists to the white lace curtains of the window facing the street.

Our other neighbors had come to regard us as a menace and were quite tried by us, resorting at various times to bribery in the form of sweets and ice cream in an effort to improve us. Emilia and I never hesitated to accept the bribes. If we had consciences, they were not in evidence, and at age ten we looked at the world as a vast playground and everyone in it fair game for our practical jokes and base humor.

Cora's parents, however, seemed to fear us, and that made us afraid. Not once did we ring Cora's doorbell and run to hide, giggling hysterically, behind the nearest tree. Nothing would have induced us to let the air out of Cora's car tires or work loose the tiles of her front pavement. When the iceman came by in his horse-drawn cart, he could leave a slab of ice on Cora's windowsill without any warning to Emilia and me that if he heard the next day that we had unwrapped it, he would take a belt to us both. We would no more have unwrapped Cora's ice than we would our own.

From Emilia's window or from the branches of the poinsettia tree, we would watch, fascinated, as Cora left her house, always in the company of both her parents. She walked between them, eyes lowered, dress immaculate and starched, a perfect rose protected on both sides by her small parents with their half smile, afraid to offend. They were inadequate as protective thorns and seemed to know it. The sole fact the neighbors were able to unearth about them was that the Allenbergs were Jewish refugees.

Emilia and I had decided to risk rejection and knock on

Cora's front door when the whole city was electrified with the news that the police had made a startling discovery on the border with Brazil. A man had been found inside a trunk, his corpse cut into several pieces. He was a former Nazi and had lived, it turned out, not far from us, in an apartment overlooking the river.

Soon after the story broke, a car drew up outside the Allenberg's, and two men in shiny suits got out. The Allenbergs did not often have callers, and when they did, they looked nothing like these two brawny fellows who glanced suspiciously up and down the street before knocking at the door and being admitted. They left a few minutes later, and the *barrio* buzzed with the news that the car had been an unmarked police car.

My father shrugged when my mother told him about it. "Everyone knows who did it," he said.

"Who, *papá?*" I asked. "Who cut up the man in the trunk?"

"The Jews."

"I suppose the police have to appear to be investigating," my mother said.

"They'll ask a few questions while people are talking about it, then let the matter drop."

"Why were they at the Allenbergs'?" I asked.

"Because Mr. Allenberg is a Jew. They know who's involved."

"You mean Mr. Allenberg cut up the man?" I gasped.

"No, no, of course not," my mother said, glancing reproachfully at my father for putting such ideas into my head.

"During the war, Magdalena," my father said, "the Nazis did some terrible things to the Jews. A lot of Nazis escaped to South America. So did a lot of the Jews they had persecuted. Every so often, the Jews find the Nazis and revenge themselves."

Emilia's father, I discovered, was convinced that Mr. Allenberg had been involved in the murder and looked at his small neighbor with increased respect.

"*Papá* says that the Jews lure the Nazis over the border into Uruguay all the time," Emilia told me, "because here the police don't investigate such cases too much."

It was difficult for me to imagine Mr. Allenberg as a murderer, but stranger things happened in the Hollywood movies we saw in marathon sessions on Sunday afternoons and evenings at the Casablanca, our local cinema.

Our imaginations were unhampered by the fact that we lived in the suburbs of Uruguay's tranquil capital city, on a quiet, shady side street providing a harbor in the busy flow of embassy life surrounding it. An island of local anarchy in a sea of diplomacy, my father said proudly.

Round one corner was the Czechoslovakian Embassy, secreted behind a high fence, with the house itself on a low rise, surrounded by flowering shrubbery. Nearby were the Italians. The fence surrounding them was of wrought iron in inviting designs of flowers and birds. Their gate was always open, giving the impression that visitors were welcome to join them for spaghetti at any time. They often gave large parties, and Emilia and I would climb the tree on the corner and watch the parade of expensively dressed men and women strolling up the long driveway between the rustling palms.

Round another corner lurked the Russians, behind eight-foot walls, two men in dark suits ever present at the gates. The only one ever to invade their privacy was Caramba, my parrot, who visited them regularly. The only way of luring Caramba back to her cage was to bang on the top of it with the cup which held her daily portion of *crema de chocolate*.

Josefa, the family cook, who had lived with us since my parents' marriage, was a most gregarious person, but refused to make a spectacle of herself before the grim Russians and made my mother go herself to retrieve the bird, leaving Josefa at the kitchen door, her thermos of hot water under her arm, and her gourd, packed full of green *mate* tea, steaming in her hand.

Every afternoon at four o'clock, after her *siesta,* my mother dressed for tea in a simple, elegant gown and high-heeled shoes. Whenever Caramba escaped, my mother would sigh, pick up the cage, and make her way to the Russian Embassy, leaving the air behind her redolent of Chanel Number 5. Her hair was styled by a slender artist called Ernesto, and he no doubt would have raised his dark brows in disbelief at the sight of his digni-fied client standing in front of the Russian Embassy holding a parrot cage on which she would resolutely bang a small, red tin cup, a remnant of some childhood tea set. Caramba appreci-ated the gesture and would fly back to her cage without protest, cocking her green head in apparent amazement as my mother strode past the Russian guards, eyes facing front.

If Pepe the policeman was on duty, he would offer to walk *señora* Rita home and carry the cage for her. Pepe had high hopes of leaving the streets one day and being promoted to work at police headquarters. Having friends of consequence, such as my mother, could only benefit him. The fact that he was deeply in love with Josefa made our house even more attractive to him, and if Josefa was not too busy, he would stop for a sip of *mate* and conversation with her before returning to his post.

Once a week, he accompanied us when Josefa and I walked down to the river to wait for the fishermen's boats to pull onto the beach. As we walked, we would guess whether the water that day would be gray or blue or green as it blended with the Atlantic Ocean beyond. Sometimes we found the waves crash-ing on the sandy shore, causing a commotion amongst the sea-gulls, who scurried away, flapping and complaining. Sometimes the Río de la Plata was a layer of mirrors reflecting the sun and the sky. As the fishermen pulled ashore, Josefa watched them from a distance and then chose the handsomest. He would smile at her and wink at me while filleting the fish on the seat of his little boat, sending translucent scales flying in the air, catching the sun in mother-of-pearl. Pepe would talk to the other fishermen, disguising his jealousy in loud banter.

A rain shower caught us unexpectedly on our way home from the river one mild autumn day, and when we arrived at the house, we changed our wet shoes and Josefa put the fish in the refrigerator, hurrying to make *tortas fritas*, for whenever it rained, all the maids in the *barrio* gathered in our large kitchen to drink *mate*.

"Why do we always make *tortas fritas* and *mate* when it rains?" I asked.

"Because of the moon," Josefa replied, bustling Pepe out the back door and pulling her white apron off its hook by the stove.

"The moon? What has the moon to do with *mate?*"

"Everything!" she answered, setting a large kettle to boil. Then, while she kneaded the suet into the flour, she told me how *mate* had been given to us a long, long time ago.

"The moon," Josefa said, "was like most young girls. Restless and curious. She floated in the sky looking down upon the earth and wondered how she could leave her rightful place and go traveling. Just like you are always talking of doing when you grow older. Well, the moon, who was as bewitching as most *chicas*, persuaded the clouds to give her cover, and she turned herself into a maiden and came to Earth. It happened not far from here, some say. Where the *cerros* meet the sea."

For a moment, her dark eyes looked with longing in the direction of the distant moors where she had been born. The pull of the sticky flour on her hands recalled her to her story and she looked at me and smiled. "The moon found the Earth enchanting! She saw capybaras and rheas and tapirs; she heard mockingbirds and parrots call. She decked herself in flowers and ran to look at her reflection in a lagoon. The water looked warm and inviting, and the moon jumped in and swam with the fishes. She emerged from the water refreshed and shook herself dry. She did not notice the jaguar, who had been watching her for some time, come creeping through the foliage. Just then, an old man, who had come to the lagoon for water, saw the jaguar stalking the maiden. He threatened it with his walking stick and the jaguar retreated. The moon was hungry by now, and the old man asked if she would care to come to his house. The moon accepted, and soon she was sitting by a fire eating *tortas fritas* just like these I'm making now," Josefa said, molding the dough into flat, round shapes while the oil heated on the stove.

"Did the moon like *tortas fritas?*"

"She thought them the best thing she'd ever tasted!" Josefa replied.

"What else had the moon eaten?"

Josefa wagged a finger at me. "What do I always tell you? Ask too many questions, and the devil himself will appear to answer them!" She tested the oil by sprinkling it with water. It sizzled in readiness.

I picked at the dough, liking the raw saltiness of it.

"The moon," Josefa continued, "ate until she could eat no more. When she had finished, she thanked the old man and his wife, and they introduced her to their daughter, a shy, quiet maiden, who kept her fingers out of the dough," Josefa said, slapping my wrist lightly, "and her eyes lowered and her voice soft when speaking to her elders."

"Like me, eh, Josefa?"

Josefa laughed so hard she almost forgot the *tortas fritas* bubbling on the stove.

I loved to hear her laugh. She did so with abandon, and the years and the cares all seemed to leave her at those times.

"*¡Ay, ay, ay!*" she said, wiping her eyes with the back of her hand. "*Sí, m'hijita,* just like you! Anyway, this shy maiden was lonely, like the moon herself, and the two of them went walking in the jungle, speaking of the things maidens speak of."

"Boys?"

"Boys, and dreams, and heartaches, and longings with no name. The moon and the maiden had, until that moment, thought themselves alone with their feelings. The moon confessed that she had always longed to be free of the sky, and the maiden told her she had always felt imprisoned on Earth. They talked almost all night, until the moon noticed that the stars were blinking at her, signaling for her to return, and she bade the maiden good-bye. The maiden cried, thinking she would never see her friend again. She did not know that friends, like guardian angels, never leave us. Their love becomes a part of us and is the blessed soil in which all future friendships blossom."

Josefa took the golden *tortas fritas* from the oil and placed them in the oven to keep warm. After adding two more to the pan, she put me to work packing the *mate* gourd with the coarsely ground green tea.

"The next night," she said, "the moon looked in on her friends and saw them sitting sadly round an empty table. 'Why are they so sad?' she asked the clouds.

"'They used the last of their flour to make your *tortas fritas,*' the clouds replied. 'Now they are hungry.'

"The moon was very upset. She had not realized that flour was not abundant. 'You must help me one more time,' she said to the clouds. 'I will seed you with a very special rain, which you must rain only around the old man's hut.'

"The clouds did as the moon requested, and the next day,

trees like no others in the jungle grew around the hut. They were covered in white flowers, and the old man's daughter discovered that she could make tea out of the leaves. Soon, people were coming from all around to buy her tea, and the maiden called it *mate.* The moon made her immortal, and from that time to this, the maiden has traveled the world, giving *mate* to everyone she meets. For *mate,* when prepared with respect and shared in a generous spirit, makes brothers and sisters of all who drink it."

I was quiet for a long time after Josefa told me this story, which is probably why she had done so. She knew the effect of her stories on me. I would retell them to myself several times, act them out, embellish them, and then write them in an old school notebook I kept in my bedside table.

Before I could get away to do this, Josefa handed me a three-tiered cake-server and told me to arrange the tea cakes on it while she finished making the *tortas fritas.* She called Lucía, a maid who had only just joined our household, and told her she would be in charge of serving tea to my aunts, who were gathering that day at our house.

Lucía would much rather have stayed with Josefa in the kitchen drinking *mate* and eating *tortas fritas,* but Josefa was not to be argued with.

Three

My *tías*, arrayed for tea, were a formidable sight. I did not know whether my mother's hairdresser, Ernesto, did their hair also, but he would have been proud to shake the hand of the person who did. As the late afternoon sun shone through the delicate stained glass of the tall drawing-room windows, its rays touched their glowing curls and waves. Some were a glistening auburn, others a silky brown with the richness of a bird's wing, and the eldest a pearly gray, swept softly behind into a thick French bun. Ensconced in the comfortable easy chairs with the large floral print or perched on the delicate Chippendales, their ankles crossed gracefully above the English rug, they cheerfully dissected their friends and relations, alive or dead. On their laps lay the tiny tea napkins with lace borders on which they wiped their fingers after touching the sandwiches and cakes. In one hand they held, in perfect symmetry with their bosoms and each other, a cup and saucer of fine, gilt-edged, bone china, replenished often by Lucía, standing by in starched white cap and apron.

She could be seen darting uneasy glances in the direction of the archway leading to the entrance hall. It was there that Caramba's cage reposed, when not being shown at the Russian Embassy. Caramba, however, was not disposed to stay in it. She was a bird of independent character and had long ago discovered how to undo any latch invented by the brain of more restrained beings. Along with her passion for chocolate custard, she had early on developed a liking for tea, which she preferred out of a Royal Doulton saucer. She loved my Uncle George, who regularly joined the aunts at tea and had a bald dome on which Caramba was fond of perching, her slender green tail pointing delicately toward his nose.

As soon as tea was served, Caramba went to work on her cage door until it opened. She then preened herself thoroughly, well aware, I felt certain, that she was about to join august company. Her toilet complete, Caramba took to the air, crossed the entrance hall, and flew through the arch, the embodiment of Lucía's worst fears. Lucía need not have worried. The conversation never faltered. The high voices twittered on, not a drop of tea was spilled, and the *tías,* as one body, raised a hand above their heads and chatted on until Caramba decided whom to settle on that day. They then wiped their fingers and helped themselves to more cake. All but the chosen one, who gently lowered Caramba to her shoulder and offered her some tea, which Caramba accepted with manners that belied her ancestry in the noisy eucalyptus groves of Uruguay.

"Have you heard? Castro is coming!" *tía* Catalina exclaimed as soon as Caramba had finished drinking.

"Castro who?" my mother inquired.

"*Fidel* Castro! Who else?"

"To Uruguay?" my mother asked in horror.

"Yes. Fresh from his victory in Cuba."

"Oh, how the Communists must be gloating!" *tía* Josefina said.

"Why should they?" *tía* Aurora asked.

"Well, everyone knows they were behind it."

"Everyone knows no such thing," *tía* Aurora argued.

"The Americans say so, and they should know," *tía* Catalina said firmly.

"What does Miss Newman think of all this?"

"Miss Newman has not mentioned Castro at all. Have you all heard the latest about our American friend, by the way?"

"About her wearing trousers to mass?" my mother asked.

"No, no, that was two weeks ago," *tía* Josefina answered.

"This is worse," said *tía* Aurora.

Tía Josefina giggled. "Much worse!"

"She could get herself killed," *tía* Aurora added.

I was particularly fond of my Aunt Aurora. Her morose personality and predictions of impending doom reminded me of Eeyore the donkey, our favorite character in the books from which she said she had learned all the English she knew.

"Well, what has she done?" my mother asked impatiently.

"She has taken to answering *piropos.*"

There was a moment of stunned silence. Only *tía* Aurora continued to chew and sip.

"But . . . but . . . ," my mother finally stammered, "what does she say?"

"Well, what I've heard is that when a man pays her a compliment on the street or whistles at her, she stops dead in her tracks and responds in kind."

"Or worse," *tía* Aurora added. "Makes references to their private parts."

My mother looked at me sharply. "Magdalena, please tell Josefa we need more hot water."

I was familiar enough with my mother's ruses to nod politely and leave the room, taking my customary place behind the door.

"Someone will have to talk to Miss Newman," my mother

said sternly. "She must understand that *piropos* are a compliment.
She should be flattered to receive them."

"She finds it insulting," *tía* Aurora sighed.

"Insulting! Doesn't she understand what's being said to her?"

"Oh, yes!" *tía* Josefina chirped. "She speaks Spanish
beautifully."

"Then what is she so upset about?"

"She maintains," *tía* Aurora explained, "that in Uruguay a
woman can't walk down the street without every male out of dia-
pers feeling it his God-given right to comment on her appearance. Without, of course, her having the right to reciprocate."

The good intentions of the street flatterers were staunchly
defended for several minutes, with allusions made to the fact
that only in the Río de la Plata would compliments delivered
on the street have risen to an art with its own name. The *piropo*,
after all, was supposed to be poetic, even delivered in rhymed
verse by its more accomplished practitioners. I sensed a certain
nervousness creeping into the conversation, however, as it always seemed to do whenever male rights were questioned. If we
behave ourselves, the women implied, and let the men carry on
as usual, then they will compliment us; if we don't, they may
take it upon themselves to teach us how to be women.

I had often heard the *tías* discussing how men ridiculed
women who cut their hair short or wore low heels to parties.
How they pointed out to one another any defect in dress or
grooming and never hesitated to tell the women they knew
whether in the man's opinion she looked heavier or lighter than
at their last meeting, and most importantly, whether or not he
approved of the change. No subject was too intimate for them
to voice an opinion on, and they gave advice quite freely on the
shaving of armpits and legs and the unsightliness of any female
body hair except on the head and one other part of the body

the men did not name but nudged one another about knowingly. Miss Newman, it appeared, had once offered to donate
the shavings from her armpits to the bald man who had the
effrontery to comment that she should not appear in public in
a sleeveless dress if she was not willing to comply with the standards they considered basic to feminine grooming.

"American women are very aggressive, of course," *tía*
Catalina said.

"I wonder if that's why American men are so peculiar?" my
mother asked.

"American men are not peculiar," *tía* Aurora stated. "They
are simply shy." Since she was the only one in the family who
had ever visited the United States, her authority on the subject
was never questioned.

"Not like John Wayne?" *tía* Josefina asked.

"More like Mr. Magoo. They seem quite oblivious to what
is going on around them. As for sexual relations . . . I doubt
they know any more than their wives do."

"How comforting," my mother sighed.

Tía Josefina laughed. "Now, now, Rita, you know you fell in
love with Javier precisely because he's so attuned to women."

"I do think Miss Newman is partly right. Men do take great
liberties with us on the street." *Tía* Catalina lowered her voice.
"I don't mind the *piropos* so much, but I do wish they wouldn't
touch us."

"Especially on the . . . ," *tía* Josefina began. "It can be awfully
distressing," she finished.

"I hit a man who did that once," *tía* Aurora said.

"So did I," *tía* Catalina seconded.

Tía Josefina sighed. "They don't like it, you know."

"Of course they don't like it," my mother snapped, "but occasionally we have to do something or . . ." She poured herself

another cup of tea. "Do you think Miss Newman is . . . ?" she allowed the question to hang provocatively.

"Is what?" *tía* Josefina asked.

The others glared at her. "You know . . . ," they said.

Tía Josefina looked bewildered. "No . . . ," she said. "What?"

Some whispering ensued and *tía* Josefina suddenly squealed, "Oh! Oh! No, no! Surely not!"

I had no idea what they were talking about. I returned to the drawing room hoping to be illuminated, but as soon as they saw me they shut up tighter than oysters. Their conversations often ended in this unsatisfactory way. Today, however, *tía* Aurora went a step further.

"Perhaps," she said, "Miss Newman doesn't need her femininity verified by every penis she passes."

"Aurora!" the *tías* gasped.

"Magdalena," my mother said, "leave the room at once!"

"But, *mamá*, I already heard it!" I cried and ran to tell Emilia.

She was not at home. Only her mother, Lilita, was there, sitting in the semidarkness of twilight in her tiny living room under a picture of Donatello's Mary Margaret, a wood carving I believed resembled Lilita's sad and tortured soul. Her dark eyes had shadows under them, and a strand or two of her fine hair had slipped from her hair net and curled like mist around her pale cheeks. She was slender and round shouldered and kept her hands close to her body as if she was afraid they might do wild things if she let them go.

"Emilia's at the gym. She'll be home soon," she said. "Would you like a Coca-Cola?"

"Yes, please," I said, following her into the kitchen. "Oh, *señora* Lilita, you'll never guess what my *tía* Aurora just said!"

Lilita laughed with delight when I told her and clapped her hands. "Every penis she passes!" she covered her mouth and stamped her feet in an uncharacteristic fit of pleasure. "Oh, Magdalena, how I hate men!" she sighed suddenly, as the Coca-Cola burst from the bottle and spilled over her hands.

"Why?" I asked, afraid that Lilita might realize whom she was talking to and change the subject, as my own mother often did.

"Because they're free. Free, Magda! They come; they go; they say whatever they want. They choose a woman, win her, have children by her, and their life continues, while ours. . . . They think they know more about being a woman than we do. They even tell us so. Have you heard them talk? 'Women like this' they say or 'They don't like that' or, worse, 'Women don't know what they want until we show them!' And they laugh at us and mock our confusion because we really don't know what we want. How can we know when our lives are dedicated to the wants of others?"

I was tempted to ask Lilita if her husband laughed at her, if those were his words she had quoted. Emilia had always spoken of her father as a mild-mannered, gentle man. He had sat by her bed every night when Emilia had the chicken pox, making sure she did not scratch in her sleep. And on the first day of every school year, he walked his daughter to school, proud of her neat appearance and her excellent grades.

I was about to ask Lilita about this when Emilia burst in at the door, still in her exercise clothes.

"Emilia!" Lilita cried. "Go and change at once, you'll catch pneumonia in those sweaty clothes!"

Emilia laughed. "It's hot out, *mamá*. Can I have a *Coca*, too, please?"

"As soon as you've changed. Go, go!"

Emilia paused in the doorway to her room. "How are you feeling now, *mamá?*"

"Better, much better. I had a headache today, Magda," she explained. "It's my liver."

"And the men, Lilita?" I asked.

Lilita smiled, a smile that made her whole face light up. She pinched my cheek. "You are full of insolence. What if your mother heard you being so familiar?"

"She would frown, like this," I said, pursing my mouth and raising my eyebrows, "and tell me that in her day they didn't call their elders and betters by their first names."

"Being called *señora* Lilita makes me feel old," Lilita sighed. "So don't tell her, and it will be our secret."

❧

A few days after my Aunt Aurora's comment, I was conducting one of my regular searches for articles of possible interest in my cousins' rooms, when I came upon a book. It was evident to me that since it was hidden in a shoe box, the book must contain information Emilia and I would appreciate having.

My twin cousins Sofía and Carmen had been orphaned at age seven when my father's brother and his wife were killed in a car crash. Shortly after the crash the twins came to live with my parents, who had been married for ten years by then and given up all hope of having children of their own. I was born a year later.

A small dressing room with a wrought-iron balcony connected Sofía's bedroom with Carmen's, and it was here that the two of them exchanged confidences and sought each other's advice.

Emilia and I had discovered that by climbing the *estrella federal* we could reach the balcony and hear everything my cousins said. Our sex education, such as it was, took place entirely on this balcony, and we retired there with the book and closed the French blinds behind us.

The book I had found was a novel written in such flowery prose that it required several readings for us to grasp that it opened with a description of the sex act. The only thing clear was that the couple were unmarried. The author felt that the young woman should have sufficient moral strength to refuse the young man; and he, sufficient respect for her to satisfy his base passions elsewhere. I paused in my third reading of this passage. If it was all right for men to have sex before marriage, I asked Emilia, but it was wrong for women to do so, whom could they be having sex with? In a fit of absolute hilarity, Emilia suggested that perhaps men did it with each other. Next time my cousins were in a receptive mood, we concluded, we would pose this difficult question to them.

I was not a great favorite with my cousins at the best of times. Recently, I had made myself entirely odious to them by pouring water from the balcony onto their heads as they sat in the garden below necking with their boyfriends. Occasions for necking, as I would discover in due course, were few and far between, since Josefa saw it as her duty to protect our good names and was given to lurking about in the garden behind the shrubbery to ensure that decorum was maintained at all times.

We were just turning back to the book when voices raised in anger reached us, and the door to Sofía's room was slammed with such vehemence that the blinds on the balcony rattled.

We closed the book hastily and were about to climb back to the shelter of the poinsettia tree when my mother's voice reached us.

"You were seen! You were seen, Sofía!" she was shouting.

"So what? So what? So what?" Sofía screamed back. "Do you think I care what a pack of jealous old maids thinks?"

"Don't you talk that way about your father's sisters!" Josefa scolded, her arm around my mother's waist. "They were godmothers at your confirmation!"

"Sofía, try to understand. You were seen by our Cousin Delia and her aunts leaving a *casa de cita.* There is only one thing you could have been doing in such a place! If you have no regard for your own future, you could at least have thought of me! Your father's side of the family has always criticized me for being too lenient with you! What am I to say to Javier when his sisters tell him they saw you leaving a house of assignation?"

Sofía's laugh was an ugly sound. "As if he never used one!"

Josefa gasped and crossed herself.

"It is different for men!" my mother said imploringly. "Please try to understand that. Every conquest that adds to their reputation, deprives a woman of hers. And you are nothing without your reputation! I am nothing if you lose it."

"*Tranquila, señora* Rita," Josefa said gently. "Sofía will never disgrace us."

"She already has!"

"Oh, *tía,* stop being so dramatic. We don't live in the Dark Ages any more. Men have sexual needs, and we must acknowledge it or lose them to someone who does."

"They can have cold showers," Josefa declared, "or go with other women."

"The decent ones do," my mother added.

Sofía uttered a cry of disbelief and stamped into the dressing room, flinging her coat to the floor.

Emilia and I receded into a corner of the balcony.

"And what of my sexual needs? Am I to go with other men?"

There was a moment of silence. We held our breath, eyes

fixed on the half-open slats through which we could just see the room beyond.

"Women are different," my mother said firmly.

Josefa picked up the discarded coat and folded it neatly, her movements controlled. "We must decide what to do about *el señor* Javier," she said quietly.

What she did not know and Emilia and I did was that my father had arrived a few moments previously and was making his way up the stairs. By the time he reached the dressing room, he had his belt off and in his hand. My mother took one look at him and stepped in front of Sofía. Josefa spread her apron before them both.

"This is a matter for me to deal with, Javier," my mother said.

"And a fine job you've done of it. My brother's daughter is a *puta!*"

"And you a whoremaster!" Sofía spat over my mother's shoulder.

"Sofía, *callate*," Josefa said shakily.

"No, I won't be quiet. He can hit me if he wants to. It's just the kind of thing that would make him feel more like a man. Go ahead, *tío* Javier, hit me for doing what you do every day of your life."

My father dropped the belt and left the room. Sofía and my mother fell on the bed, sobbing in each other's arms, while Josefa locked the door as a precaution against my father changing his mind. Her cheeks were wet with tears as she came over to the balcony door.

Emilia clutched my arm, expecting to be discovered, but I knew that that was not Josefa's intention. She had felt my presence and my distress as tangibly as if I had been in the room with her and she wished to comfort me. Her eyes met mine for the briefest moment before Emilia and I climbed over the railing onto the poinsettia tree below, where we sat in silence for a long time, holding hands.

I wished that Josefa had not cried. Her tears were a gift of caring wasted on Sofía's anger and my mother's pride, although I knew Josefa would never think so. She gave because it was in her nature to give, just as the Río de la Plata flowed and the *estrella federal* flowered.

In the stillness of the *siesta* hour we could hear the breeze rustling the tree's heavy leaves. Emilia raised her head and gave a small cry of surprise.

"Look," she whispered, and pointed to a branch high above us.

One perfect star had bloomed a bright, piercing red.

Four

Emilia and her parents lived in the single apartment building in the neighborhood. It was a small building, presided over by a man called Basco, who appeared in public in his undershirt, leading the neighbors to conclude that Basco surely entertained hidden vices. What these might be, Emilia and I were not told. We were warned, however, that under no circumstances were we to be alone with Basco. Emilia needed no reminders of this warning. She avoided Basco, knowing instinctively that she was afraid of the way he moistened his heavy underlip whenever he saw her, rubbing his thighs with his hands. If her father was present, Basco did not even look at her.

Señor Mario strolled by my house every morning on his way to buy the daily paper. He returned home to lunch and left for his civil service job in the afternoon, while Lilita waited anxiously by her front door for her elderly father, who came every day to visit her.

Lilita was determined that Emilia, her pride and joy, would marry a millionaire or, if not a millionaire, a man of such repute that money would be meaningless. To that end, Emilia was taken several times a week to exercise classes, dance, English, and piano lessons. Lilita deprived herself of every luxury to make these lessons possible. She had a small silver box in which she stored every *peso* left over from her housekeeping money and the occasional gifts made to her on her birthdays by her father. This money, she told Emilia, was to outfit her suitably when the day came that she met a man worthy of her.

Emilia, I knew, would have liked to spend it on a Great Dane.

During the winter of 1959, Emilia and I celebrated our twelfth birthdays with a trip to the amusement park at the Parque Rodó and teas with our relatives. The trip to the Parque Rodó we made together; the teas were given separately. Emilia's cousins came from all over the city bearing gifts and food, and Emilia had a new dress of dark blue velvet, trimmed with shiny red ribbons. *Tía* Josefina baked me a splendid chocolate cake, covered with spun sugar seashells in pale shades of pink and lavender, and my grandmother gave me a twelfth *esclava*. The first of these gold bangles, given to me on my first birthday, lay in a box in my dresser, along with several of the ones that followed. I could still wear five of the others, and they jingled against one another as I opened the box containing the twelfth one.

Cora also celebrated her twelfth birthday that year, a fact I discovered because flowers were mistakenly delivered to our house with a large card on which the number twelve and the words *"¡Que los cumplas feliz! Tío Alberto"* were written in bold purple letters.

My mother asked Josefa to deliver the flowers immediately to the Allenbergs, and I seized my chance. I followed Josefa to the kitchen.

"I'll take them, Josefa. You're busy with lunch."

"Yes, I am, and your mother doesn't like it if I serve it one minute after one o'clock." She looked at me severely. "However, I know you very well, Magda. You will run off to get Emilia, and by the time these flowers are delivered to the *señora* Allenberg, they will have frogs in them."

I was offended. "I was eight years old when I put frogs in *tía* Catalina's flowers, Josefa. I am twelve now, please remember."

Josefa shook her head, her neat black braids swinging at her back. "I'm blessed if I can see any difference, *niña*. Look at your clothes. Your jeans need patching again, and if I had my way, *señor* Ernesto would have been given free rein to cut that hair of yours above your ears! Anybody lucky enough to have hair the color of newly polished copper should be thankful enough to take care of it. As for—"

"Josefa," I said, kissing her, "I promise to let you brush my hair if you'll let me take the flowers. That is, I'll let you brush it after Pepe leaves this evening. You can borrow my perfume if you want."

"Borrow your perfume!" Josefa laughed. "The last time I saw it, you were putting it on the dog." She disentangled herself from my embrace. "Promise me—no tricks, and you may take the flowers."

"I promise, Josefa."

Emilia and I held the huge bouquet carefully between us. It was wrapped in white paper with a design of pink flowers stamped on it, and from the partly open top, we could see twelve bird-of-paradise thrusting their flowery beaks out of a bed of white baby's breath. We crept up to Cora's house, eyes fixed on the open window at which Cora and her mother sat, busy on a work of delicate embroidery.

"We beg your pardon," I said. "These flowers for Cora were delivered to our house by mistake."

Cora's mother put her embroidery down hastily. "How kind of you to bring them. You should not have bothered. We would have fetched them. I'll be down directly."

"We're twelve too!" I said as Mrs. Allenberg disappeared.

"Is your birthday actually today?" Emilia asked.

"Yes," Cora answered. "When was yours?"

We told her and asked if she liked going to the cinema.

"I love it! Especially when Lassie is on!"

"Do you have a dog?" Emilia cried.

"I can't. My father suffers from allergies."

This rapid exchange came to an end as the door opened and Mrs. Allenberg reached gratefully for the flowers. "Thank you so much," she said, taking the colorful bouquet.

"Not at all, we were happy to be of service," I answered.

"Good-bye now," Mrs. Allenberg said pointedly. She closed the door and reappeared moments later at the window.

"Can Cora come out to play?" I asked.

Mrs. Allenberg looked alarmed.

"Can I, Mamma?" Cora asked, in a voice so sweet Emilia and I felt we could never speak again.

"No."

"Why not?"

"They will call you a Jewess."

"That's what I am."

"Not in the way they'll mean it, child," and Cora's mother closed the window and released the blinds. The house's one eye on the street was sealed, and Emilia and I were left staring up at it.

For days afterward we imitated Cora's gentle voice, until our mothers talked of calling the doctor. This threat was enough to make us decide that the time would come soon enough when we would really have to lower our voices and behave like my cousins Sofía and Carmen, wearing high heels and monopolizing the bathroom as they conceived of ways of escaping their chaperones. Compared to the secret mischief they could get into, anything I did was mild.

After the recent quarrel with Sofía, it had become evident that my mother's preoccupations were exclusively over her. I was ordered from the room more frequently. Tears and door slamming punctuated the family's daily life, and my father, whose presence could be counted upon only at Sunday lunch, started absenting himself even from that ritual. When the women gathered to talk over the garden gates or across the low walls separating their houses, they spoke in soft voices with much gesturing and sighing and often patted my mother gently, assuring her that Sofía would be married soon and then she, too, would understand what it was to manage a family.

It was evident to Emilia and me that something happened between the time a young man and his beloved courted and the years after they were married. The grim husbands leaving every day for work, paunchy and careworn, bore no resemblance we could see to the exuberant young men who clustered on street corners, scrutinizing every woman who walked by and emanating an aura I could not have described then, but which I knew frightened me.

Boys, however, were not predominant in our thoughts. We were much more interested in romance, and none of the males we knew remotely embodied our idea of it.

Cora was the closest thing to romance we could imagine. At the time, the idea of being kept sequestered behind a stone wall and appearing in public immaculately groomed and chaperoned seemed romantic to us.

"It must be so wonderful to walk out with one's father looking so proud," I said, remembering my father's disappointment that I had not been a boy. When Josefa telephoned him in Buenos Aires with the news of my birth, he had exclaimed, "A girl?" and gone back to sleep. My mother had laughed when she told me this story, not knowing that I would never forget it.

"And to be taken care of that way," Emilia sighed. I knew that she was thinking of how often it was she who washed and ironed and starched her mother's clothes, while Lilita sat silent,

lost in some private labyrinth of sorrow. She had often told me
of Lilita's nighttime excursions, when she slipped out of the
apartment thinking Emilia was asleep. Emilia would lie in her
bed trying to sleep, but the night was not her friend, she said. It
robbed her of the security of her mother's presence. It brought
thoughts of death and feelings of abandonment, fears without
the words with which to express them. She would stifle her
cries in her pillow until her mother returned and then hate herself for being angry. For hours, she had longed to hear Lilita's
footstep, the sound of her key in the lock, and when it came,
Emilia was furious. Furious at the sleepless hours, the wet pillow, herself, her mother, and whoever it was Lilita went to see.
I told her that perhaps Lilita was earning the money to buy
the house the two of them dreamed of, but Emilia shook her
head impatiently and said there was much more to her mother's
secrecy than a mere job.

Not even our families, however, could mar the wintry beauty
of that day, and soon Emilia jumped up.

"Let's go fishing!" she said.

We changed into our old shoes and ran the two blocks to the
beach. All we ever caught were minnows, but we always made it
a point to visit one of our favorite spots along the river, a small
peninsula on which stood a fishermen's shelter, made entirely
of spreading bushes, hollowed and trimmed into the shape of
a long, low house.

We entered the shelter through one of several openings cut
in the shapes of doors in the closely growing shrubbery. On
the inside, the bushes were used to provide seating. With all
the lower foliage removed, the thick trunks and branches were
shaped to resemble chairs and, along the outer edges, places to
hang clothes, nets, and fishing gear. The fishermen were friendly,

although they never invited us to join them in their boats, as Emilia and I hoped.

On rainy days, we enjoyed looking up and hearing the patter on the thick leaves, watching in wonder as the world above us turned to gleaming crystals when the sun came out again.

No one lived there, except for several cats and one dog, to whom we gave one of the bread-and-butter sandwiches we had brought for our lunch. Then we took our glass jars, string, and stale bread for bait and sat among the rock formations on the point, catching minnows and throwing them back into the river until the bread ran out. We walked home along the shore, gathering treasures washed up by the tide—shells the size of pinheads; bird feathers; fish bones; and deflated, white rubber balloons, finding their way back to shore from the sewers that emptied out at sea. Why such a quantity of white balloons occasionally adorned our shores, we never inquired, but accepted them along with everything else the river offered and stored them in an old shoe box under my bed with the idea of blowing them all up one day and selling them. Our plan never materialized.

One rainy day, when we were playing *conga* at the dining-room table, we heard a scream from upstairs and dropped our cards, running to see what had happened. My mother, pale and shaken, was sitting on my bed, the balloons scattered at her feet.

"What's wrong?" I asked.

"Get these out of here!" my mother gasped.

"They're just balloons," I said, as Emilia stooped to collect them.

"Don't touch them!" my mother screeched.

Emilia and I exchanged confused glances. "How else can we pick them up?"

"Use a cloth, a newspaper, anything, but not your hands!"

my mother answered, rising unsteadily. "And never bring one of these foul things home again!" She staggered away.

"*¡Idiotas!*" hissed Carmen from the doorway. "Don't you know what those are?"

"*Claro,*" I answered. "Balloons. I didn't know *mamá* disliked balloons."

My cousin laughed. "You're even stupider than I thought. They're rubbers! Men put them on their thingies and pee into them!"

Emilia and I glanced down in horror at our hands, heaped full of used rubbers.

"I will never, ever, ever, eat anything you've touched, ever, ever again!" Carmen added and went to comfort my mother.

Emilia and I were debating one day whether, now that Carmen had spread our balloon story all over the *barrio*, we would ever succeed in persuading Cora's mother that we were fit companions for her daughter, when Miranda appeared. Miranda was a *criada*, a young girl brought from the orphanage and allowed to live with a family in exchange for light housework.

Miranda worked in the big house on the corner, where the eldest daughter, Cristina, was an invalid. I thought Cristina very beautiful in her tall, slender paleness, as she moved like a ghost about the house. Her father doted on her and rented films for her entertainment. Every so often, Emilia and I were invited to watch these films, and Miranda approached us with just such an invitation that day. We ran to wash our hands and brush our hair, then climbed the marble steps leading to the large double doors of Cristina's house. We were ushered into the hall by a uniformed maid who led us upstairs into the movie room. This was a luxury for us, and we appreciated it.

Here, on a small screen, in this upstairs ballroom, we allowed ourselves to believe that we could tap dance our way into a man's heart or, barring the availability of lessons in that particular skill, pad our shoulders and proceed to make millions in the business world.

Cristina always wore white and rarely spoke. She had shoulder-length brown hair and very large dark eyes. I could not remember ever having seen her smile. She was extremely elegant and would gesture for her guests to sit in the chairs provided for the small audience. We would listen in awed silence as the movie projector whirred and watch, usually Fred Astaire, Cristina's great favorite, embodying a mobility she would never enjoy.

We were not sure what illness Cristina suffered from. It was not discussed in our presence, and we assumed that, as was usual, the adults supposed us too young to be told.

Today, as we took our seats silently, we looked around us and saw Cora waving to us from the next row. In the pause while the movie was being prepared, we slipped toward her.

"What are you doing here?" we whispered in surprise.

"Cristina's father persuaded my father to let me come. They do business together."

"Who's your favorite actor?"

"Randolph Scott," she giggled.

"Mine is Gary Cooper," Emilia added.

"Tyrone Power," I said.

Cristina glanced over her shoulder at us, raising one long finger to her fine lips.

We stopped talking, but not even Fred Astaire could distract us that day. We were anxious for the movie to end, and as soon as it did, we thanked Cristina hastily, while Cora kissed her hostess and slipped a small package into her hands.

"These are not balloons, I hope?" Cristina asked, winking at Emilia and me.

We were too embarrassed to appreciate that this was the only lighthearted remark we had ever heard Cristina make.

Cora looked puzzled and told Cristina that the package contained unleavened bread.

Realizing that Cora had not heard the balloon story, Emilia quickly took her arm, and the three of us hurried away.

"What kind of bread was that you gave her?" Emilia asked as we went down the wide staircase to the front door.

"Unleavened bread. She's very fond of it. I don't know why she thought I'd brought balloons! And in a package—"

"What does unleavened bread taste like?" I interrupted.

Cora shrugged. "A little like *galletas.*"

Anxious to keep away from the subject of balloons, I asked if her mother would let her play.

"I doubt it. But if I invite you to my house, she can't turn you away! Do you want to come?"

Emilia and I did not need to be asked twice. Cora led the way into her house and into another world. The entrance hall we stepped into was tiled from floor to ceiling in blue and white squares with windmills painted on them. Potted ferns hung like delicate green clouds above our heads.

Cora gestured for us to follow, and we entered the little front room in which she and her mother did their handwork. Every surface was covered in a riot of embroidered flowers, cascading to the floor in exquisite bouquets or lying in peaceful garlands on the armrests of the chairs. In the corner stood a mannequin wearing a wedding dress made entirely of lacework so filmy it seemed as if someone had taken cobwebs and spun them into froth. Emilia and I stood before it hardly daring to breathe.

"It's for my cousin Rebeca. She's getting married next week."

"I've never seen anything so beautiful," Emilia sighed.

"No one makes lace like Mamma. She was famous for it in Holland."

Just then, Mrs. Allenberg entered the room. "Cora, I didn't know we had visitors."

"We've only just arrived. May we have some lemonade? We're thirsty after that long movie."

"Of course," Mrs. Allenberg answered politely. "We are leaving in half an hour to dine at your uncle's, but there's time for some lemonade. Would you like to go into the patio? It's still quite warm there."

Most of the houses on the block had patios, places where grapevines grew and children raised nestlings found floundering on the ground, where wine was brought out in large demijohns at family gatherings and couples found occasional moments of privacy in the tangled vines tumbling from the high walls. The Allenbergs' patio had only the Uruguayan weather in common with its neighbors'. Here at the center of this house, whose contents reflected no touch of local culture, tulips flourished in neat rows all along the walls. In the center was a tiled pond full of goldfish. White wrought-iron furniture was arranged under a spreading oak tree whose boughs were trimmed to fit perfectly into the small space. The lemonade was brought to us by a small, painfully thin woman, dressed entirely in black. Her blonde hair was pulled back into a tight bun, and her hands shook slightly as she filled three glasses.

"I hope you've kept some for yourself, Hannah," Cora said.

The woman did not answer, but patted Cora's shoulder gently as she left.

"She's just arrived in Uruguay," Cora whispered. "She was in a concentration camp for two years."

Emilia and I wanted to ask what a concentration camp was, but Mrs. Allenberg looked out a window at that moment and said something to Cora in Dutch.

Cora laughed. "Mamma strikes as regularly as a clock. I have fifteen minutes left, she says."

"Would she let you come to the beach with us now that she's allowed us in the house?" Emilia asked.

"I doubt it."

"Is she afraid something will happen to you?"

"It's hard to explain. My parents had to escape from Holland in a hearse, pretending to be dead, you see, and they had to leave everything—their house, their furniture, everything."

This was more thrilling than we could have imagined. "In a hearse?" Emilia whispered in awe. "Why?"

Cora shrugged. "I don't understand why. It had something to do with money."

"Do you have a lot of it?" I asked.

"I suppose so," Cora answered. "We must have if they wanted to kill us for it."

Emilia wanted more details about the hearse, but Cora could not tell her much more.

"Where were *you?*" I wanted to know.

"I hadn't been born yet. I was born later, in Paraguay."

Cora told us how different it was there. She had had a nanny, an Indian woman who had taught her to speak Guaraní. She missed her greatly. Uruguay, her parents said, was so European by comparison.

"Say a few words!" Emilia cried. "I love Guaraní. We hear it on the radio sometimes, in songs."

Cora laughed. "I don't know what to say."

"Say good-bye," her mother's voice came from the window. "I'm sorry, girls, but Cora must get ready to go to her uncle's. See our neighbors to the door, dear."

"We're always around, you know," I said. "Can you wave a handkerchief from the window or something if we can come and see you?"

Cora's face brightened. "Yes! Now that Hannah's here, Mamma sometimes goes out!"

"We'll look for it!" I promised. "Every day!"

We raced down the front steps and turned the corner of the brick wall at full tilt, colliding with our neighbor, Mr. Stelby, who reached out and grabbed us.

"Little hooligans!" he said. "If you were boys, I'd take a stick to you! I slid on the pavement again today and don't think I don't know why! I've seen you soaping it before I go for my walk!"

Emilia and I regularly soaped the pavement in front of Emilia's building. Our intended victims, however, were not our neighbors, but the frail widows, dressed in black from head to toe, who went to daily mass at the church around the corner. They were craftier than Mr. Stelby, however, and invariably crossed the street before reaching the stretch of pavement we had soaped to slimy perfection. Not once had we had the satisfaction of seeing anyone slide on the mess, as happened in the American cartoons we wanted to test.

Emilia and I apologized for Mr. Stelby's accident and wriggled free. Mr. Stelby frightened us. I was better acquainted with his type than Emilia was. At the private school I went to, the feeling that the British teachers there would have enjoyed beating the pupils into immobility was never wholly absent. They were prevented by strict Uruguayan laws from touching the students, a fact the teachers bemoaned every day in the staff room, outside of which I stood for many hours each month as punishment for my transgressions, the principal one being my refusal to speak English during break time.

Business investments had brought the Stelbys from England to Uruguay thirty years previously, and for reasons no one could fathom, they had decided to remain in a country they never stopped reviling. Neither of them had succeeded in mastering Spanish, nor could they understand that animals did not hold quite the same esteemed place in local culture as they did in England. Their neighbors had been horrified when Mr. Stelby curtailed his dog's sex life by neutering it. These same neighbors, as Mr. Stelby pointed out to my mother, would think little of abandoning a litter of puppies by the roadside. My mother tried to explain to the Stelbys that a different set of values operated in Uruguay, but they simply snorted in disdain and answered with their favorite expression when referring to anything Uruguayan, "Typical!"

Mr. Stelby's nemesis, the dogcatcher, drove by our neighborhood in his square, gray wagon at least once a week. He was looking, as Mr. Stelby had soon learned, not for stray dogs, but for those evidently well fed and wearing expensive collars. "Typical!" Mr. Stelby had exclaimed. There was no profit in picking up strays. It was a certainty that no grateful owner would come to collect them, tipping the wardens who had cared for their pet in captivity. There was no better place in Montevideo to get an idea of the thoroughbred pet population than the pound. Owners of thoroughbred dogs walked them warily, casting suspicious glances over their shoulders at the sound of a car engine and unleashing their pets only when on the beach.

Since dogs were not allowed there except during the winter months, when the beach was unused by people, thoroughbreds led sheltered lives.

Apart from his dog, Mr. Stelby was devoted to a small Scottish lavender bush he had planted in a square of earth on the pavement near the curb. He kept it neatly clipped; admired the subdued tone of its flowers; and watered it every day from an old aluminum watering can that had, along with its owner, seen better days.

The riotous colors and uncontrolled growth of the local flora offended Mr. Stelby's sensibilities. In summer, when the heady camellias and the gentle jasmine permeated the streets with their scent, he walked his dog with a handkerchief sprayed in lavender held firmly to his nose. When the poinsettias burst in the winter sun, he would sometimes pause by the tree in our garden, shaking his head in disbelief that any flower could be so passionate, and in the winter time too.

A few days after our visit to Cora's, Mr. Stelby's dog appeared unaccompanied by Mr. Stelby and began its self-appointed round of all the trees in the neighborhood, leaving Mr. Stelby's bush to last. Just as Waldo was returning home, tail held high, right ear cocked, left ear hanging limp, the dogcatcher rounded the corner and spotted him.

Waldo looked unconcerned and trotted on toward his owner's prized bush.

The dogcatcher smiled and started twirling the rope over his head.

We should have warned him, but we were mesmerized by the rope and Waldo's impending doom. We simply knelt where we were, our mothers' bars of washing soap in our hands, and stared.

The dogcatcher broke into a trot and threw his lasso at the

same moment that his feet hit the pavement we had been busy soaping.

As the dogcatcher's black patent leather shoes made contact with the soap, he and his lasso flew simultaneously, he to land on his ample behind on the pavement with an amazed air, the lasso neatly falling around the lavender bush beneath which Waldo had crouched. At that moment, Mr. Stelby emerged. He saw the lasso, Waldo, and the dogcatcher's van and scooped Waldo up in indignation. He then approached the dogcatcher, who scrambled to his feet and locked himself in his van.

"*¡Usted es un rata!*" Mr. Stelby shouted. "*¡Esta perro es mía!*"

The dogcatcher, bombarded with mixed genders, took off at top speed, still holding tightly to his end of the rope. Mr. Stelby stood frozen as his bush was torn out by the roots and dragged ignominiously away in the wake of the dogcatcher's van.

"Look on the bright side, Mr. Stelby," Emilia comforted him. "It could have been Waldo . . ."

Five

Señora Francisca lived across the street from Cora's, and she and her family intrigued us. Like all the fathers on our street, *señor* Rubén was only a figure in a suit, coming and going at predictable hours, raising his hat to the ladies, and exchanging a courteous and brief good morning with his fellows. *Señora* Francisca, however, was different from the rest of the mothers in that she kept almost entirely to herself. No one questioned that Cora's mother should do so. That was to be expected from a lady who kept the Sabbath and in whose home Hebrew was spoken. The Jews had suffered much, and if they chose to keep to themselves, who could blame them?

The only explanation for *señora* Francisca's aloofness was that she considered herself superior and that made the mothers on our block irate. Nothing they could dig up revealed any reason for *señora* Francisca's superiority. Her father had been a dentist and her mother a Gómez Pérez. No reason there for her puffed-up attitude, they said. Her daughters, Raquel and Margot, were admittedly more stylish than the other girls on the block, but she had no sons. Marco's mother, *señora* Marta, who had three, was fond of stressing this particular point, to be strongly seconded by my mother, who thought Sofía and Carmen every bit as handsome as the Arteaga girls, even if their clothes were not bought at exclusive boutiques in the summer resort town of Punta del Este.

Whenever Emilia and I were privy to these discussions, we would interject that not only were we extremely good looking, but planning professional careers. Whenever we brought this up, a collective sigh would arise, and if one of our mothers was present, she would be patted sympathetically as she regarded us with melancholy eyes. Since Emilia and I ranked high in our own esteem this response irritated us.

We had been interested in *señora* Francisca from the moment she and her family had moved into the house across from Emilia's building. She was a lovely lady, with a broad, pale face, wavy auburn hair, and hazel eyes. She wore high heels and straight skirts that set off her long, slender legs, and she smoked dark cigarettes in a white ivory holder. Her black sealskin coat and matching sealskin shoes were the envy of my cousins, who pleaded with my father to buy them something similar. While having no principles on the subject of fur coats in general, my father objected to sealskin. My mother claimed it was because he had once been responsible for saving a beached and wounded seal and handing it over to the zoo. It had been this one show of sentiment toward something other than the females of his own species that had first endeared him to my mother.

Apart from the sealskin coat, *señora* Francisca and her daughters were quietly stylish and unobtrusive.

One evening, when no one was out, I saw Lilita trying to reach the Arteagas' front door without any of the neighbors seeing her.

It was a chilly evening, and a misty drizzle shimmered in the bright rings cast by the tall streetlights. Blinds were down, and curtains drawn against the upcoming night. I saw Lilita walk past the Arteagas' front door. Pausing behind a large tree, Lilita glanced quickly toward her apartment building, back-tracked, and disappeared into the Arteagas' house. It was not surprising to me that Lilita and *señora* Francisca should have something in common. Long before the *barrio* discovered it, I suspected that *señora* Francisca kept to herself because she was afraid and that Lilita understood why. What puzzled me was the secrecy of Lilita's action. What could either of them be up to that required their friendship to be so private?

At that moment, I saw Emilia running down the street and went to intercept her.

"Come with me quickly and don't make any noise!" I said.

"Why not?" Emilia whispered, following me down the street. "Who can hear us? No one in their right mind is out on a night like this!"

"Shh! Your mother has just gone into the Arteagas' house!"

"What for?"

"I have no idea! But I'm going to find out."

"How? This sounds just like another of your crazy—"

Putting a finger to my lips, I moved silently forward, hugging the wall until I reached the Arteagas' house. Emilia followed reluctantly. I reached out and tried the front door. It opened easily, and I pulled Emilia into a small, bare, entrance hall. From a room at the top of the stairs, light spilled into the passage, and the murmur of low voices mingled with the sound of rain whispering in the ivy covering the front of the house.

"Look," Emilia said.

"At what?"

"The dining room. It has a table and four chairs."

"Yes . . . ?"

"That's all there is, Magda! And there's nothing in the hall. That fireplace looks as if it has never been lit."

I stopped for a moment, nodding slowly. The house appeared unlived in.

There was no evidence of real people inhabiting this place.

No sign of personal taste or eccentricity. I thought of my own house where Josefa's flower arrangements reveled in every nook and cranny, where my father's racing-car models often littered the dining-room table, making my mother click her tongue impatiently at this boyish hobby.

Emilia moved silently on, drawn in by her curiosity at the lack of all the comforts she felt essential to well-being. "There isn't a single picture on the walls."

"No ornaments anywhere," I added. "And look at the kitchen!"

"What a mess!"

"There's no stove!"

"Do you think she does all her cooking on that little Primus stove?"

"She must. They can't afford a maid," I said. "My mother told me they could if *señor* Arteaga ever gave his wife any money."

Emilia shivered. "My mother says he takes a belt to Margot and Raquel if he thinks they behave like his whore."

"Sofía told me he hit them for wearing makeup last week and for sitting out on the balcony with it on. She said they usually wash it off before he gets home, but that day he was early." I looked around once more. "It's a stark and desolate place."

"Don't be so dramatic. Obviously, *señora* Francisca has no idea of how to decorate. It's just an empty old house."

"This house is more than just empty."

It was uncared for, neglected. Life seemed unwelcome and intrusive here. Heavy blinds over the windows kept out the light, and a deep hush prevailed. I felt the house would shudder if something as vital as Caramba were suddenly to enter it.

Emilia's hand touched the banister and her eyes met mine.

With a brief nod, we crept up the stairs. The stair treads creaked under our weight, and we held our breath, expecting someone to emerge at any moment and confront us. The voices, however, continued unabated. We reached the top of the stairs and huddled together on the step. We could smell *señora* Francisca's cigarette and see the smoke wafting out the open door from which the voices came.

"Where is he now?" we heard *señora* Francisca asking.

"In Paraguay," Lilita answered softly.

"Fighting?"

"Always. Always fighting."

"It's a lonely life," *señora* Francisca sighed.

"Don't we know it, Francisca? Imagine how much lonelier if we hadn't recognized each other that night at the meeting?"

"If it weren't for the meetings, I couldn't go on."

"Do you think the day will ever come when we can fight openly?" Lilita asked.

"Yes, I do. I have to believe it. They tell us it's just a matter of time. All the groups are so at odds!"

"They agree on the ends."

"But not on the means. And until we agree on that, we won't get anywhere."

"There are a few who say it is time to merge or give up," Lilita sighed.

"Meanwhile, the guns are difficult to hide," *señora* Francisca laughed.

Emilia gasped and her hand closed around my arm with such force that I almost cried out.

"Do you still have them in the basement?"

"Yes, under the one thing Rubén will never touch again."

"What's that?" Lilita asked.

"My wedding dress."

Emilia could bear no more. Pulling me after her, she tiptoed quickly down the stairs and eased open the front door. Once outside, we breathed with relief as the cool rain hit us. We stood for a few moments, letting the drizzle cool our faces. Our hearts were beating fast.

The wind blew the gate shut behind us, making us both jump.

"Guns!" Emilia exploded.

"Perhaps they're going to hold up a bank!" I said eagerly.

Emilia looked at me impatiently as she dragged me across the street. "Don't be such a turnip! They were talking about revolution!"

"You mean against the government?"

"Of course! And can you imagine how crazy their friends at those meetings must be if they're all like my mother and *señora* Francisca?"

"Lilita isn't crazy, Emilia. She's just sad sometimes."

Emilia laughed bitterly as we entered her apartment and took off our wet shoes. "You don't live with her."

"No, but—"

"She's crazy! You have no idea. I've never told you."

Seeing tears in Emilia's eyes, I realized for the first time that what I had always taken to be Lilita's sadness had a darker side where Emilia was concerned. "Tell me now, Emilita," I said, sitting on the dark little sofa and gesturing for Emilia to join me. I was beginning to regret having followed Lilita.

"You know that she leaves the house in the middle of the night. Once she came home with her clothes torn. Another time, two men came to my school and followed me. When I stopped to cross the street, they came up to me and told me not to be afraid, that they had some questions to ask me about my mother. One of them looked like a foreigner. His clothes were expensive, and he had a large gold ring on one finger."

"What did you do?"

"I kicked him in the shins and ran."

"Did they chase you?"

"I don't think so. I didn't look back until I was almost home."

"Have you told your father?" I asked.

Emilia looked startled. "No! He'd put *mamá* in the insane asylum! She told me once that he's just waiting for her to die so he can marry his kept woman."

"Do they all have them, Emilia?"

"I suppose so."

"Why?"

"Oh, Magdalita, how should I know? I suppose it's because our mothers don't know how to make them happy."

For the first time in my life, I was conscious of feeling afraid. I could not have expressed why exactly. I suspected that if Lilita's sorrow was really despair and *señora* Francisca's pride really secrecy, then a door was opening into a world I did not want to enter. The *tías* often hinted of their knowledge of such a world, but the *tías* were safe and predictable, their talk as airy as Josefa's meringues.

I suggested to Emilia that we make hot chocolate and listen to the Platters, and Emilia looked at me with such seriousness that I felt I had failed her in some way.

I asked if she would prefer to run out and ring doorbells, since no one would expect it on a rainy night.

"It's time we stopped doing such stupid things," she said.

I was too hurt to answer. We had been ringing doorbells and making mischief for as long as we had been friends.

Unspoken between us had been the understanding that such acts of trivial naughtiness were necessary to keep at a distance the shadows that were a part of our lives. So long as we could laugh together, we could forget Lilita's moods and my mother's preoccupation with her teenage nieces.

When Emilia called our fun stupid, I wondered if she thought me stupid, too, for enjoying such things and for suggesting them that day.

I thought I was going to cry, so I said good-bye and ran back home, leaving Emilia desolate in the dark.

Six

The next day dawned clear, with my favorite winter brightness in the air—a sharpness that made me want to open my eyes as wide as they would go and take in all the beauty of the day at once: the poinsettias nodding in the breeze; the late blooming laurels in their crimson and pink plumage; and the glitter of the river, dancing like a liquid diamond under the cries of the soaring gulls.

I was about to run down the stairs and ask Emilia to go fishing with me when the memory of how we had parted the night before settled in me like a tangible weight. Perhaps Emilia no longer wanted to fish either, perhaps that, too, would seem stupid in her eyes. I sighed and walked down the stairs, my hand squeaking on the banisters as I drew it slowly along the dark, polished wood.

I made my way outside and sat on the top step, looking across the street at Marco and his brothers who were lying under their car, banging tools noisily on the pavement while the radio played tangos at full volume.

All three of them suddenly stopped what they were doing, their eyes fixed on the corner of the street.

I saw a stranger standing there, looking up at the dark blue street plaque with white lettering. The stranger was dressed in black from head to foot, but nothing about her suggested mourning. This was the black of riches, the black of ebony and ostrich feathers and Chinese lacquer. Her lips were painted a brilliant red and so, I suspected, were her nails, tucked into a pair of short, black lace gloves. Her eyes were invisible behind her dark glasses.

The Pereira boys froze in mute admiration as she walked past them and approached the Arteagas' house. She rang the doorbell decisively and stood, tapping her small patent leather bag against her thigh.

Seconds later, she was admitted.

Minutes after that, she made a hurried exit.

The blinds of *señora* Francisca's front window were violently flung open and she stuck her head out, opened her mouth, and wailed in a deep, wounded voice that made the hair rise on my arms.

Lilita hurried out, took one look at her friend, and ran down the street, closely followed by Emilia. Marco and his brothers withdrew into their house, and soon *señora* Marta emerged and joined my mother tentatively approaching the Arteagas'. As they neared her house, *señora* Francisca disappeared, and soon various articles were flying out the window—men's suits, shirts, ties, underwear, shoes, a tennis racket—all falling in a heap under the tree outside the front door.

When the rain of objects came to a halt, the women walked slowly into the house, too unnerved to notice that Emilia and I had followed them. Huddled on the floor in a corner of her empty living room, her knees drawn up to her chin, *señora* Francisca rocked, tears soaking her clenched hands.

The women knelt round her and let her cry, occasionally reaching over to wipe her nose or caress her hair. When it seemed that the worst was over, they closed like petals around her sorrow and held her close. She rested her head, exhausted, on Lilita's breast, and *señora* Marta left to make *mate.* A few minutes later she returned, poured the boiling water from the kettle into the large thermos under her arm, and stirred the tightly packed gourd with the silver *bombilla* through which the tea would be filtered as the gourd passed from hand to hand.

"Now tell us who she was," *señora* Marta said, and I wondered if she, too, like Lilita, had been conversing secretly on intimate terms with *señora* Francisca all along.

"Rubén's *puta*," *señora* Francisca sighed.

"Why did she come to you?" *señora* Marta asked in amazement, exchanging glances with the others.

Such things were not done, even by whores.

"He's left her for a younger woman."

"And this was her revenge?" Lilita asked.

"Rubén told her that if ever I found out my daughters live in an empty house because of her, I'd kill him."

"And she hopes you will?" *señora* Marta asked in awe.

Señora Francisca smiled. "Yes." She looked around her as if seeing the room for the first time. "But I won't. You shall see. I will buy furniture instead and make this house look like hers, the one she just showed me pictures of."

For the second time in as many days, Emilia and I slipped out of the Arteagas' house at a loss for words.

"Want to go fishing?" Emilia asked, glancing casually toward the river.

"I'll get my things!" I grinned and raced home.

We walked to the rocks by the river and threw our small jars, baited with bread, into the water.

"I used to think I wanted to grow up soon," I said, as the minnows started circling my jar.

"Me, too," Emilia answered.

"It seems very complicated though."

Emilia shrugged. "It's not easy being any age, I suppose."

"But such decisions . . . I mean, what will *señora* Arteaga do? How will she live with her husband now? And how can she live without him?"

"I will never allow that to happen to me," Emilia said. "I will always work for myself."

I was silent for a long time. "Emilia," I said at last, "is anyone you know happy?"

Emilia considered this. "Like in the movies, you mean?"

"Yes. You know how in the movies problems seem so . . . so . . ."

"Simple?"

"Simpler to solve anyway. Ours are so complicated, so big."

Emilia looked at me. "I always thought you were happy."

I nodded, unable to explain the weight that hung within me, the responsibility I felt for not having been born a boy, able to save the family.

"There was a time," I said, "when I didn't think much, *sabés?* When the family's problems had nothing to do with me. But one day I heard Sofía and Carmen talking, and now I know that it's my fault my mother and father are always worried."

"What have you done?"

I shrugged, remembering my cousins' words.

"*Tío* Javier told me that we can't go to Copacabana with our friends this year," Sofía had said.

"Why not?" Carmen asked.

"He says he has to save up for our weddings. And I imagine that even Magdalena will find someone to marry her when she's old enough. Anyway, *tío* Javier has to pay for it all, and he says he can't if he sends us to Copacabana every year."

"I wish Magdalena had been a boy," Carmen sighed.

"So does everybody."

"I think I've been a burden," I said to Emilia. "They wanted a boy."

In the days that followed, the *barrio* was unusually quiet, the neighbors treading round the Arteagas' with the care and delicacy accorded a family when it went reaping in the pastures of its private sorrows.

Eventually, *señora* Francisca gathered her daughters to her and told them about their father. Together, they went to Montevideo's most expensive antique dealer and furnished the house in the bygone finery of old Spanish mansions. As soon as the furniture had arrived and the bills had been delivered to *señor* Rubén's place of business, they had the locks changed and forbade him the house.

He stood for a long time one night, knocking softly on the door, pleading with his wife to let him in. Several pairs of eyes watched from darkened rooms in the houses all around. When he received no response, he adjusted his hat, put his hands in his pockets, and went whistling down the street toward the river.

From that day forward, *señora* Francisca worked every day. She learned to knit on a machine—sweaters, cardigans, shawls, dresses, and scarves. She was up before light to knit until it was time to see her daughters off to school. Then she sat at her machine until dark, using every *peso* she made from the sale of her wares to provide the family with the comforts they had lived so long without.

Seven

As winter gave way to spring and the climbing roses in our garden covered the walls with bursts of pink, it was possible to imagine that summer would come again, and with it the blessed release from school. Meanwhile, Emilia and I had to be content with spending as much of each weekend together as family obligations permitted.

One Saturday morning, as I was leaving my house to pick up Emilia for an outing to the zoo, I saw a small white hand-kerchief waving from Cora's window. I waved back and ran down the street.

Cora leaned out. "Mamma has gone shopping for the day! Hannah is left in charge and says I may play outside on such a beautiful day!"

I gave a whoop of delight and clapped my hands. "Emilia and I are going to the zoo!"

"I will come with you!"

She disappeared for a moment and then emerged from the front door dressed beautifully as always, in tailored pale gray slacks with matching jacket trimmed in black velvet.

We ran up the street toward Emilia's apartment and knocked on her door. Lilita opened it. A handkerchief was tied around her head and an apron hung limply from her thin waist.

"¡Lilita, mirá! ¡Es Cora!"

Emilia joined her mother at the door, and I thought she

looked tired. There were dark circles under her eyes and she did not smile when she saw us. I wondered if Lilita had been out again the night before.

Lilita returned silently to the kitchen as Emilia slipped out, closing the door behind her.

"Cora can come with us today!" I said. "Did you remember the bread?"

Emilia held up a paper bag. "Did you remember the fruit?"

I patted the pockets of my coat. "Bananas and grapes."

We jumped on a bus and rode the short distance to the city zoo. There were few people there. We walked slowly round the sunken enclosure where the rheas lived, then leaned over the rock wall and fed them bread crusts before moving on to see the hippopotamus lying in his pool, his ears, nose, and eyes partly visible above the murky water.

The seals were barking, and Emilia and Cora wanted to watch them being fed.

"I must see Tomasito first," I said.

"Who is Tomasito?" Cora asked.

"The elephant."

"He is Magdalena's *novio*," Emilia said.

Cora laughed. "Then I must meet him! When is the wedding, Magdalena?"

I did not like being teased about the elephant. I had never been able to make Emilia understand the special bond I felt with him. He had been born here in the Montevideo zoo and all the schoolchildren had been invited to participate in a contest to name him. I had just started school then, and the birth of the little elephant and thinking of a name for him had been the only things that made school bearable.

As soon as he saw me, Tomasito moved away from his house and came toward us.

"Watch out! Watch out!" Emilia said. "He's coming across the moat!"

I waved my banana.

"Magdalena!" Emilia implored. "Stop it! He's going to cross the moat!"

I laughed, peeled the banana, and threw it to Tomasito. The elephant took it delicately in his trunk and put it in his mouth.

Emilia was livid. "That was irresponsible, Magdalena. He could have come across and then what would we have done?"

The elephant finished eating and renewed his cautious testing of the moat. Emilia jumped back. "He thinks we have more bananas! Run! Run!"

I shook my head. "He doesn't think that." I jumped over the low rail and reached across the moat until the elephant's trunk touched my hand. The warmth of his breath on my palm made me oblivious to Emilia's distress.

"Magdalena, come back here!" Emilia was crying now. "I'm getting a guard!" She raced off down the graveled path with Cora following.

"*Hola,* Tomasito," I whispered. "How are you? . . . Yes, I know. It's the same with me. . . . But they don't know. . . . Yes, I hear him too. I'll see you next week."

With a farewell puff of breath, the elephant turned and moved calmly back into his house. I climbed back over the low railing and stood, holding my hands together, treasuring Tomasito's soft touch.

Emilia and Cora returned with a guard, and I turned to face them. "I want to see the elephant," I protested. "Why won't he come out?"

The guard looked surprised and glanced suspiciously at Emilia from under his dark eyebrows. There were crumbs on the front of his shirt, and I suspected he had been interrupted during his *mate* break.

"Did you climb over this?" he asked, gesturing at the rail.

"I can read!" I replied, looking affronted. "It says here: 'Be so kind as to remain on this side of the fence.'"

The guard pulled my hair playfully and smiled, revealing a large gap between his front teeth. I smiled back. *"Bueno, preciosa,"* he said. "Throw a rock at him or something, maybe he'll come out then." He walked off whistling, and Emilia turned on me.

"You just made a fool of me!"

"I didn't mean to, Emilia."

"Just because men get stupid when they see you, you think you can do anything you want!"

"No, I don't! What are you talking about?"

"You know perfectly well. When men get around you they become idiotic. You could have asked that guard to *let* you in there and he would have done it!"

"No, he wouldn't!"

Emilia turned away in exasperation. "Sometimes you make me so angry I could kill you. Why do you always have to visit the elephant?"

"I understand the elephant, Emilia. He likes me. I can't come to the zoo and not see the elephant. We know each other."

"That is ridiculous! Elephants are dangerous! You have no sense of danger! Do you even know what I'm talking about?"

I was surprised by her anger and shook my head.

"It's the same at the beach! You swim out too far. The waves don't scare you. You ride your bicycle in front of buses!"

"Do I?"

"Yes! Yes! You do!"

"I didn't know it worried you."

Emilia burst into tears. "If you get killed, I will have no one!"

Cora put her arms around Emilia and looked at me in surprise.

I was puzzled. "Emilia, I won't get killed."

"That's what you think! You think people don't die!"

"No, no, it isn't that. Of course we die. But, Emilia, I'm not going to. Not for a long time. Not until you don't need me any more. I promise you."

"You are so ridiculous! How can you make such promises? You aren't God!"

"Oh, but I am," I said, and Cora gasped. "I know it sounds like blasphemy, but I don't mean it that way. That's why I love the elephant. Because he knows he's God too, like I am."

"Sometimes I think you're crazy, and then because I'm your friend, I think I'm crazy too," Emilia sighed. "You're always getting us into trouble. One day you'll get us killed."

I laughed. "Let's show Cora the rest of the zoo! She can't be gone all day like we can."

Cora, however, had lost interest in the zoo. She wanted to go to the beach and make plans for future escapes. "I have decided," she said, "that I will simply have to start lying to my mother, like the maids do when they want to see their *novios.*"

⁂

"I don't think I like Cora any more," Emilia confessed a few days later.

It took me some time to understand from what Emilia then told me that she had had high hopes that Cora would be like her. She had thought her a quiet, studious girl until that day at the zoo.

"But now I think Cora is just like my mother and you! I don't understand her at all! She has a nice, safe home with predictable parents whose only interest in life is Cora, and here she is planning to lie to them and get herself into God only knows what kind of trouble! And she looked so smug when she told us that her parents would never punish her if they found out! She thinks there's nothing to be afraid of here, that it's not like Europe."

"As she said, here even the elephants are tame," I laughed.

"Magda, I want you to be serious for a minute. Do you know how she got out that day?"

I shook my head.

"She took a large dose of her mother's sleeping medicine and put it in that poor woman's tea. What was her name? The one who'd been in a concentration camp?"

"Hannah?" I said, trying not to laugh.

"That's right. Hannah. She'd been left in charge of Cora while her parents went out, and woke up twenty-four hours later, having no idea what had happened to her! Oh, I know you think that kind of thing is very funny, but I don't! The only thing Cora and I have ended up having in common is our desire for a dog!"

Like Mrs. Allenberg and Lilita, my mother also resisted having pets for many years. Her English father had been fond of animals and her childhood home was overrun with dogs, parrots, and assorted wild species roaming the large garden. It had seemed to her that my grandfather made more fuss over the litters of puppies born all over his house than over his own daughters. My grandmother explained that he could wrestle with the puppies, tumble in the grass with them, and let them lick his ears, while his daughters, in their fine laces and starched eyelet, seemed unapproachable.

My mother as a child had been chased by rheas and soaked by capybaras, shaking themselves after a swim in the stream that ran through their estate, and she was determined that when she married, her home would be a tasteful place, with a white Persian cat on a red velvet cushion perhaps or a canary singing in an arbor. There would be no room there for frivolous flamingos or spiny armadillos. In her home, only humans would breed and never, under any circumstances, would there be cause to discuss the extermination of either fleas or lice.

Sofía and Carmen had convinced her that goldfish neither bred in captivity nor carried fleas. While the latter proved true, the former came into serious question when the aquarium soon contained several more fish than the original four my mother had consented to. My father, who before his marriage had been interested in animals only as hunting trophies, was drawn by his now famous rescue of the seal into a zoological society whose aim was the preservation of the quickly disappearing local wildlife. As a result, my mother had had to accommodate a *chaná* in her patio. Josefa had taken one look at the large bird, with claws on its shoulders and the eyes of a basilisk, and decided to visit her relatives in the interior, leaving my mother temporarily without the help upon which she had relied for almost thirty years.

Josefa told me that she had no objection to *bichos*, she respected all wild creatures, but she had no wish to share her living quarters with them.

Shortly after the removal of the *chaná*, spiders had appeared in the bathtub, and my mother, Sofía, and Carmen could stand no more. My grandmother, *Mamasita*, came to the rescue.

Mamasita told my father that he was a fool for having subjected the women in his house to visiting *bichos* when he knew as well as she that Sofía and Carmen screamed at sight of a cockroach, let alone spiders the size of partridges. She made room for his collection in her capacious house in town and since then an assortment of *bichos* had been lodged there awaiting transfer to the society's preserve.

Mamasita believed that no home could be considered complete unless it was shared by at least one member of another species. Her country estate, Caupolicán, was surrounded by eucalyptus trees, where the green parrots that often plagued farmers lived in large communal nests. At Caupolicán no one was allowed to shoot them, and they multiplied accordingly. Every year, several nestlings fell out, and *Mamasita* raised them on the porch from which they soon flew back to the eucalyptus trees. One bird had been reluctant to return to his noisy home and was given to me on my fifth birthday. My mother's dreams of a tasteful, tranquil home were relegated along with her childhood possessions to one of *Mamasita's* cavernous wardrobes.

When the task of seeing her nieces into established womanhood was absorbing my mother's every waking moment, I brought Pepita home. Pepita had wandered into the grounds of my school and been set upon by a group of boys who thought teasing a puppy a relief from the tedium of having to watch their mates beaten at rugby by a visiting school team.

I had rescued the puppy and brought it home on the school bus. My mother's resistance was weakened by a recent fight with Carmen, and Pepita was soon installed in the house, adding to the general cacophony by barking at Caramba and anything else that moved. Pepita grew exuberant, friendly, and large. When seated, she was regal. Her coat was black and glossy, her ears erect, her paws neat. When in motion, she was the embodiment of chaos.

My cousin Miguel saw her for the first time on one of the rare occasions when Pepita was seated. Miguel was wearing the latest summer fashions and looked resplendent in a suit of ivory-colored linen with a brilliant cravat in my favorite shade of blue. He was not aware that the last time he had called on us I had heard him telling Sofía that he thought me prettier than she was, a remark Sofía considered beneath her notice.

Miguel was leaning on the fireplace looking admiringly at Pepita. "Nice dog," he said, looking down at her from his lofty six feet.

"Yes, she is," I replied.

"Yours?"

I nodded.

"Seems a well-behaved *bicho.*"

I looked at Pepita and believed the dog smiled at me. "Would you like to walk her?" I asked Miguel.

Miguel was a fashion buff, and I had observed him looking through foreign magazines where young men like himself were depicted walking elegant breeds or hunting wild fowl with a trusty canine at their side. We had both inherited our grandfather's light coloring. Miguel flaunted his European heritage and was openly contemptuous of his fellow countrymen, to whom he referred as "the natives," a term which, when used by Miguel, was meant to be derogatory. He was *tía* Aurora's youngest son and a prodigy in her estimation. Those able to view him through less loving eyes found him a wonder only in his monumental self-centeredness. It was widely accepted that he could do much "if only he would try." Miguel rested on this dubious laurel and made no effort in any discernible direction other than his unflagging pursuit of the opposite sex.

He had recently developed an interest in Raquel, who, with her father banished, was sitting on her balcony openly painting her toenails, a fact Miguel would not have failed to notice.

"Do you have a leash for her?" he asked, stooping to pat Pepita on the head.

"A brand new one. I've never used it."

This should have served as a warning to Miguel, but he was too intent on the figure he would soon cut to heed it. I handed him the leash, and he attached it to Pepita's collar. She stood up as he pulled on it and followed him out the door.

Pibe, Marco's dog, happened to be out that day too.

Pibe was also large and exuberant, with ears that flapped when he ran and paws the size of saucers. Just as Miguel stepped outside with Pepita and struck a nonchalant pose on the top step, dangling the leash in one hand, Pibe spotted his rival, the family cat. She did exactly as usual, ran up a tree with a large fork in its trunk and watched from a high branch as Pibe chased her, leapt up the tree, and got stuck in the fork. The effect of the chase on Pepita was electrifying. When the cat rushed by her with Pibe in pursuit, Pepita leapt forward, dragging Miguel with her. He went by Raquel in an ivory streak, his cravat in disarray, and was propelled around the tree at such speed I thought he would turn to butter.

Pibe, meanwhile, started howling. It was his way of calling Marco, and Pepita was driven by the sound to further displays of frenzy. She shot across the street once more, dragging Miguel through a manure patty, up the curb, and back to Pibe's tree. A window was raised at the Pereiras' and Marco looked out.

"What are you doing to my dog?" he shouted at Miguel, who was beyond answering as he tried to disentangle himself from the leash pulled tight across his wrist by Pepita, who at that moment was trying to join Pibe in the tree.

Marco grasped the situation at last and disappeared, soon
to emerge, stepladder in hand. Pepita saw him, recognized a
friend, and calmed down, going up to him to be petted. Miguel
disentangled himself and staggered to my house, where he
collapsed in an easy chair, calling for water.

I decided to make myself scarce and followed Marco into
his house.

The moment I stepped in the door, I smelled *señora* Marta's
mouthwatering pizza.

Señora Marta was an ample woman, voluptuous and pretty,
with a wide, laughing mouth and dark hair, which she wore in a
loose braid down her back. She was a poet and a playwright who
wrote soap operas as a means of augmenting the meager allowance given to her by her husband. She was a gentle dreamer
who had read only Shakespeare during her pregnancies so that
her children would come into the world with a ready appreciation for the finest literature. She had blithely named her
sons Marco Aurelio, Orsino, and Basanio, after characters in
Shakespeare's plays, with no thought for the black eyes, bruised
shins, and missing teeth these names would cause her sons and
any who dared laugh at them.

Her equanimity was unshaken even by her husband, who, in
a parody of old-fashioned lord-of-the-manor behavior, forbade
her soon after their marriage to leave the house unless in the
company of relatives.

Colonel Pereira had recently retired from the army. He was
a large man, tall and broad shouldered, with a black mustache
that hung below his chin, giving him the air of a melancholy
pirate. An ill-advised acquaintance once made the mistake of
complimenting *señora* Marta in her husband's presence and
turned to find himself reflected in horror on the wide and
glistening blade of Colonel Pereira's knife.

Señora Marta and I were great friends, and she greeted me with a cry of joy and a hug.

"I'm sorry about Pepita, *señora* Marta."

"Pepita?" *señora* Marta asked vaguely, extricating some pages of her latest manuscript from the rising pizza dough.

"She chased Pibe again."

"Oh, Pibe . . ." said *señora* Marta, her thoughts elsewhere. "Do you think that a *chica* of say fourteen or fifteen could fall in love with a man of forty?"

I thought of the men that age I knew. "No," I answered.

"Well, my heroine must in order for my ending to work," *señora* Marta said. "What if he were handsome, rich, and kind?"

I thought again. "Do you know anyone who fits that description?"

Señora Marta laughed her wondrously rich laugh, a laugh as generous as the dough she was kneading and as perfumed as the herbs she scattered by the handful into the bubbling mixture on the stove. "No!" she chortled. "If I did, I would have married him myself!" She kissed the top of my head. "You are always a help to me. Did you know that I acknowledge you in the introductions to my plays?"

"Me?" I smiled.

"Yes, you. You'll stay for pizza, no? Marco, come and help Magdalena lay the table."

"You don't have to, Marco, I can do it," I said as he appeared reluctantly in the doorway. He was so handsome that he intimidated me. He had his mother's dark hair, only his was curly and framed his head with a softness I had seen only in old paintings. His long, dark lashes and finely shaped eyebrows set off the amber of his eyes, but it was his mouth I could not help staring at. At the time, I was too young to understand the hunger it evoked in me. I knew only that in Marco Aurelio Pereira's presence I felt inadequate and plain. Sometimes, if he was absorbed in a task, I would find myself staring at him, wondering how anyone could be so perfectly beautiful as he and so unaware of it. He gave no sign of noticing me, and it would be many years before I discovered that he often lay on his bed, his window blind cracked open, watching me as I ran down the street to Emilia's or sat in the poinsettia tree drying my hair in the sun. He would tell himself that I was only fourteen and he nineteen and he had no business thinking of me at all, but logic had not helped to curb his desire.

"Marco Aurelio is taking me to the Cerro this afternoon," *señora* Marta said. "Would you like to come?"

I had not been to the Cerro since my escapade there at age nine. "I'd love to!" I said.

"When we've had lunch, go and ask your mother. We'll leave at four."

Marco left the table to refill the water jug, and I lowered my voice. "Why does Marco look so sad today, *señora* Marta?" I asked, helping myself to a large slice of thick pizza.

Señora Marta sighed. "I should never have named him after a tragic hero. He takes it to heart."

"I do not, *mamá.* My name has nothing to do with how I feel," Marco said, putting the jug down hard and spilling water on the checkered cloth.

"I should have named you Hamlet. You are just as moody. But I imagine you'd object to being named after the greatest hero in the English theater!"

"A spoiled prince who sees ghosts and is jealous of his uncle is not my idea of a hero," Marco answered, making me stare as he put a tumbler to his lips and opened his mouth to drink.

"Youth!" his mother said contemptuously. "What can you know of Hamlet's feelings?"

"He must have been about my age when he went *loco*.
I probably understand him better than you do."

"Who *is* your idea of a hero, Marco?" I asked.

"Harriet Tubman."

"What can a woman who helped escaped slaves possibly
have to do with you, Marco Aurelio?" *señora* Marta said, clicking her tongue impatiently. "This is all because he's upset at his
father," she said to me.

"Are you, Marco?" I asked, wondering if it was Colonel
Pereira who had inflicted the dark bruise under Marco's
right eye.

Marco looked at me directly for the first time since he had
joined us at the table. "He wants me to go into the army."

"And you don't want to go?"

Marco shook his head. "I want to study political science."

"And reform us all," his mother sighed.

"What's wrong with the army?" I asked. "It must be fun to
be a soldier."

"Marco Aurelio doesn't want to have fun. He wants to make
Communists of us. Like those dreadful Tupamaros."

There was a moment of silence. The word *Tupamaro* was
usually spoken in quiet and careful tones. No one quite knew
who the Tupamaros were, but their crisscrossed star with a T in
its center was seen more and more frequently emblazoned on
walls and underpasses. It was rumoured that the Tupamaros
were some of the most ruthless and well-educated men and
women in Uruguay and that their numbers were growing daily.
Their aim was to take over the government.

"Do you really want us to become Communists, Marco?"
I asked with awe.

"Of course not," Marco answered. "Although there are many
worse things we could be."

"Oh?" his mother asked. "Such as?"

"We could be right-wing fanatics, like you."

"He calls me a fanatic because I see through Communism."

"The only thing you see through are the rose-colored glasses you wear."

"I, Magdalena, believe that the United States wants genuinely to assist us. Look at all the loans they wish to make to us so that we can join the twentieth century and become civilized. Marco Aurelio is a cynic. He thinks the loans are motivated by greed."

"I think worse than that, *mamá*."

"What could be worse?" I asked.

"Manipulation. Rockefeller isn't offering to lend us money because he thinks we'll use it to improve ourselves. He's mortgaging our future, ensuring that we'll be too poor to rule ourselves, leaving our resources free for him to plunder."

"Cynical, cynical! I don't know where he gets it," *señora* Marta cried.

⚜

My mother had no objection to my visiting the Cerro with *señora* Marta, so I changed from my blue jeans into a pair of black trousers and pulled a red cotton sweater over my head. Then I looked around my room for something to take to Gabriela. Ever since I had seen her hut, I had appropriated every household item my family discarded, hoarding it in my room until I saw Gabriela and could present it to her. Over the years, I had given Gabriela rugs; chipped china; a pipe rack one of the uncles no longer wanted; a chess set with a missing rook; and last year, when *Mamasita* had ordered a new eiderdown for me, I had taken great delight in handing my old pink-and-white flowered one to Gabriela and imagining it brightening her hut and warming its occupants.

There was not much for Gabriela today. In my closet lay a hat Sofía had discarded and a pot with a broken handle. Neither seemed appropriate, and I did not want to go to the Cerro empty-handed. Nor did I want to take discards today, much as Gabriela rejoiced in receiving them. I opened the top drawer of the little night table by my bed. I had been saving my money to buy Elvis Presley's new record. Half of what I had would buy a big bunch of flowers. I suspected that no one had ever given Gabriela flowers. I hesitated. It would take a long time to save up that money again. I fingered the five hundred *pesos,* imagining Gabriela's delighted face. Then I brushed my hair more carefully than usual and ran round the corner to the florist. He had been selling my family flowers for most of his life and took a personal interest in our affairs. He always asked for details regarding the occasion and the recipients of the flowers before recommending something from his stock. When I told him who the flowers were for, he was puzzled. He put his hands in the pockets of his gray flannel trousers and swayed back and forth on his heels, surveying the overflowing receptacles full of bird-of-paradise, carnations, roses, lilies, and camellias.

"Does she own a vase?" he asked.

"I doubt it," I replied.

"So do I," he said, eyeing the stately lilies. "I carry no plastic flowers . . ."

I shook my head. "I don't like them anyway."

Suddenly his face brightened. "*¡Sí!*" he cried. "*¡Claro! ¡Las flores mejicanas!*" He held up a finger, asked me to wait, and disappeared through a door behind the cash register.

Moments later, he stuck his head back in. "Now, *señorita*

Magdalena, you will never have seen anything like this. Your lady mother would never consider them for your home, but—" and with a flourish he jumped out of the door almost concealed by a bunch of the largest, most brilliant flowers I had ever seen. They were made of paper and resembled no real flowers I knew of. There was no doubt that they were just the thing.

"They will last forever!" the florist laughed. "And nothing could be more *alegre* than these colors. It will be like bringing *Carnaval* to her."

I nodded with delight. "But how much do they cost?"

The florist looked at me from under his black eyebrows and then glanced at the flowers. "I have had them for a long time . . . They are too garish for my clientele . . . How much do you have?"

"Five hundred *pesos.*"

"For five hundred *pesos* you can have half of them. How is that?"

I smiled. "Thank you, *señor* Paredes. Half is about all I could carry anyway!"

I chose six gigantic blooms in mixed colors of yellow, red, purple, pink, bright blue, and orange. Several people turned to stare as I walked back to *señora* Marta's.

Señora Marta emerged looking comfortable and cool in a long silken poncho that billowed in the wind as she walked down the street, giving her the appearance of a majestic ship in full sail. She gasped in amazement at sight of the flowers. They were magnificent, she said, and she would go to *señor* Paredes herself tomorrow and acquire the rest of his stock for her writing room. Marco said nothing, but smiled at me in a way that made me blush with pleasure.

At the corner, we boarded a crowded bus, and *señora* Marta

and I sat together at the front while Marco found a seat toward
the rear. The flowers excited much commentary, and I had to
explain several times where I had bought them. *Señor* Paredes
might find himself doing a brisk business in paper flowers,
señora Marta said.

As we wound our way through the outlying neighborhoods,
I studied the houses. They were as well maintained as my own,
smaller and more crowded perhaps, but clean and neat. It was
not until we reached the hill itself that the poverty became ob-
vious. Almost from one block to another, the houses lost their
solidity. Crumbling walls sagged under the weight of vines
gone wild, and grasses grew between the broken tiles of the
pavements. Horses, set free to forage, crossed the streets in
search of food. Lean and small like the inhabitants of these
neighborhoods, they bore the same look of sturdy independence. They were confined only when in harness, and I had
sometimes seen them, after the day's work was done, being led
by their owners into the river for a swim before resuming the
long trek back to the mountain.

"Do you remember the day Gabriela brought me home
with Emilia and you went off with the baby?" I asked, turning
to *señora* Marta.

Marco, who as the bus emptied had joined us in a seat behind
ours, leaned forward. "She thought we'd taken him."

"Poor people," *señora* Marta sighed. "Poor, poor people.
Imagine believing that someone could take a baby and not
return him."

"She believed it," Marco said, "because it happens."

"But your mother would never do such a thing!" I cried.

"No, but there are those who would."

"Who, Marco?" I asked him. "Who would steal a baby?
And why?"

"That baby would have fetched four thousand *pesos* on the adoption black market."

"Marco Aurelio," his mother sighed again, "how is it that you know such things?"

With a sudden jolt, the bus stopped at the foot of the Cerro, and Marco got off first to help his mother and me down. We stood together for a moment as the bus pulled away, looking up the steep street leading to the fortress on the hill. Marco and I each took one of *señora* Marta's arms, and the three of us climbed the mountain.

When we reached the walls of the fortress, *señora* Marta took a notebook and pen out of her capacious bag and went to talk to one of the soldiers guarding the entrance. I saw him grin as *señora* Marta told him she would base one of the characters in her next *radio novela* on him.

Marco went to sit on a large rock overlooking the huts. He sat still for so long that I wondered if he had fallen asleep. I approached him quietly, but he did not move, and to my surprise, I saw that there were tears in his eyes. Not knowing what else to do, I made a crown out of the tiny wild daisies growing all over the hillside, and when I had finished, I put it on his head. He used it as an excuse to wipe his eyes and turn away, laughing.

"Marco," I said, "how did you get that bruise on your cheek?"

He shrugged. "At school. I got in a fight."

"Did you march with the strikers again?"

Marco sighed. "Yes. We marched with the sugar cane workers."

"My mother says if they keep on making the American owners angry, they might stop buying our sugar cane, and then where would the workers be?"

"You're too young to understand, Little Lion," he said, leaning over to pull my hair.

"It's time you stopped calling me that," I said, slapping at his hand. "I can't even remember why you started."

Marco reminded me that years before, when the Russians invaded Hungary, the high school and university students massed in large numbers around the Russian Embassy to protest the act. I clearly recalled angry groups of young people running through the streets near my house avoiding the police and how the wife of a Russian official had been caught outside the embassy compound. I had often seen her walking by in her outdated clothes and old-fashioned hairdo, her gray coat flapping in the wind, tight braids firmly in place, haloing the round, pretty face. The woman spoke no Spanish as far as I knew, but she would wave shyly if she saw me in the poinsettia tree and had once offered me a sweet out of the shopping basket hanging on her arm.

A group of angry students had cornered her, shouting insults, and backed her into the gate leading to my front garden.

"You came out of the house like a maniac," Marco said, "telling them to leave her alone and pushing them away."

"They laughed at me."

"Yes, Little Lion, because you were so small and so fierce, but they also backed off."

"*You* laughed at me, Marco."

"I was a clumsy boy of fourteen who didn't know any other way of showing my admiration for you than by nicknaming you Little Lion and laughing at your ferocity."

I felt myself blushing. It was the first time Marco had ever paid me a compliment. "Tell me about the workers and about Gabriela's baby," I said, changing the subject.

Marco looked down the hill at the huts. "Remember how she hugged Gervasio and cried?"

I nodded.

"Next day, when she came to our house, I tried to talk to her, but she was afraid of me."

"Why? Did she think you'd sell her baby?"

Marco smiled sadly. "No. She could think of only one reason why a man of my class would talk to her."

I looked away.

"I am embarrassing you. I'm sorry."

I shook my head. "Ignore me. I really want to know."

"What I wanted," Marco said, "was to understand how I could help her. Did she want to work? How did she get reduced to begging? Where were her parents? Who was Gervasio's father and where was he? I don't know why I am so curious about the poor. My earliest memories of these cardboard tenements are crystal clear. Unequivocal. I have always known that I belong here, Magda, not in Pocitos with its tree-lined streets and uniformed maids. That's why I want to study political science. I want the power to help. Remember Battle?"

"The president?"

"Yes. He came to power fifty years ago, after the civil wars. His social programs were models of equality, of opportunity."

Marco told me of Battle's national health program, of his pension plans and child-welfare projects. Of how he had wanted to guarantee birth-to-death security for every citizen. He told me how, even now, when the promise of those enlightened social programs lay unfulfilled in the huts scattered like forgotten debris on this Cerro, he believed that Utopia had been within our reach, and he wanted to know where we had gone wrong. Marco wanted to understand how a country like ours, with a free university education guaranteed to all its citizens, with a stable population in spite of the dictates of the

Catholic Church, with a climate congenial to all life, how such a country could be slipping gradually into foreign debt and losing the support of its people.

I had no idea what to answer. Marco looked at me and seemed convinced that I was listening with an intensity equal to his. He turned to face me, and I felt for the first time the full force of his personality.

"Sometimes, when my father takes me to visit our family's land in the interior, and the *cerros* roll away, far away, to the horizon, I feel such pain that I can't breathe. I have to ask my father to stop the car so I can get out and listen to the wind whistling in the valleys. The only sign that human beings have been there is that narrow, dusty road, winding and dipping its way as far as my eyes can see. Above me, the *gavilanes* soar on the wind; below me, the grass ripples, dotted every so often with sheep, bleating to one another across the green divides. My father sees it only as a place to plunder. I see Eden and want desperately to protect it. My father is a predator." Marco stopped and looked at me intently. "Do you have any idea what I'm talking about?"

I nodded slowly. It was very important to me to say the right thing. I wanted to be honest, but I was afraid that if I spilled my own thoughts too hastily, if I let him know how like him I felt myself to be, he might think me childish and turn away from me, leaving me without the clarity and passion of that moment when I felt so close to him.

"I understand the pain. I feel it when we travel inland too. Once, when I was at my grandmother's, I went exploring by myself up a small river. I saw a turtle, and fish swam right up to my legs to see what I was. I lay under a tree and felt as if I'd found something very precious that I wanted to protect. I didn't know anyone else felt things that way."

"My mother thinks it's melancholy. Really, it's despair. Because, you see, Little Lion, sometimes I think we're beyond help. I think we've gone so far along the path of our own destruction that no one can save us. And yet, whenever I come to the Cerro, I know that I must try."

"Is that why you march?"

"It's why I live, Little Lion. Because helpless as we are, we are each other's only hope. During the last march, a child died. Of malnutrition. 'Impossible!' the politicians say. 'Such things do not happen in Uruguay. We are the Switzerland of South America!' Do you know what the workers are demanding? An eight-hour workday and a livable wage."

"Why are they not getting it?"

"Because cheap sugar is vital to the economies of the North, and the men making fortunes out of imported sugar from Latin America do not give a damn about the people who work in the cane fields. Slavery may be outlawed, but the slave owner's mentality is not. And in the North, they have discovered two kinds of sugar. The kind we produce, which sweetens what we put into our stomachs, and the kind they produce, which poisons our souls."

"Explain that to me."

"I believe, Magdalena, that the reason Americans and Europeans are so successful is that they have found a way of dulling the senses by satisfying them. If you can persuade people that what they need in order to be happy are material possessions and then you make those possessions available to them, enriching yourself in the process, you have found a way of controlling people's minds that any ideologue would envy." Marco stood up suddenly. "Enough. I am getting carried away." He laughed. "My brothers tell me that when I start on this subject I bore them to tears. And I would not bring tears of any kind to eyes that are the color of the sky over the moors at twilight." He turned away. "Which is Gabriela's house? It's time we took her these," he gestured to the flowers on the grass by my side.

I was not ready to stop. We had only just begun. I wanted him to sit on the hillside and talk to me forever. But I did not know how to make him stay.

Together, we gathered the paper flowers, and I reached up to remove the crown of daisies from his head and put it on the ground. I walked ahead of him and did not see him pick it up and slip it into his shirt pocket. That he would tell me much, much later.

I had not visited Gabriela in the years since I had hidden with Emilia in the cart and did not remember which house was hers.

Marco laughed and kept walking down the hill. He was soon surrounded by children and began to distribute *caramelos* from his pockets. The children unwrapped the sweets and popped them in their mouths, reaching out their hands for more. Several of them had red hair. I asked one of them where Gabriela lived, and the child pointed to a small hut nearby.

Memories flooded back, and I found myself wondering if the little plates still hung on Gabriela's wall. I was surprised at the pang with which I remembered them.

We found Gabriela at the back, washing baby clothes in a tub. A toddler played with a puppy nearby, and a baby lay on an old towel at Gabriela's feet. I had lost count of her children by now. She herself had changed little over the years. Her body was as lithe and her hair as red as ever. The only difference was in her eyes, grown more tired since I first knew her, and in her smile, which she now hid behind her hands. She had lost several teeth, one for each baby, she always said.

She dried her hands on her apron when she saw us and came to greet us. She was so delighted with the flowers that she ran to show them to her neighbors, leaving the children in our care. When she returned, we sat on the grass, drinking *mate*, until Marco glanced up at the fortress and saw his mother waving.

As Marco and Gabriela walked ahead, I allowed myself to slip behind, pretending to play with the puppy, and glanced quickly in the window. The plates were still there, as were all the things I had given her over the years, including the pink-and-white eiderdown under which two children slept in the chill of evening.

Eight

And then, Che came.

He was to speak at the University, and I was determined to go. My parents forbade it. Che Guevara was a revolutionary terrorist they said, and trouble followed wherever he went. I pleaded with Marco to escort me, but he was equally adamant in his refusal.

"No, Little Lion," he said. "I will not take you to see Che."

"How am I to become a better citizen if you protect me this way, Marco?"

He smiled his irresistible smile. "By listening to me."

"You are not Che Guevara."

"I'm a better dancer," Marco laughed.

"Be serious, Marco."

"I am serious all the time. When I'm with you, I like to laugh."

"Am I so funny?"

Marco shook his head. "No, Little Lion, but there is a fountain of joy in you that brings out the joy in me."

"And it would make me very joyous to hear Che," I insisted.

"Listen to him on the radio."

"It's not the same, Marco."

"It is safer."

"What could happen?" I pleaded.

"Magda, listen to me. The University is very different from

the world you inhabit. You're not old enough to encounter such differences yet."

"You only say that because now you go to the University and you think you're so smart!"

"I am smart. Smart enough to know that at this event things will get out of hand. Rocks will be thrown; windows broken. The police will crack a few heads. The Americans will see to it that a visit from Che Guevara does not go peacefully. And I will see to it that yours is not among the heads that will be broken."

"If I'm with you, you can protect me."

Marco laughed heartily. I believed he was laughing at me because he thought my desire to see Che Guevara naive and pretentious. What Marco did not know was that I was aware that the police would be watching him very closely. He was well known to them already, and while he thought it was just his good fortune that had prevented him from being arrested or beaten up, *señora* Marta told me one day that her husband was exhausting his contacts and his influence to keep Marco out of jail and that she was not at all sure how long she could count on him to do so. Colonel Pereira was saying it was time to let Marco learn a lesson. I was angry enough at Marco to tell him this, until the memory of our afternoon at the Cerro returned. I remembered what he had said about bringing tears to my eyes and knew that I would never knowingly hurt him either.

I was determined, however, to hear Che, so I tried to talk Emilia into accompanying me. Emilia was not only disinterested in Che, she was vehemently opposed to him. Lilita's nighttime excursions had stopped not long after the conversation with *señora* Francisca that we had overheard, and Emilia believed her mother had withdrawn from her secret activities. She wanted to do nothing to rekindle Lilita's interest in

revolution. Only the discovery that her mother had actually
been assisting in planning Che's visit made Emilia agree to ac-
company me. She overheard a telephone conversation regarding
these plans and confronted her mother, who insisted that
Emilia had misunderstood. The plans she had overheard had
nothing to do with Che, Lilita assured her. Emilia did not believe her. She decided to come with me, hoping to catch her
mother red-handed.

I told my mother that Emilia and I were going to the
Rambla to have tea at one of the tea shops there. To appease
Emilia's conscience, we really did have tea before taking the bus
downtown.

❧

Banners of welcome were flying for *el* Che, many of them con-
demning *Yanqui* interventions in Latin America. Some made
references to the CIA, an organization about which Emilia and
I knew nothing.

The crowd of students outside the University buildings was
euphoric. They climbed on the lamp posts, the statues, the
marble columns, waving flags and cheering as Che Guevara,
handsome and austere in his olive drab uniform, made his way
to the auditorium. We followed the crowd inside, and for several minutes, the cheering was so loud that Emilia covered her
ears. As Che raised his arms high above his head, a silence fell
on the crowd, and only the occasional creaking of a door broke
the stillness that followed.

"*Compañeros,*" Che said, and the cheering broke out again and
again. He would say a few words, and the room would ring
with voices hungry for the power he represented. He encouraged us to stand up and say no to the rich and their interests, to

the military "gorillas" and their Nazi methods, and to the giant that crouched far to the north, always ready to crush the voices of the people whenever its profits were threatened.

Then he grew quieter and so did the crowd, sensing that he was about to say something important.

"*Compañeros*," he began, "in spite of all that we have suffered, in spite of the wrongs done us daily, in spite of having to stand by and watch hunger and poverty lay waste our nations, in spite of all this, while there are legal methods of reform available to us, it is wrong for us to take up arms. We must care for this democracy and not fire the first shot."

The crowd sighed as if in pain.

"We want to," he continued. "Oh, how we want to do unto others as has been done unto us and rip the boot of oppression from the foot of the *Yanquis* and their flunkies. But we must not. Not while we can talk like the civilized people we are. Not while we can live the letter of the law of the *Yanqui* Constitution while its representatives violate it daily on this continent. Not while we can stand proud and say—we are a free people! The image of instability and democratic ineptness with which we have been painted is an image created by the painter—the *Yanqui* painter who interferes daily in the politics and economic stability of the great nations of Latin America and supports only those who spout the ideology they wish to hear, turning a blind eye to the human rights' abuses of which they are daily guilty. Let us show them that we understand the precepts of democracy far better than they do and shall use their very forces against them in our peaceful struggle for liberty and justice for all!"

Che's speech drew to a close, and the cheers rang out as people hugged one another and threw their hats to the ceiling. Che relaxed and smiled for the first time. As he waved farewell

to the jubilant crowd, a shot reverberated through the hall and
panic spread among the students. Emilia and I were far from
the stage and could not see who had been shot. The crowd
around us turned and surged out into the lobby, down the
broad steps of the University building, and into the street. The
mounted police, thinking a riot had broken out, went into action. Hooves clattered on the pavement, sabers were drawn, and
Emilia and I were borne forward in a flood of humanity.

As the chase intensified, those in the rear fell or ran away
from the crowd. The hooves and the cries grew nearer and once
we were almost separated as a panic-stricken woman tried to
run between us. We hung onto one another and managed to
keep running together until we passed a dark side street. I
swerved and pulled Emilia into it. We almost fell over a girl
hunched on all fours in the gutter. Emilia and I froze for a moment, mesmerized by the blood dripping from the girl's head
into a glistening pool at our feet. As we took her arms and
tried to raise her, we saw that it was Cora.

"Go away! Go! They'll come after you!" Cora urged us.

The sounds of screaming and horses' hooves rang out again
behind us.

"Go! Run!" Cora said, but Emilia and I hung on to her, half
pulling, half pushing her into a sheltering doorway. People ran
past us, throwing rocks at the infuriated policeman bearing
down on them. They disappeared round the next corner, and
the three of us huddled, shaking with cold and fear, until the
noises died down in the distance.

"What shall we do?" Cora whispered.

"We can't stay here," Emilia said. "You need a doctor."

I stuck my head out of the doorway. "I'll try to find a taxi."

"I'll come with you!" Emilia cried.

"You mustn't leave Cora. I'll find help. If a policeman sees me, I'll tell him I was shopping and got caught downtown when the riots started."

I stepped out into the dark little side street. I saw the moon, ominous and cold, shining in a pool of Cora's blood, and I shivered, drawing my coat tightly around myself. Most of the streetlights had been shattered and there was darkness everywhere I turned. I believed that 18 de Julio lay to my left. The main avenue leading through the downtown area was usually a place of bustling activity until the early hours of the morning. I conjured up a picture of its friendly street vendors and laughing crowds to give myself the courage to step into the forbidding darkness ahead. My heels clicked noisily on the tiles as I approached the plaque on the wall above me. I looked up and read the street name. I had been right. 18 de Julio lay ahead and to my left. I walked for two blocks without seeing anyone and was beginning to feel calmer when a motorcycle roared up behind me.

"¡*Alto!*" the policeman said. "Up against the wall! Now! Move!"

"I'm lost!" I cried. "I got caught up in the crowds. What has been happening?"

"The wall! Now!" and the policeman took me by the wrist and swung me against the rough concrete. "Spread your legs!"

"Officer, I—" I stopped, a cry of surprise caught in my throat. His hands were under my skirt, groping between my legs. The sting of his fingers penetrating me made me turn and hit him with all my strength with the brass buckle of my handbag. He reeled in surprise and fell, a hand to his bleeding mouth. Before he could recover, I kicked him in the stomach, discarded my high-heeled shoes, and ran along the broken pavement toward the lights ahead.

"Here! This way!" a voice called from an open doorway, and

without a thought, I threw myself into the dim opening where a group of people huddled together. They hushed me as I fell, and the door eased shut behind me. Moments later, the sounds of a motorcycle could be heard outside the window just above our heads. I froze in fear and looked around me to see how the others were reacting. Two young men and a woman stared back at me from the narrow lobby in which we crouched, their eyes as fearful as mine.

As the sounds of the motorcycle died away, a sigh of relief escaped us, and we moved for the first time.

"I have to get help," I said, "my friend is hurt."

"Where?"

"A few blocks down, on Gaboto."

"We'll walk you there," one young man said. "Where are your shoes?"

"I kicked them off so I could run."

"Here, Laura, give her yours," the boy said, turning to the young woman.

"Oh, no, please, I can walk barefoot," I said.

Laura laughed. "On the beaches of Punta del Este perhaps."

"*Vamos,* Laura, she's just a kid."

"The rich ones learn how to take advantage of us early."

"*Dale,* Laura," the other young man intervened. "You live nearby, and the kid's feet are bleeding."

Laura tossed her hair out of her eyes and stooped to remove her shoes. In the dim light I could see that the sneakers were cheap and well worn. This pair of shoes might be the only ones she owned. "I will return them," I said. "Where do you live?"

Laura looked at me with eyes as old as poverty. "Nowhere your mother would let you visit."

"Let's go," the boy repeated. "*¿Julio, venís?*"

"Vengo, Fernando," he replied, taking the shoes from Laura and putting them on my feet. *"Bueno, nena,"* he said gently as he tied the laces.

The shoes were too small for me, and I winced as the three of us emerged carefully onto the street. In my effort to escape the policeman, I had not been careful where I stepped and my feet were cut by broken glass from the shattered streetlights.

"Who will see Laura home?" I asked.

Julio laughed. *"She* was protecting *us!"*

"I have to find a taxi."

"Forget that. They'll all be home, listening to the riots on the radio. Where do you live? Carrasco or Pocitos?"

"In Pocitos."

"You'll have to walk. How badly hurt is your friend?"

"I'm not sure. Her head is bleeding."

"I'll have a look at her," Fernando offered.

Julio laughed again. "He thinks he's a doctor already. He's in his second year of Medicine."

We walked in silence, hugging the wall, checking every few seconds over our shoulders for signs of others on the street.

"Who was shot today?" I asked. "Not Che?"

Julio shook his head. "One of us. Were you there?"

"Of course! What happened?"

"The Russians will say the Americans did it," Julio answered with a shrug.

"And the Americans will accuse the Russians," Fernando added.

"But why? Why was a student shot?"

"Because Che came advocating restraint. If we succeed in doing what he asks and redistribute the wealth without bloodshed, then all of Latin America will fall to the people."

"So who shot the student?"

Julio and Fernando glanced at each other. "The powerful," they said.

This answer did not satisfy me, and I wanted to know more, but we had arrived at our destination, and I could see Emilia's worried face peering out at us from the doorway.

"Where's the taxi? What happened?"

I told her.

"You saved my life tonight," I said, turning to the two young men.

They grinned. "Not your life, but your honor certainly! That cop was hot!"

Shame overcame me, and I felt myself blush. "You saw him—?"

"Oh, no, not clearly, no, no!" Fernando said hurriedly. "We saw him stop you and we knew . . . You see, you're a girl and . . . Well, we knew, that's all."

I took their outstretched hands. "Thank you."

"What's your name?" they asked.

"Magdalena Ortega Grey."

"Ortega Grey? Like the landowners?"

"Yes."

"*¡Ay, ay!* We'd better not tell the others!" They laughed. "Well, beautiful girls have a right to be rescued, even if their name is Ortega Grey! Be careful now. Stick to the side streets where there are shadows and hallways."

Fernando glanced briefly at Cora's wound. "She'll need stitches, but she can make it home."

They waved and disappeared into the night.

"Do your parents know you're out alone, Cora?" I asked, as the three of us walked arm in arm into the bitter wind.

Cora shook her head. "Of course not! I told them I was going to the synagogue."

I noticed that her voice had changed and remembered how, long ago, Emilia and I had tried to speak as Cora used to do, with a lilting softness. Now her voice sounded harsh and angry.

"I had to see Che! This was a historic event!"

"Why does he interest you?" Emilia asked. "He seemed rather odd to me."

Cora looked at her in surprise. "I am a socialist. We all are in my family. The socialists saved my parents in Holland. They risked everything to get them safely out of Europe. When I knew Che Guevara was going to speak, I had to come."

"What did he have to do with the war in Europe?" Emilia persisted, still puzzled.

"Nothing. But he stands for the same things the socialists there did."

"We're all going to be in a lot of trouble," I sighed. "Our mothers think we're having tea with friends."

We passed under a street lamp and I saw that Cora was very pale. "Emilia, there's a bench over there. Let's stop for a minute."

"We'll freeze!"

"Cora needs to rest." I took off my coat and covered Cora's legs with it as we sat huddled together in a small, dark plaza. I could hear Cora's teeth chattering.

"Magdalena, it's very late," Emilia pleaded. "I have to get home."

"I'm sorry," Cora said. "It's all my fault that you are in this much trouble. You'd have been home already if you hadn't had to bother with me."

I helped her up. "We haven't seen you for so long. It's nice to be together again. Even like this. We'll be laughing about it in a few days."

"If your parents ever let us see you again," Emilia added grimly.

"Oh, they will. I'll tell them you saved my life. Besides, they let me go out a little more now because Pappa wants me to work with the ladies' society at the synagogue. I use the opportunity to go to the public lectures at the University."

We walked for over an hour, and Cora's head started to bleed again, staining her pale yellow angora sweater. I was trying to ignore the sting I still felt from the intrusion of the policeman's fingers. It was the first time I had allowed myself to think of what he had done. His hands had been rough, and the speed with which he had moved aside my underclothes and penetrated me with his fingers left me dazed. I wanted to wash away the burning pain of his touch and never think of it again. I was grateful for the cold, for the wind that made my ears hurt. Emilia seemed lost in her own world; Cora too weak to talk any more. My borrowed shoes had chafed my cuts, and I limped as I hung onto Emilia's arm. Her nose was running and every so often she swiped at it angrily with her gloves.

We left the side streets to take the nearest route home along Bulevar España. The boulevard was quiet that night, traffic scant. A few pedestrians passed us, and one or two stopped to offer assistance when they saw Cora's condition. I accepted the third offer we received and asked for help in finding a taxi. Emilia gave the driver an address a block from our homes. We wanted to do nothing that might attract attention to our arrival in the *barrio*.

Once there, we were forced to walk once more. We had made it this far, and now that final block seemed to stretch before us into infinity.

"Come on," I said. "It isn't far." I led them forward, and we did not stop until we reached the corner. My house was ablaze with lights. "Oh, my!" I said. "They are waiting for me."

"My apartment is dark," Emilia said.

"There's one light on at my house," Cora sighed.

We hugged one another, wanting to reach the warmth and comfort of our homes, but in need of one another.

"We have to face them sometime," I said.

"Will you come and see me tomorrow?" Cora asked.

Emilia and I nodded. "And phone us tonight if you need to."

With a final pressure of hands, we separated. Cora, holding my scarf to her head, hurried toward her house, her heels clicking on the pavement. She turned once for a last wave and disappeared.

I sighed and shrugged. "Here goes," I said, and hugging the garden walls, I made my way home as Emilia unlocked her apartment door and stepped into the darkness.

I was sent to bed at once with a hot-water bottle while Josefa prepared a tray for me. My father, I was told, would be informed as soon as he came home of what my behavior had been that day. This meant simply that my mother was relieved that I was home and had no idea how to deal with my transgressions. My father might not be home for days, and by then, all would have been forgotten.

I spent a long time in the bathroom washing myself, but the burning sensation between my legs would not go away. What if he had torn something? Would I bleed? If I did, I would have to see a doctor, and how could I tell him what had happened to me? Would he want to look? I felt humiliated enough already.

No matter how much I washed, I felt soiled. The telephone rang while I was dousing myself with talcum powder, hoping its fresh scent would make me feel cleaner. Eventually, I gave up the effort and settled down in my bed, wishing I could warm my feet on the hot-water bottle Josefa had provided, but the cuts were too painful. My mother joined me as I was finishing my cocoa.

"That was Mrs. Allenberg on the phone. They are taking Cora to the hospital. She wanted to thank you for helping her home." She sat down on the bed.

I was unaccustomed to such close scrutiny from my mother.

"What happened, Magdalena?"

"It's a long story, *mamá*. Can I tell you tomorrow?"

My mother seemed about to insist on an answer when a siren split the silence of the night. For one eternal moment, I thought it was the police coming to arrest me for what I had done to one of them. My mother walked quickly to the window and looked out. It was an ambulance, she said, stopping at Emilia's apartment building. I jumped out of bed, threw a coat over my nightdress and was out the door before my mother could stop me.

As I reached Emilia's building, a stretcher was carried out. Emilia walked, crying quietly, beside it.

Lilita's small face was visible above the dark blankets, her eyes closed, her mouth sagging open. I ran to Emilia as my mother joined us.

"What happened?"

"I'll tell you later," Emilia answered.

"Do you want me to come with you?"

"No. Stay and tell *papá* we're at the Italian Hospital." She stepped into the ambulance behind the stretcher and was driven away, looking old beyond her years and irremediably tired.

My mother and I went into the apartment and sat in the chairs by the front door.

"Magdalena, what exactly happened tonight?" my mother asked again. "No evasions this time."

"To Lilita?"

"No. I think we both know what happened to Lilita. I mean to you."

I surprised myself by telling her everything.

"Is that all he did?" she asked.

"Yes."

"How I'd like to get my hands on him! The bastard! I'd kill him."

"It's over now, *mamá*. I'd like to forget it. I won't have to see a doctor, will I?"

"We'll see how you are tomorrow. I hope it was a lesson to you. You were lucky those students didn't finish what the policeman started. Did he know who you are? Did he ask for your *cédula?*"

"No. Anyway, I didn't have it with me."

"It might have stopped him. You should never go out without your identity card. Still, as things are, it's better that our name didn't come out. The press would have had a field day with it."

"Why should they care?"

"You are very naive, Magdalena. Why do you think those students helped you?"

"They had no idea who I was when they helped me."

"They can tell you're not one of them just by your clothes and your manners. One of them will probably show up tomorrow wanting your father to give him a job."

"Do you really believe that?"

"I've lived a lot longer than you, Magdalena. I know these people. They take advantage of everything and everyone."

We heard *señor* Mario's key turning in the lock. He looked

surprised to see us and took his hat off hurriedly. My mother told him that his wife had been taken to the hospital. He ran a hand through his thick, dark hair. "I am sorry you were troubled," he said. "Emilia should have left a note."

"It was no trouble," my mother said. "Is there anything more we can do?"

"No, no. I shall take care of everything."

"Would you like something to eat?"

"No, I've eaten, thank you."

"Then we'll go home. Please let us know if we can be of any assistance."

"Yes. Thank you again. It's most kind of you."

My mother and I walked home in silence. She waited until I was in bed again and kissed me good-night.

"You're right," she said. "It's best to forget what happened."

But I found forgetting impossible. Not only could I not obliterate what had happened to me, but I kept remembering Emilia's terrified face as we ran with the crowd. I knew that I would never have forgiven myself if something had happened to her because of me.

The next day, I went to visit Lilita in the hospital and found her looking frailer than ever. Emilia had spent the night in her clothes, and her usually neat coat and skirt were creased and rumpled. She looked away when I arrived and busied herself counting out coins for the bus. "I am going home to change. Can you stay until I get back?"

I nodded. "For as long as you like."

We walked out of the room together. "What happened, Emilia?"

"She tried to kill herself. I should have been there. I don't know if I can be your friend any more, Magda. You're always doing such crazy things."

"You told me Lilita wasn't going to be home yesterday!"

"*Ya sé, ya sé.* I know I said that, it's not your fault, really, but—"

I put a hand on her arm. "Go home and change. I learned a lesson yesterday too, Emilia. I won't ever endanger you again. I promise."

Emilia smiled weakly. "I am going to make you keep that promise, Magda."

There was an ethereal quality to Lilita's room. Plain white curtains were drawn across the window, and the evening sun filtered through them onto the white walls and the blanket covering Lilita's slight body. Her dark hair seemed to float on the white pillows, and her eyes had a shadowy, elusive quality as if she were looking at me under water. I took her cold hands and kissed them. Her veins stood out in sharp contrast to the pallor of her skin.

"They killed him, Magdalena; they killed my Juan," she whispered.

"Who was Juan, Lilita?"

"He was my friend. The only man I've ever completely trusted. My parents didn't approve of him, so we met at the library, to talk. I loved him very much. And he cared about me so much, Magdalena. He worried if my feet got wet or if I cried at the movies. And they killed him, Magda; they killed him!" she sobbed.

I lay on the bed and took Lilita in my arms, feeling her spine like a row of pebbles under the soft fabric of her hospital gown. "Who killed him, Lilita?"

"Stroessner's men. He went to Paraguay to fight with the rebels and they caught him."

I searched my mind in some confusion, wishing I had paid

more attention at school when we covered Paraguayan politics. "Who is Stroessner?"

Lilita shuddered. "A devil. A dictator, beloved of the Americans, hated by all freedom-loving people." She sat up suddenly and pulled me up to face her. "Things are happening here. Important things. One day, you will have to make a choice. When that day comes, I want you to remember how Juan died."

"Yes, Lilita."

"They put a hook through his jaw and flew him, hanging from an airplane, over the jungle where his companions were hiding. And they dropped him there."

Tears ran down Lilita's cheeks. "Can you understand how stupid I am? Have you ever heard of raising one's only child with the belief that marriage to a rich man is the only safeguard, while fighting to bring the rich down?" She laughed wildly. "No wonder my husband thinks I'm mad!" She clutched my arm. "Listen, Magda. Terrible things are going to happen here. I've heard you and Marco Aurelio talking. You are just the kind who will not be able to stand by and watch it happen. I was like you once, and I know. But Emilia could. She doesn't have the sense of outrage necessary for revolution. Marco Aurelio does. You don't know it yet, but so do you. Will you promise me that you will prevent Emilia from ever joining you?"

"I have already told Emilia that I will never endanger her again. It was because of me that she was out yesterday."

But Lilita was not listening. "Promise me!" she cried, her nails digging into my arms.

"I promise."

Nine

Our fifteenth birthdays, one of the most important rites of passage for young women, were almost upon us. It was an event Emilia and I had been looking forward to since we were children. We had watched Sofía and Carmen and Emilia's many cousins preparing for this celebration, choosing gowns, printing invitations, rehearsing the opening waltz with their fathers, and being the center of attention for months before and after their parties.

Since our birthdays were only days apart, Emilia and I suggested to our mothers that they plan a joint *fiesta de quince* for us. They agreed more readily than we had imagined. With inflation at 422 percent, the prospect of sharing costs for the party was welcome to my mother. For Lilita, there was the relief of joint responsibility. She had left the hospital so thin that her skin was almost translucent, and I could see Emilia glancing at her often as her mother sat at the table toying with her food.

"How thrilling!" *tía* Catalina exclaimed, as the *tías* prepared to consume Josefa's tea cakes. "The last of my nieces to celebrate her fifteenth birthday! We must make it especially memorable!"

"It's a rather medieval rite of passage, I think," *tía* Aurora said.

Tía Josefina gave a peal of laughter. "Uruguay didn't exist in medieval times!"

"Of course it existed, *tonta*."

"Not as a civilized country, I mean!"

"Does it exist as a civilized country now?" my mother asked grimly.

"Be that as it may," *tía* Aurora said, "Spain and England did. And that's where these so-called civilized traditions came from."

"Was this supposed to be a *Carnaval* tea?" *tía* Catalina inquired.

"What on earth is a *Carnaval* tea?" my mother asked.

"I don't know," *tía* Catalina answered. "I only wondered because Aurora came in costume."

Tía Aurora put her teacup down slowly. "Look again, Catalina. In case it has escaped your notice after living here for sixty-odd years—"

"Fifty-eight," *tía* Catalina corrected.

"Fifty-nine, surely," *tía* Josefina said. "I'm fifty-eight and we're not twins, you know. At least, I don't think we are . . . *Mamasita* never mentioned—"

"As I was saying," *tía* Aurora continued, "in case it has escaped your notice, *bombachas* are worn here."

"Not by women, they're not."

"You are mistaken, as usual, Catalina. Women often wear gaucho pants for riding."

"Did you arrive on horseback? If so, I missed it."

"Miss Newman and I have decided that it's high time women started dressing comfortably. And there's no garment more comfortable than *bombachas*."

"Miss Newman?" my mother exclaimed. "I thought she was dead!"

"Dead?" *tía* Aurora said. "Whatever gave you such an idea?"

"You did. I distinctly remember you saying her lover had killed her."

Caramba flew in at that moment and the *tías*, my mother, and I raised our right arms over our heads. Caramba seemed unsettled and flew around longer than usual.

"So Miss Newman has become a fashion consultant? Was it also her idea that you dress entirely in black in the middle of summer?" *tía* Josefina inquired. "She should have stuck to teaching."

"She has stuck to teaching, as you so crudely put it," *tía* Aurora answered irritably, throwing a napkin at Caramba, who settled on the tea cozy. "Stupid bird. Now my shoulder aches. I am wearing black in opposition to our government's decision to break off diplomatic relations with Cuba."

"Why should you care?" *tía* Catalina asked in surprise.

"Because it is yet another indication that we are under the thumb of the United States."

"That's what the Communists always say every time anyone takes a stand against them," my mother said.

"This time, *hermanas*, it would behoove us to listen. Remember Panama."

"What has Panama to do with us? It's hundreds of miles away!" *tía* Catalina said.

"The U. S. charges ships for going through the Panama Canal," *tía* Aurora answered impatiently. "That money is used to finance the School of the Americas—a cover for the training of future military leaders ready to overthrow anyone who threatens U. S. profits in Latin America."

The *tías* gasped and were silent.

"Be careful of where you say such things, Aurora," my mother finally said.

"People will think you're a Communist!" *tía* Josefina cried.

"If Panama is too far away to alarm you," *tía* Aurora continued, "think of Brazil. No sooner had President Goulart announced his plans to nationalize the oil refineries and reform the country's agrarian policies than he was overthrown! The same happened in Bolivia! What will it take for us to come to our senses?"

"Could we return to planning Magdalena's birthday?" my mother inquired of her sisters.

Tía Aurora threw up her hands in despair.

"I shall pay for the invitations," *tía* Josefina said. "Do you want silver or gold lettering, dear?"

"Emilia and I want gold please, *tía* Josefina," I answered.

"Who is Emilia?"

"My friend, who I'm celebrating my birthday with."

"Oh, yes! The one whose mother tried to do away with herself," *tía* Josefina said happily.

The others sighed.

"I shall pay for the rental of the English Club," *tía* Catalina said.

"Emilia's parents will share all of these expenses, of course," my mother added.

"I shall pay for the band," *tía* Aurora put in. "At least that won't be money totally wasted. It's important to support artists."

"Have you designed your dress yet, Magdalena?" *tía* Catalina inquired.

"Perhaps we should consult Miss Newman first," *tía* Josefina added.

"We have the material," I said. "It's very pretty. Filmy, and with flecks of silver in it. I'm not quite sure of the style yet. Something cut low in the back, I think, and with a wide skirt."

"What photographer will you use?"

"We haven't decided. Can you recommend anyone?" my mother asked.

"Miss Newman takes excellent photos. It's her hobby," *tía* Aurora said.

"Really?" my mother said nervously, obviously wishing she had not asked.

"And while she doesn't approve of this *fiesta de quince* nonsense, she has offered her services and considerable talents free of charge."

"What doesn't she approve of, *tía* Aurora?" I asked.

"The whole thing. Money being wasted parading a poor girl before a bunch of ogling boys. Wearing virginal white. Waltzing with one's father and having the men cut in. She says it has sexual overtones."

"What does she mean by sex—"

"Never mind," my mother interrupted. "Magdalena is having a fifteenth birthday party, no matter what Miss Newman thinks."

"I'm surprised Javier can afford it. I hear he sold off a lot of land just recently," *tía* Catalina exclaimed.

"His investments haven't been paying off very well lately," my mother said.

"Does he still have a racing car?"

My mother glared at her sister. "I believe so. A man is entitled to his hobby."

"You were saying that Miss Newman wouldn't charge us, *tía* Aurora?" I asked. "It would be a great saving, *mamá* . . ."

"It would indeed. The prices photographers are asking for these days are quite outrageous! But I haven't seen any examples of Miss Newman's photographic talents."

"You have, Rita," *tía* Aurora said. "Remember that collection of photos from the Prado exhibition? The ones you saw at my house?"

"Oh, yes!" my mother said. "They were extraordinary!"

My mother had told us all about the magnificent photos she had seen of the gauchos and their horses, of the prize cattle and sheep, and of the visitors to the exhibits. The photographer had captured the character, atmosphere, and tone of the annual show in a way my mother had never seen before.

It was not difficult therefore to persuade her that Miss Newman would do justice to Emilia and my *fiesta de quince.*

"Who was that young man we saw you talking to as we arrived, Magdalena?" *tía* Josefina asked.

"Marco Aurelio Pereira. Our neighbor."

"Oh, one of those poor boys with the mad mother!"

"She's not mad, *tía* Josefina. A little eccentric, perhaps."

"My dear, my maid listens to her radio plays. I assure you, the woman's quite mad," *tía* Josefina insisted. "Only the other day there was an episode about a soldier taking his *novia* into the fortress in the dead of night so he could make love to her on one of the cannons. We all know what *that* symbolized . . . !"

"I don't," I said.

"I should hope not!" *tía* Catalina interposed.

"I was with her when she interviewed the soldier," I said.

"It's a true story?" *tía* Catalina gasped.

"I don't know," I answered. "I couldn't actually hear their conversation. Marco Aurelio and I were talking."

"Marco Aurelio again. Well, apart from the absurd name and the mad mother, he is quite something!" *tía* Josefina giggled.

The *tías* all murmured their appreciation of Marco's physical qualities.

"What does his father do?" *tía* Aurora asked.

"He's a retired army colonel," my mother answered.

"Could be worse. Is he mad too?"

"He *is* rather odd," my mother said. "Horribly jealous. Won't allow his poor wife to leave the house alone, that sort of nonsense."

"Can't say I blame him if she acts like the characters in her plays," *tía* Catalina said.

"She should shoot the monster," *tía* Aurora declared. "Do they have other children?"

"Two other sons," I said.

"Are they *churros* too?" *tía* Josefina asked eagerly.

"They are very handsome," I answered. "But not as . . . not as. . . ." I could not find the right words with which to say what Marco was. "They are not as unusual," I finished.

"Will you be going to many parties this *Carnaval*, Magdalena?" *tía* Catalina asked.

"I hope so!" I answered.

I had high hopes for *Carnaval*. Since my encounter with the policeman the night of Che Guevara's speech, I had felt unclean. Perhaps the water fights would cleanse me, return to me a sense of adventure; perhaps at the costume parties, I could mask the shame that often overtook me when I remembered the episode, making me blush for no reason.

I had always loved *Carnaval*. The family album was full of photos of relatives transformed by *Carnaval*. My mother dressed as a gypsy, with gold coins sparkling from the red bandana tied around her dark hair; Uncle George as Genghis Khan, the tips of a black mustache hanging to his chest; I myself as a baby chick in a bright yellow bodysuit and hood covered in soft and tiny feathers.

A long time ago, Josefa had told me all about *Carnaval*.

I had gone to the kitchen hoping to be allowed to lick the

bowl after Josefa put a cake in the oven. Instead, I found myself
facing a stately woman sitting by the patio door.

"Magdalena, this is my mother, *doña* Azul," Josefa said.

I went up to *doña* Azul and kissed her cheek. "Why are you
called blue when you are such a shiny brown?"

Josefa and *doña* Azul laughed like echoes of the same song.

"I was born blue, my mother said. So she named me Azul."

"My mother is here to dance in the *corso.*"

Doña Azul sighed. "For the last time. This year the parade
will finish me. Next year, I'll be buried."

"She says that every summer, Magda," Josefa reassured me,
as she saw my eyes widen.

"This time it's true. Josefa will inherit my costume," *doña*
Azul said, pointing to a large cardboard box under the kitchen
table.

"May I see it, *doña* Azul?" I asked.

Doña Azul walked over to the table and lifted the box onto
it. A dozen brightly colored bracelets jingled as she moved, and
I noticed how tight her skirt was and how long her legs. She
untied the string and lifted the lid. I stood on a stool and
looked inside the box. I gasped. It was not the first time I had
seen a traditional *Carnaval* costume, but I knew at first glance
that there was something very special about this one.

Doña Azul lifted out a feathered headdress as tall as I was,
running her long, red fingernails caressingly over the white and
yellow plumes. "My great grandmother left me this."

Josefa's hand reached over my shoulder and touched the
beadwork where the feathers nested. "The feathers have been
replaced many times, Magda, but the beads are as old as memory." She took my hand and placed it on the wooden beads.
"My great-grandmother's great-grandmother was wearing these

when her village was raided. She was brought here more dead than alive in the hold of a slave ship."

I looked up into Josefa's serious face. "What became of her?"

"She was sold, along with all the others. She and several of her village remained here in Montevideo, and they found ways of keeping their village alive with music and dance. Once a year, at *Carnaval*, their owners allowed them several days of freedom. They gathered to cook and sing and dance and to remember their ancestors and their stories. The masters liked the food and the music, and so they gave the slaves the things they needed to make the costumes and the drums. That is how the *candombe* and the *murgas* were born."

The *candombe*, I had long ago learned, was a dance that could coax indulgence from the sternest bodies. Every year, just as summer drew to a close, the *tamborileros* came down from the hill and out of the northern *barrios* to fill the streets of Montevideo with a flavor of the past. Sometimes, they were groups of men, all playing the long African drums of their ancestors. Sometimes they were mixed, with female dancers leading the way. It did not matter. Windows and doors flew open, and people streamed out to let the *candombe* take them. Hips flew and feet hissed on the pavements; bosoms bounced and arms invited as matrons, men, young women, and children melted into the pounding invitation of the drum. The *candombe* could be danced alone as a solitary pleasure; it could be a flirtation or a consummation. Dancers who gave themselves entirely to it could never relinquish it, *doña* Azul told me, for the *candombe* speaks to something intrinsic in human beings and is as visceral as a heartbeat.

That year, when the drums sounded in the distance, I

jumped from my bed and flung open the shutters. The late morning sun streamed in, making me put a hand up to shield my eyes. They were coming! I threw on my clothes and ran down the stairs to the kitchen.

"Josefa! The *tamboriles* are coming!"

"I heard them! I heard them! I'm just finishing the *crema de chocolate* for Caramba and I'm coming!"

Caramba loved the drums, too, but not enough to forego her custard. She was pacing up and down on her perch, and I opened her cage door as I ran by. "It's the *tamborileros*, Caramba!"

Caramba flew out into the kitchen, where she circled Josefa's head until the cook poured the custard into Caramba's cup and gave it to her.

"Let it cool! Let it cool, Caramba! You'll burn your tongue!" Josefa admonished, flinging off her apron.

The drums got nearer.

Emilia was out, leading Lilita by the hand.

Marco and his brothers had their shirts off and were undoing their shoelaces on the curb. *Señor* Mario emerged, straightening his tie. It was time for him to leave for work, but the drums were almost there.

Cora was at her window, pleading with her father.

Mr. Stelby was closing his shutters.

The *tamborileros* turned the corner as *señora* Marta emerged in full *Carnaval* costume. Her generous bosom was encased in a bright red top glittering with sequins. On her head was a feather headdress several feet tall, with a rainbow of ostrich plumes quivering in the breeze. From her waist hung a skirt of layer upon layer of ruffles blending into one smudge of color as she twirled into the street, her sons dancing around her like a ring of fire with her at its center.

For a moment, I thought I would not be able to dance that

year. The place within me the policeman had violated with his rough fingers burned for an instant hotter than ever. Then I saw Marco. The drums and his beauty were a force so cleansing that I threw my arms above my head and let my hips take me. With every beat of the drums and every move I made, the burning cooled, replaced by a healing sweat.

Lilita passed me, laughing with her husband. She looked young and carefree, and I knew as I watched her that I wanted that rare image of her to remain with me always.

Marco took my hand and made me twirl until I had to rest my head on his shoulder for a moment to catch my breath. With every movement we made, I wanted to blend more closely with him. I could no longer tell if it was my body or his that kept the beat, if it was his skin or mine radiating heat whenever we touched. At times, he kept a tantalizing distance, smiling at me as he laced his fingers with mine and brought me closer, where he could put his hands on my waist and feel my hips moving as my skirt brushed his bare legs. Once we were crushed together by the line of dancers, and I felt the feathery flame of his breath on my shoulder as he brushed my skin with his lips. I leaned into his touch but the snaking line was moving too fast, and we were separated as the entire gathering danced in and out amongst the lampposts and the trees, passing Cora's door as she and her father came out to join it. Mr. Allenberg looked bewildered, but *señora* Marta took his hands and placed them on her hips and from that moment he was one of us, his small feet barely grazing the pavement as he was swept along under his wife's delighted smile from behind her lace curtains.

Laughter rang among us, and as if the drummers felt a hidden need for healing on this street, they prolonged their departure and moved on slowly, leaving the memory of release and the smell of sweat in the air and taking the heartbeat of Africa to another neighborhood to remind the people there of the origins of humankind.

⚬⚬⚬

In the weeks before the *fiesta de quince*, Josefa had accompanied me to weekly fittings at the dressmaker's. She made appointments with Ernesto and dealt with the caterers, sleek, fat, and quick as flies, who swarmed round, waving pictures of delicacies only they knew how to produce.

Josefa chose *empanadas* the size of large coins, the pastry fried to golden flakiness, the sweet meat inside cooked to perfection; *milanesas* cut into tiny squares, covered with bread crumbs fine and crisp, the beef so tender it melted like butter in the mouth; minute hot dogs; and finger sandwiches on fine white bread, filled with everything from paper-thin ham to creamy corn; individual seafood casseroles in seashells; and *masitas* of every description—from the heart-shaped sticky *palmitas*, to my favorites, the *milhojas*, layer upon layer of transparent pastry stuck together with *dulce de leche*, made by cooking milk and sugar together until they caramelized and turned the consistency and color of peanut butter.

Emilia and I arrived early and were surprised by the flash of a camera as we stepped out of the taxi.

From what my aunts had told me about Miss Newman, I had envisioned her as a robust woman with a brash demeanor. I was surprised to be greeted by a petite blonde with a radiant smile. Miss Newman loved our dresses, thought our coloring in charming contrast, and made us pose against the black wrought-iron railings fronting the club's entrance.

As we entered the club, we saw that *señor* Paredes had

outdone himself. Garlands of camellias scented the air over our heads. White carnations and red roses were woven together down the center of the long serving tables, and lilies stood tall in every corner.

Emilia and I retired to the ladies' room to make sure our hair spray had survived the wind that blew across the Rambla where the club was located, and Miss Newman followed us.

"I've taken some of my best photos in bathrooms," she said.

Emilia and I looked at her in surprise.

"Oh, don't be shocked," she laughed. "I don't mean while people are in the stalls! But what they do in front of bathroom mirrors is very revealing."

Emilia and I murmured something about this being most artistic and left the bathroom quickly to join Josefa. She was dressed in her finest dark blue taffeta and was ordering the musicians to start playing while she organized the family pictures. Feet tapped and hips swayed, but under Josefa's watchful eyes, no one dared to dance until Emilia and I opened the ball by waltzing with our fathers. Josefa was determined to follow all *fiesta de quince* traditions and soon put a stop to Miss Newman's idea that we pose informally in small groups. Josefa posed us first with our family, then with each other, and told Miss Newman she would have plenty of time for her modern ideas later. Miss Newman got her revenge by photographing Josefa herself as she directed the proceedings, and by the time visitors started arriving, the two of them were openly at odds.

The invitations read eight o'clock, which meant that most of the guests got to the club between eight-thirty and nine.

I was eight years old when Sofía and Carmen celebrated their *fiesta de quince.* My father had looked exceptionally handsome in his dark suit and white shirt, twirling the twins in turn around the ballroom. When my time came, I had always

thought, I would be as perfect a dancer as he, and my father
would say of me, as he did of my mother, that it was like dancing with his own shadow, so perfectly could I follow him. But
the telephone had rung the day before. My father was detained
on business in Rio de Janeiro and would not be with us.

When my mother broke the news to me, I pretended not
to care. I continued revolving slowly, as the dressmaker knelt at
my feet adjusting the hem of my dress, and shrugged. "Who
will we get?"

"I suppose we'll have to press poor Uncle George into service," my mother answered.

Uncle George, in spite of his aversion to dancing, did his
duty manfully and escorted me on to the dance floor beside
Emilia, whose father was beaming proudly and mopping his
forehead with a dazzling white handkerchief as the orchestra
broke into the "Blue Danube." To my uncle's relief and my
own, he was not forced to suffer long. As tradition demanded,
the young men present cut in, one after the other, and Emilia
and I were whirled around the floor by at least a dozen of them
before the waltz reached its final chords.

Marco was my first and last partner, and as we finished
dancing, he kissed me lightly on the cheek and wished me a
happy birthday. I had not seen him for several weeks. He had
finished his two years of *preparatorio* and entered the army, for
the colonel had issued an ultimatum. His patience with
Marco's political escapades was at an end. Either Marco joined
the army, or he left home. *Señora* Marta had broken down and
pleaded with her son. What could he lose, she asked, by trying
it for a year or two? If he really hated it, they would work
something out. Meanwhile, by humoring his father, he could
remain at home like a proper young man and not be an outcast
from his own family. Marco had relented and agreed to do as

his father wished. I teased him about his short hair, and Miss Newman snapped a picture of him running a hand over his cropped black curls.

He grinned. "Wait till I'm an officer; then I can grow it out a little."

"Oh, and when will that be?" I asked him.

"Sooner than you think. If I'm to be stuck in the military, then I intend to do it right."

Emilia and I fox-trotted, tangoed, and rock and rolled our way through the rest of the evening. Every so often the couple dances were interrupted by a *farándula*. The dance started in one long chain, included everyone present of every age and size, and evolved into a huge circle with Emilia and me in the center. We each chose a partner and left him to rejoin the circle while he chose another dancer from it and in turn left her to do the same. Even Miss Newman was drawn into this dance, and it was the only event of the evening not recorded in photos. The music was fast moving, and after it, large quantities of cider and Coca-Cola were consumed while the dancers caught their breath and the orchestra took a break. The men congregated outside to smoke and loosen their ties, while the women crowded into the bathroom to refresh makeup, repin loose curls, and take off high heels for a few moments of relief. Some of the most endearing photos of our friends were taken at this time as they laughed gleefully at the idea of a photographer following them into the ladies' lounge and snapping pictures of them massaging their feet.

While attendance at these balls was by invitation only, it was not unusual for young men to come accompanied by an uninvited friend. If he was properly dressed and behaved himself according to the rules governing these occasions, the friend was made welcome. Young men were occasionally known to be perverse and refuse to dance, so the matrons chaperoning these events were always on the lookout for potential new partners for the wallflowers.

One such young man arrived quite late and stood unnoticed by the food table, calmly smoking a cigarette until he spotted Marco. Marco was delighted to see him and gave him a quick embrace. He found Emilia and me and introduced us.

My heart beat unexpectedly faster. Jaime Betancourt was as tall as Marco, slender and very dark. He had strong, delicate hands and a tentative smile, which he flashed cautiously and not very often. He had a serious air about him, and his eyes, light green and rimmed in dark lashes, were warm and open as he shook my hand and asked for the next dance. He smiled slightly as he put his arm around me.

"You're in the air force, Marco tells me," I said.

"Yes."

"Do you like flying?"

"Yes."

He seemed content to dance, and I made no further effort at conversation. Clearly he had asked me to dance out of politeness, not out of any desire to know me better. This suspicion was borne out when he led me back to Marco and asked Emilia for the next dance.

"He's not a great conversationalist," I said peevishly to Marco.

"Oh, but he is, when the subject interests him! He's brilliant, and a master chess player."

"Well, obviously, I am not among the subjects he's interested in. He said all of two words to me."

Marco looked at me attentively. "He's not the man for you, Little Lion."

I blushed. "How dare you! Who are you to say what kind of

man is right for me?" The pain of my words registered like a blow on Marco's face, but I was too ashamed by the transparency of my emotions to apologize for the anger.

I was amazed to receive a letter a few days later, posted from the air force base near Montevideo. The envelope was a plain white one, with my name and address on it in neat block letters.

Jaime Betancourt wrote briefly to thank me for the party and to say that while he imagined we would have little in common, he could not help being attracted to me and would call during his next leave. I laughed outright at his presumption and did not write back. When he telephoned the following weekend, I was not at home, and several weeks went by before I heard from Jaime again. A large bunch of flowers arrived with an invitation to go dancing the following Saturday night. He would call on Friday to see if I was available.

Much to my surprise, my mother gave her permission. Sofía had recently broken off with her latest boyfriend and Carmen had acquired a new one. My mother was in constant demand to soothe one or another of them and had no time to ask questions regarding my outing with Jaime. She assumed we were going out chaperoned by a group of friends and thought no more of it. I took full advantage of the situation. I made an appointment with Ernesto and had my unruly curls styled into immobility. When Jaime telephoned on Friday, I was ready for him. "You're right, of course," I said. "We have nothing in common. Are you sure you want to waste your time taking me dancing?"

His laugh was surprisingly spontaneous. "Yes."

"Well, once can't hurt."

He called for me at ten o'clock the following night, and we rode in silence in the back of a taxi for several minutes before

pulling up in front of a narrow building with no windows. I
was determined not to be the first to talk, and Jaime appeared
to have no need to do so. Although it was my first visit to a
boite, I had been prepared by Sofía for the pitch darkness I
would encounter inside. Around the small dance floor, tables
and booths disappeared into the dark recesses of the club, and
a band played against the back wall. Jaime chose a booth toward the rear and ordered two Coca-Colas.

"I was hoping you'd wear your hair loose," he said.

I was speechless. My hairdo had cost me my allowance for
the week, and I expected to be told I looked regal, majestic,
pretty, at the very least.

Jaime took my hand and led me to the dance floor. The
band was playing the Platters' song "One in a Million" and the
lilting beat made my heart sway with it. It seemed completely
natural that Jaime should hold me very close, his cheek warm
against mine. As the song drew to a close, he opened my hand
and kissed my palm. By the time we returned to the booth, I
had the gratification of seeing he was as overcome as I by the
sudden passion that had run between us when we touched. The
darkness engulfed us, and as his mouth closed on mine, I let
myself go and kissed him strongly. Jaime pulled away.

"That's enough," he said and reached for his drink, his hand
shaking. "Let's get out of here." He threw some bills on the
table, and we left in silence.

We walked out and crossed the wide Rambla onto the
beach. The river glistened in the moonlight with a cold, un-
friendly glow. I had never seen it look so uninviting.

"I'm not ready for any involvement," Jaime said. "Especially
not with you. You stand for everything I find most reprehensible in this country."

"How can you possibly know what I stand for?" I asked.

He laughed bitterly. "A dance at the English Club. Every big landowner in the country present. A private school. What do you know about anything?"

"Tell me what you think I should know."

"My father is a tailor. If your father knew that, I wouldn't be allowed in the door again."

"So what did tonight prove to you?"

"That I'm an even bigger fool than I thought I was."

"Well, I suppose I must be one too. I don't know why you're so angry, Jaime, but I wish you'd kiss me again."

❧

In the weeks that followed, he opened up to me all the hidden store of rage he had treasured as a spur to his ambition. He told me what it was like to be born so poor he wore newspapers to school under threadbare sweaters to keep out the cold. What it was like to know himself more intelligent than his teachers, to receive grade after outstanding grade, and yet to see that the only avenue open to him for advancement was the military. He had wanted to be a doctor but decided that he could not put such a financial burden on his parents.

"The University is free," I said.

Jaime laughed bitterly. "Yes, Magdalena, but food, clothes, and supplies are not."

"Oh." I looked down in embarrassment. Hadn't I been listening? Yes, but he had been talking about the kind of poverty I could not even begin to understand. For a brief moment, I considered asking him not to call me again, but when I turned to him, he was looking at me and all his anger had evaporated.

He took my face in his hands. "I knew the moment I saw you that I was lost. Every time I touch you I alternate between panic and desire. The panic I'm used to; the desire frightens me."

"And me," I whispered, confused by this mixture of love-making and analysis. What did he want from me?

"If I were to ask you, would you marry me?" he asked.

"Is that a question or a proposal?"

Jaime laughed with sudden delight. "Just a question!"

I sighed in frustration. "Then I don't have to answer."

Part of his immense attraction, I realized, was his unpre-dictability. Just as I thought I knew him a little better, he would reveal a side of himself I had never seen, drawing me farther into the maze of his personality. That a man so complex should find me interesting made him irresistible.

We were walking in the shallows of the river again, and a part of me wanted to run away from Jaime, but my feet were deep in the wet sand, and all I felt able to do was shake it off impatiently and walk away from the water's edge. "Tell me about flying," I said.

"Flying is like making love. It gives one release. The plane becomes a part of me, and I can make it do whatever I want. I can gentle it above the clouds or thrust it into somersaults. I can make it soar with just a touch. And the freedom of it! Especially when I fly solo. I could take off and fly until I ran out of fuel and then just lose myself in the sea. And one day, if I don't get what I want, that's just what I'll do."

"What do you want, Jaime?"

"Money. Power. Money."

"How do you intend to get it?"

Jaime let the sand run through his long fingers. "I don't know. I will go to the U. S. I will not be poor all my life."

I wondered then whether he was courting me as a means of

bettering himself. I felt obliged to tell him that my family was facing some difficult financial times. Jaime laughed, making me realize once more how relative my statements to him were. Compared to his family, mine was still a rich one.

My mother had no doubt what he was after. She knew we had something beyond price: an old and distinguished family name and influence—the kind money alone could not buy. It was the influence of ties as old as the Spanish colony itself; of a family network that stretched into the uppermost reaches of government, finance, and diplomacy. My mother and Jaime both knew that with a few telephone calls she could arrange for him to meet the people who could facilitate his move to the United States and his introductions to those who could secure visas and interviews for him once there. They spoke little, their enmity absolute and undeclared. Jaime asked for permission to place his relationship with me on a formal footing. My mother consented to a weekly two-hour visit, but I noticed a new wrinkle appear between her eyes. It was not often that she came face-to-face with a determination as rigid and inflexible as her own. She had taken one look at Jaime, had her penetrating and critical gaze met by his equally arrogant one, and dubbed him a social climber. Jaime represented everything she mistrusted; she represented everything he loathed as unwholesome and degenerate.

My mother had a way of lifting her nose ever so slightly when she spoke of Jaime, as if he exuded an unpleasant odor she would have liked removed from her presence. He would crack his knuckles as if preparing his supple fingers for her aristocratic neck.

I was most frightened when they smiled at one another. It was more a show of teeth than a smile. I came to wonder if either of them loved me, so intense was their struggle over me.

They seemed quite unaware of how it wounded me to think that winning their personal battle was more important to them than I was.

Marco was away during the months of Jaime's courtship. I missed him so profoundly that I would simply sit under the *estrella federal* and stare at his house, hoping that he would magically appear. He rarely did. His mother told me he was busy at the army base, recognized as a potential leader and being groomed by his father's friends for promotion. Then I would remember our final words at my *fiesta de quince* and wish I could take them back. What had he seen in Jaime and in me to make him say what he had?

It had not crossed my mind that a young man five years older than I could be in love with me. Jaime was three years older, and even that seemed a great difference at times. Besides, Marco was so perfect—handsome, intelligent, funny, and gentle. That I could be loved by someone like him seemed impossible. I thought he would marry one of the beautiful, dark-haired beauties I envied, like Emilia. The confident ones who walked the beaches of Punta del Este as if they owned the world and deserved to. Perhaps that is what attracted me to Jaime. He saw me as one of those proud, confident ones, whereas Marco looked right through me to my frightened core. I had not looked closely there myself yet, and I was afraid and mistrustful of someone who seemed to know me better than I knew myself.

Very few words were needed for Jaime to understand that his dream of flying for an American airline company was obtainable, at a price. If he gave me up, my mother implied, she would do the rest. Jaime considered the possibility of complying with my mother's wish, making his fortune, and marrying me anyway. He tried to persuade me to tell my mother that I had broken off our relationship but still wanted her to help him obtain a visa. I refused. Despite the fact that my family seemed to regard me as some sort of afterthought, a person by whose presence they were constantly surprised, as if I had appeared in their midst unexpectedly and without the proper introductions, I cared profoundly what they thought of me, and I wanted to please them. What exactly prevented me from succumbing entirely to Jaime's influence I do not know, but it drove him to question me mercilessly. Would I leave my family for him? Was I brave enough? I always avoided answering his questions by repeating that, given time, my family would accept him.

Jaime was about to deliver his ultimatum and take my mother up on her offer when he was visited while on leave from the base by two Mormon missionaries. They spoke very little Spanish and were delighted when Jaime was able to respond to them in the English he had been perfecting with my help.

Mormon missionaries were unmistakable in Uruguay. No matter how hot it was, pairs of males would stride through the streets of Montevideo wearing dark suits of American cut, white shirts, and lace-up shoes. They sported crew cuts, not in fashion among Uruguayans, and rarely spoke Spanish, certainly not with sufficient fluency to make coherent religious arguments. They lived together in a large, expensive housing complex in the most exclusive suburb of the city and sent their children to the costly nearby English school. There they befriended other foreigners, since their lifestyle was so incomprehensible to Uruguayans that most young people were not allowed to socialize with them.

Jaime was not the least bit interested in religion, but he never let an opportunity of practicing English pass him by. He asked them in, and during their visit, they unwittingly revealed that some of their converts had obtained U. S. visas. They were with Jaime for two hours and left feeling encouraged.

Converting to Mormonism would be a tricky move. His family would be appalled, and his few friends would consider that Jaime had lost what little sense they deemed him to have. If he was persona non grata with my mother now, I told him, embracing Mormonism would convince her beyond any doubt of his unsuitability to join our family.

My mother, meanwhile, was making plans of her own. Tradition dictated that I should be sent to Europe. Sofía and Carmen had already traveled there, under *tía* Josefina's chaperonage, and I was certainly old enough to do the same. My father, in an unusually tightfisted mood, said he could not consider a European tour for me just then. My mother fumed for a day or two and then, dressed in her most elegant Chanel suit in a deep shade of rose that made her brown hair gleam, she visited the American ambassador, who was pleased to inform her of the available opportunities for participation in foreign-exchange student programs.

She then decided that I would be happier in my travels abroad if Emilia accompanied me, so after a chat with the Lanconis, Emilia and I were presented with foreign-exchange student application forms, and my mother made sure that they were completed correctly.

I was confused. I had never considered going away from home to further my education. Sofía and Carmen's trips to Europe had been purely for pleasure. The United States had never before been viewed as an educational mecca for the Ortega family. A few of my male cousins had studied in England, one had even ventured to Australia, but we had no link with the United States. My mother, however, seemed bent on the idea. And Emilia was thrilled. Without the exchange program, it was unlikely that she would ever visit the United States.

After delivering our application forms personally to the Youth for Understanding offices, my mother even smiled at Jaime when he arrived for his evening visit. She also contrived to spend a few moments alone with him while I fetched him a glass of water. Jaime reported to me later that my mother had told him that if he stopped me from going to the States she would make sure he never saw me again.

"What did you say?" I asked him.

"I told her that I have no intention of preventing you from going. She informed me that you are no fool and that one day you'll see right through me. I know exactly what she meant. She thinks I'm a fortune hunter, a social climber. I was angry, Magdalena, and I told her so. Not for me. I have no fear of what you'd see if you could look right through me, as your mother wishes. You would see ambition, yes, but you would see love too. And I am angry because she doesn't realize that you are loved for your own sake, not for the money and the social standing she values so much. You believe me, don't you? You've never thought—" He saw me look away and turned me to face him. "Magdalena . . ."

"I know you love me, Jaime," I said, "but I have wondered . . ."

"Her influence is that strong?"

"Put yourself in her position, Jaime. You haven't made much of an effort to be liked. She barely knows you."

"I will give her credit for knowing me a little," he smiled. "She said that she had mentioned my name to the American ambassador and that if I request a visa during the time you are away, it will not be granted."

"Were you planning to do that?"

"Of course! We could be married in the U. S. and never come back here!"

"Jaime, that's crazy!"

"Well, it's not possible now anyway. But your mother also told me that the ambassador has a close friend who is an executive in a major airline, and if I apply for a visa once you're back . . ."

"It will be issued unquestioningly?"

"The ambassador could make no such promise, but—"

"Let me guess. If your visa is granted next year, the ambassador is willing to introduce you to his friend the airline executive?"

"Precisely!"

Ten

As soon as the news of my impending visit to the United States became public, the *tías* convened to offer their insights into traveling abroad.

"I, for one," *tía* Catalina declared, "keep all my old underwear for just such occasions. Washing and drying clothes can be dreadfully inconvenient when one is traveling. I simply toss my old unmentionables overboard each day."

"Difficult to accomplish on an airplane, Catalina," *tía* Aurora commented.

"Oh, is Magdalena flying?" *tía* Catalina asked in surprise.

"Yes, *tía* Catalina," I replied.

"Oh, well, then, I have no more to say on the subject."

"I shall lend you my money belt," *tía* Josefina said. "You can carry all your jewelry there, and no one can take it from you unless they knock you out first."

"Thank you, *tía*," I said.

"They have no *bidets*, you know," *tía* Catalina said, sipping her tea.

"No *bidets*?" *tía* Josefina repeated in wonder.

"No," *tía* Aurora verified. "Miss Newman tells me that one sees them only occasionally in the homes of the very rich."

"What are you taking your family as gifts, Magdalena?" *tía* Catalina asked.

"Don't take tea cozies," *tía* Josefina interjected. "Aurora, for some absurd reason known only to herself, since Americans drink only coffee, as anyone with half a brain knows, took tea cozies, and the Americans thought they were bonnets and wore them."

"Sad, but true," *tía* Aurora sighed.

"I believe *mamá* is sending things typical of Uruguay."

"I didn't know we could package strikes and inefficiency," *tía* Josefina said.

Tía Aurora glared at her. "They occasionally have strikes there too! Your conversational skills," she said, turning back to me, "will be greatly challenged. You must steer clear of religion and politics."

"And sex," *tía* Josefina added.

"What else is there to talk about?" *tía* Catalina wanted to know.

"You will also find," *tía* Aurora continued, "that Americans will ask you the most personal questions within moments of meeting you."

"Miss Newman asked me whether my father had had more than one mistress," *tía* Catalina said primly. "She did not believe me when I told her he had had none."

"*Mamasita* would have killed him, I suppose," I laughed, thinking of my indomitable grandmother.

"You will also find," *tía* Aurora persisted, "that if you make even the briefest comment on an American man's car, you will receive an exhaustive history starting at the invention of the automobile and listing every advance up to the present. If at this point you are still awake, he will proceed to give you a blow-by-blow account of the history of each part of his particular automobile."

"American women, as we have learned from our dear Miss

Newman," *tía* Josefina said, "have a profound preoccupation with themselves."

"Rightly so," *tía* Aurora said defensively, "no one else gives a damn."

"You will find their English quite appalling," *tía* Catalina added. "They take no pride in education. Their goal in speaking appears to be to ignore the basic rules of grammar as much as possible."

"We should help Magdalena by talking to her only in English until she leaves," *tía* Aurora stated. "At least when *Mamasita* isn't here . . ."

The *tías* were all fluent in English, a language they spoke at the insistence of my grandfather, who had been born in London. I had often been told the story of how he had left England as a young man, fed up with the constraints placed upon him by a family determined to see him enter the clergy. He had persuaded his father to entrust him with an annuity of several thousand pounds sterling, which he was to come into the following year when he reached the age of twenty-five, and then hopped on the first ship he saw that looked seaworthy to his inexperienced eyes. When the captain told him its destination, Ernest Grey shrugged and said that the Río de la Plata sounded as good as anywhere.

When the ship docked three months later, he knew he had made the right choice. He had no knowledge of either the language or the culture he was joining but knew a thriving city when he saw one. In 1902, he stepped ashore in Montevideo and proceeded to buy himself a ranch. He settled down to raise beef cattle, prospered, and, a few years after his arrival, won the heart of Aurelia Ponce de Aragón, a vivacious girl of seventeen who married him in spite of her parents' objections. The two families, *Mamasita* told me, met at the wedding and, by mutual and silent consent, agreed that they never wished to repeat the experience.

My great-grandfather was appalled to find that his son's future wife possessed an education equal to his own, read extensively, and was encouraged to express her opinions in public. He concluded that marriage to such a woman could bring nothing but misery.

My English great-grandmother did not approve of the profuse affection displayed toward her by her son's new relatives. Their embraces ruffled her composure and altered the careful arrangement of her laces.

It was clear that *Mamasita*'s parents thought she was marrying beneath her, an attitude that stunned the Greys: the fact that they were English should have been enough to establish their superiority. A competition ensued over the wedding. Tradition dictated that *Mamasita*'s parents should pay for it, which they were well able and most willing to do. There was nothing, however, to prevent Ernest's parents from building the young couple a house in Montevideo.

She and Ernest, *Mamasita* revealed in an unguarded moment, laughed at it all and continued to do what they had been doing almost from the first moment they had seen each other. Every few days they met at the beach to swim naked in the Río de la Plata, making love on Ernest's cape on the sand. The moment these words left her mouth, my grandmother sat straight up in her chair and clasped my arm. "Forget I said that! What am I talking about? It is probably the only thing you'll remember about me! Never tell your mother or your aunts!"

I promised never to reveal what she had let slip, and the secret created a special bond between us that lasted until she died.

After my grandfather's death, my grandmother threatened to sell the large house his parents had built for them fifty years before and move into an apartment, but she had not done so, for I loved the house, and I was *Mamasita's* favorite grandchild.

The house was set in the middle of large grounds, surrounded by palm trees, which *Mamasita* had learned to climb from her gardener, *don* Leopoldo. It was a source of endless irritation to my mother that my grandmother had better legs at age seventy than my mother did at age fifty. *Mamasita's* legs were long, slender, and perfectly toned, while my mother disguised her rather thick ankles and generous calves by means of artfully cut skirts. *Mamasita* had offered to teach my mother the skill of palm-tree climbing, but my mother had declined.

Soon after being informed that I was to spend several months in the United States as an exchange student, I sought my grandmother out and found her standing outside the eight-foot, wrought-iron gates with don Leopoldo. She was wearing a pair of trousers and a shirt tied at the waist. Her black hair was swept gleaming into an intricate knot at the nape of her neck. A pile of *tacuara* cane lay just inside the gates, and she and don Leopoldo were involved in a lively discussion.

"Hello, *Mamasita,*" I said.

My grandmother beamed when she saw me and kissed me heartily. "*¡Hola, corazón!*" she cried. "You get lovelier every day! Your great-grandmother would have given anything if the red in her hair had been this shade of copper. Hers looked like grated carrots and had the same texture."

"What is the *tacuara* cane for, *Mamasita?*"

She pointed to the rear of the property. "We need a new fence, and Leopoldo has brought me this," she gestured with contempt at the pile of cane. "I ordered prickly pear!"

"Whatever for?" I asked in amazement. I had fallen into a prickly pear once and knew it to be an inhospitable plant.

"To keep out the *Charrúas*."

"They're all dead, *Mamasita*."

"That's what they want us to think. They're just waiting. One of these days, they'll come charging out of the *monte*, just like they used to do in the old days, mounted on their wild horses."

I exchanged glances with Amapola, *don* Leopoldo's stately mare, who was standing tethered to the gates. I smiled at her dignified expression, which challenged anyone to accuse her of being a descendant of marauders.

Mamasita turned to *don* Leopoldo. "Take it away. Bring me prickly pears. And bring Amapola round to the kitchen door. I have apples for her. There are *empanadas* for you." She strode away toward the house.

"What are you going to do, *don* Leopoldo?"

He shrugged and grinned. "Bring the prickly pears of course!"

"But there are no *Charrúas!*"

"*Doña* Aurelia says there are. Who's to say they no longer exist just because we can't see them?" He led Amapola away as I walked up the gravel drive, remembering the stories *Mamasita* had told me about the *Charrúa*.

The territory now called Uruguay was part of the lands the *Charrúa* had roamed for centuries. When *Mamasita's* ancestors, a black Irishman by the name of FitzGibbon and his wife, Isabel, had first arrived in the Province of the Río de la Plata in 1743, the *Charrúa* posed a threat to all settlers. Nevertheless, Charlie FitzGibbon had managed to build and defend a fortresslike house along the shores of the river Cebollatí, and Isabel FitzGibbon had befriended a young *Charrúa*, who

Mamasita said had been in love with her. Uncle George, the family historian, said this was nonsense, but *Mamasita* was unpersuaded. She said no man who was not in love could have made anything so beautiful as the agate puzzle she now possessed.

I saw this puzzle for the first time when I was nine years old. I was staying with *Mamasita* at Caupolicán, her country estate, while my parents were traveling in Brazil. *Mamasita* and I had spent the day riding—she on one of her *criollos*, I in the saddle with a trusted gaucho who smoked dark cigarettes and had a deeply lined face. When we returned to the house, she went to change, and when she came to find me, I was engrossed in looking at her collection of Indian artifacts: spear and arrowheads, some shell jewelry, and a few pieces of what appeared to be shriveled leather.

As I handled them carefully, *Mamasita* watched me.

"I know what these were for, *Mamasita*," I said, pointing to the shells and arrowheads, "but what is this?" I picked up a piece of leather and dropped it quickly, wiping my hands on my jeans.

"Why did you wipe your hands?" *Mamasita* asked.

"I don't know. I didn't like the feel of it."

Mamasita nodded. "It's human skin. The *Charrúa* used to skin the faces of those they killed in battle."

I recoiled from the chest containing the collection. "Why do you keep it?"

"Because it's powerful. Just like this is." She left the room and returned a few moments later with another piece of ancient leather. "Don't worry," she said. "This isn't human." She unfolded the leather and revealed several pieces of the truest blue agate I had ever seen. Blue agates were not rare in Uruguay, but these were translucent, with the clarity almost of diamonds. Every shade of blue imaginable shone in my hands as I held the pieces. They seemed so delicate I was almost afraid to breathe.

"It's a puzzle," *Mamasita* said, assembling the pieces. "Only the *Charrúa* were known to make them, and this one was made for Isabel FitzGibbon over two hundred years ago."

A star had taken shape in her hands, the smooth edges blending together to bring out the various shades of blue in the agates. I could not take my eyes off it. From that day forward, I asked to hold the puzzle every time I visited Caupolicán. It was magical for me, mysterious and revealing. *Mamasita* said the puzzle and I both glowed when I held it.

As I approached the stone steps leading to *Mamasita's* front door, I wished the puzzle were in her town house for me to hold today.

The butler was waiting and bowed as I entered.

"Good afternoon, Frederick."

"Good afternoon, Miss Magdalena. You are looking exceptionally well."

"Thank you, Frederick. How much time do I have?"

He took a gold watch from the pocket of his striped waist-coat. "Ten minutes, miss."

I walked up the staircase to the room *Mamasita* kept ready for all her granddaughters. It was a large room with two double beds and a gigantic oak closet in which hung garments *Mamasita* considered suitable for meals at her house.

I took down a white silk blouse with full, long sleeves and a pleated blue skirt; kicked off my sandals; and changed into a pair of the flat, black patent leather shoes on the floor of the wardrobe. Next door was a similar room, for *Mamasita's* grand-sons. In that wardrobe hung various suits in assorted sizes and colors. Once, when Miguel had come to dinner wearing no jacket over his starched pale blue shirt, *Mamasita* had sent him there with a simple raised eyebrow. No man had ever sat down to a meal with her without wearing a jacket, and her grandson was not about to be the first. It was an exceptionally hot day. Miguel asked Frederick for a pair of scissors, cut the sleeves off the jacket and appeared at the table wearing the remains.

At the dressing table, an assortment of silver-backed brushes awaited me. I glanced at myself in the mirror. I was looking well today. My hair curled to my shoulders; my teeth were straight, thanks to two years of wearing braces; and my lashes were darkening, making my eyes stand out. I might even be pretty some day, as Sofía had recently commented.

I descended to the dining room just as the gong sounded. The long table was resplendent in old Spanish lace and silver, a bowl heaped with red roses in the center. Since the first anniversary of my grandfather's death twenty years before, a single red rose had been delivered to *Mamasita* every morning. The family all knew that the flowers came from Brigadier General Paz, an admirer of *Mamasita*'s from her youth. He had remained unmarried as he rose in the military from the humble lieutenant who had first seen the young Aurelia at a dance, to the straight-backed, silver-haired Brigadier General so many now feared. He called on her regularly, and the vase of red roses was carried into whatever room they chose to sit in. *Mamasita* pretended not to know who sent them, and the Brigadier to be amazed by the fidelity they represented.

My grandmother and I sat at one end of the table, within easy reach of one another. She had changed into a pale gray dress with long sleeves, and around her neck, she wore a choker of ten strands of pearls.

"So. His name is Jaime Betancourt. I don't know his family."

"His father is a tailor."

"An honorable trade."

"My mother doesn't think so."

"Your mother is a snob. Does he have decent table manners?"
I smiled. "Yes."

"The air force would have seen to that if his family had not.
Does he read?"

"Extensively."

"What would you give up to marry him?"

I glanced up from my soup. "I don't know," I answered in
surprise.

"When you do, you'll be ready for an engagement.
Meanwhile, don't promise him anything."

"He is hungry for promises."

"Young men in love always are. They wish to establish quick
ownership. Don't let him. He will try to shape you, and it is up
to you to make sure you shape yourself. You are far too intelligent to marry young."

"You were seventeen."

"That was a different era. In my day, a woman married or
remained under the supervision of her family for the rest of
her life. I was lucky. I was in love, and my husband was a rich
man. Horses were my passion, and he indulged me in it. I had
everything I wanted."

"How does that feel, *Mamasita?* To have everything one wants?"

"It is humbling and liberating."

"Should I go to America?"

"Of course you should."

"Jaime is afraid I shall forget him there."

"Perhaps you shall."

"My mother hopes so."

"It is only for a year. A wonderful opportunity to be a part
of a different culture."

"Do you remember Marco Aurelio Pereira, *Mamasita?*"

She put down her spoon. "My womanhood would have to be shriveled beyond all hope for me to forget a young man like Marco Aurelio Pereira. I had hoped you might fall in love with him."

"Oh," I lowered my eyes. "I couldn't. He . . . he's so special. He'll marry someone like you. Someone purely Uruguayan, like he is."

"No one is purely Uruguayan. Except the *Charrúa.* The rest of us are a mixture. Mongrels all."

"Perhaps. But Spanish and Portuguese are acceptable mixtures. The northern breeds are not."

"Acceptable to whom, child?" *Mamasita* asked, surprised.

"To men like Marco Aurelio Pereira. To thoroughbreds."

"What extraordinary ideas you have. Perhaps the Americans, who are truly a tutti-frutti nation, will help you get over them."

I laughed. "Have you ever been there, *Mamasita?*"

"No, but I'd love to go. I admire Americans. Overgrown children at present, but one day they'll come into their own and teach us all a thing or two."

"The *tías* say they will bore me to tears talking about their cars in ungrammatical English."

Mamasita laughed. "They are proud of their toys. Their prosperity is based on having convinced themselves and others that no one should live without them."

"Marco says greed will one day destroy us."

"And so it shall. Meanwhile, you are to enjoy your stay in North America. I suspect life will be quite difficult for you when you return."

"Why, *Mamasita?*"

"Well, your school days will be over, for one thing. You will have to start assuming family responsibilities."

"I want to study psychiatry."

"Good. I hope you will. The family will need another income. You may have to work while you study. Your cousins are both looking, I understand."

I nodded. "Sofía will probably start teaching next year. I don't know about Carmen."

"Carmen is waiting for a husband who will keep her. She should have a better opinion of herself."

"*Mamá* says women shouldn't take men's jobs."

Mamasita sighed. "Sometimes I wonder how I could have had such daughters. Well, they say brains skip a generation. Perhaps you will redeem us!"

Eleven

Emilia and I soon received letters from our host families with warm words of welcome and photographs of unfamiliar snowy landscapes. Emilia was thrilled to discover that her family included a Great Dane.

Along with a hundred other teenagers, Emilia and I boarded a Pan American jet loaded with farewell gifts brought to the airport by friends and relations. Flowers wilted and balloons obstructed our vision, but travel in our part of the world was an occasion for merrymaking and gift-giving, and few families allowed themselves to be deterred by practical considerations. The terraces surrounding the airport building were crowded with people cheering and waving to us as we climbed the steps and entered the plane. Emilia and I waved back, pretending to know someone on the crowded balcony. Emilia's family had been influenced by mine and persuaded to bid us a quiet and discreet farewell in the passenger lounge, with no flowers or balloons to hinder our departure.

The stewardesses had dealt with airplane loads of exchange students before and were good-natured about the level of noise, the guitars in the aisles, and the number of us perched on the arms of the seats. The lights were turned off as the plane flew into the night, but we slept little. Some of us were homesick already.

Sophisticated as we liked to think ourselves, we gasped

aloud when we first saw New York City, stretched below us for miles, a fairyland of lights in the blackness all around. The airport seemed vast and friendless compared to our small one, and there were no waiting arms to welcome us.

Buses were waiting to take us to our various destinations, and Emilia and I parted: she to go south; I north. A quick hug was all we had time for, and then Emilia's familiar face was swept away into the grayness of old snow and a bleak sky.

The absence of natural color was something new to get used to, I thought. Billboards assaulted us from every direction, ordering us to drink, smoke, and smile a perfect smile.

For the first time since leaving home, the fifty students bound for Michigan were silent, overcome by our smallness in that vast landscape of concrete and glass. It was not until we had left the city behind and were driving through open spaces that we relaxed and started talking. We were on the bus for seventeen hours. Eventually, we slept.

When I stepped off the bus in Michigan, dressed in my light overcoat and leather shoes and gloves, the cold seemed as tangible as the gray stones of the church I was ushered into. Coffee and doughnuts awaited us, and we gravitated to the table eagerly. Some of the students brought out their guitars, and as we waited to be picked up, we sang folk songs reminiscent of home.

Soon families started arriving, and I sat nervously studying and assessing them. One of them, a man with full, downturned lips, furtively eyed the girls. I was hoping that he was not part of my new family when a tiny lady strode in. Her dark eyes flashed from a photo she held in one hand to the faces looking up eagerly around her. She was smiling, and warmth radiated from her. She spotted me, brushed her greeter aside, and took me in her arms. "Here you are!" she said. "I'm Amanda Norton, your Mom!"

I could hardly believe my good fortune. Soon my "Dad's" arms were around me, and his warmth and loving good-humor made it unnecessary for him to tell me that I might be in a foreign country, but if he had any say in the matter, I would never feel alone there.

It was January of 1964, and the United States was still reeling from the assassination of President Kennedy two months previously. The first female astronaut, Valentina Tereshkova, had made a three-day flight in space, and a military coup had overthrown the government of South Vietnam.

I found high school difficult to adjust to. Methods of teaching were different, and the material was elementary. The only unfamiliar subject to me was American government, but with the test answers provided in a multiple-choice format, I could get by with a minimum of study. Slowly, I realized that what I was learning were not facts, but a whole new way of student life and that, after all, was the reason I was there.

The first thing that struck me about my fellow students was their passivity. They sat politely, more concerned it seemed to me about their appearance and social life than about their studies. The girls wore makeup and sported hairdos that must have taken hours to accomplish. One or two were planning weddings.

Very few of the people I met during my stay in Michigan had heard of Uruguay. It was commonly mistaken with Paraguay, and all of Latin America seemed to be lumped together in people's minds into one unstable entity with dangerous leanings toward Communism.

Janet, my American sister, tried to help me. "This is a stable country, Magdalena. We haven't had a revolution since the Civil War."

"I'm not so sure that that is something to boast about."

"You think wars are good?"

"No, but revolutions can be. I wish nobody got killed during them, but rethinking the way we do things, not accepting what the government tells us, that is not a bad thing."

"Some of us trust our government. Is that bad?"

I hesitated. "No. I think it's ideal. But are you sure they're trustworthy?"

Janet shrugged. "Until they do something to make us wonder, why worry about it?"

"What about Martin Luther King and his demonstrations? Aren't they revolutionary?"

"Dr. King is a pacifist."

"I know, but what he's proposing will cause others to be violent, don't you think? President Kennedy had to call the troops out in Alabama. Tell me, have you ever been on strike?"

Janet laughed. "On strike? What for?"

"Doesn't the government ever do anything you object to?"

"Well, they raise taxes sometimes, but what good would it do for us to go on strike about it? No one cares what kids think."

I explained that student strikes were a matter of almost monthly occurrence in Uruguay as, simply as a matter of principle, we protested government policies on anything and everything, flexing our political muscle, writing slogans on city walls, marching by the hundreds, holding up traffic and defacing government property. Janet was shocked. She asked what possible effect such strikes and unruly behavior could have since I had told her we could not vote until we were eighteen. No one had ever raised that question in my presence before.

"No, I can't vote yet, but I'm not powerless, Janet!" I said. Unions were supposed to strike, and our student union was as serious as any other. Janet appeared not only unimpressed, but somehow above such things.

Not long afterward, when the war in Vietnam rocked the foundations of American society, I received a letter from Janet recalling our conversations, wondering if her trust had indeed been an illusion about the future and how assured it seemed to be. By then two of Janet's friends had died in Vietnam, and Janet herself had begun to question things in the same way I had once done.

But back then, living with that family whose patience seemed saintly to me, I allowed myself to revel in how much laughter there was in their house, how much acceptance and love. I tried to understand the rest of the American world where it seemed that a lot more freedom was available or, at least, more privacy. Young people dated and went out alone. Students held part-time jobs.

In Uruguay, school was full-time work, five and a half days a week, with several hours of homework every night, and summer school if we failed a final exam. There were no electives, except for sports, and we worked too hard at our studies to do much else, even if part-time jobs had been available.

When I told Janet that the only electives we had were sports, she could not believe it. "How does anyone graduate if you have to take four years of physics, four years of chemistry, four years of everything?"

Later, when she became a teacher herself, Janet told me she wished her students had to work harder at their studies and were less concerned about the part-time jobs they needed to support their cars.

Before my nine-month stay with the Nortons came to an end, I accompanied the family on a visit to Janet's future home on her college campus. It was the most significant event of my stay. From the moment I stepped out of the Norton's station wagon onto the lawn surrounding one of the many stately

buildings, I knew that I wanted more than anything to stay
there. The air of peace was so pervasive that for a moment I
simply breathed and shut my eyes. To me, places of learning
were places of turmoil. Our university buildings, set in the
midst of the city, were the recipients of years of anger and
frustration. Walls were covered in slogans; monuments defaced.
Buses came and went, their brakes screeching, belching black
exhaust. Horns blew, and leaves, dust, and old newspapers littered the narrow streets.

Here, students strolled in the first warmth of spring with
books under their arms and flowers blooming around them. I
wanted to study in a place like this where, for a while at least,
I could forget about human rights or injustice or oppression.
I imagined teachers with only the cause of learning to serve,
oblivious to politics.

I had criticized Janet's indifference to the world outside her
borders, feeling that she and her friends did not care about
their government's interfering policies, choosing to ignore what
was being sown in the world in their name.

For the first time, I understood why. I knew that if I lived in
a place of such comfort and ease, I, too, would lose touch with
peril and would immerse myself in explorations of the mind,
forgetting all else.

I loved to study and longed to do it where strikes would not
interfere with finals; where a student's political views were unknown to the teachers and could not influence grades; where, as
Janet had told me, one could play in an orchestra, sing in a
choir, act in a play.

I had no idea what had created the differences between our
two countries, nor any understanding as to whether one system
was better than the other, and if so, why. I only knew that for a

single moment, standing in Ann Arbor, I wished that, like Janet, I had never heard of Che Guevara.

⚜

Emilia's big discovery was that religion in America was taken very seriously. It had not occurred to us until we traveled that in Uruguay religion was a matter of extreme privacy. Emilia and I went to mass every Sunday morning only because it gave us an opportunity to observe the boys from the Catholic school. We agreed that we had always looked on nuns and priests as deprived persons who entered convents because of broken hearts or because they had no interest in sex. People we knew listened politely to their sermons and advice with the understanding that as persons retired from life, they could not possibly know anything about it. Churchgoing for us was a social occasion. No one we had ever met took the idea of hell seriously; heaven, if there was one, must surely be open to all, or what point was there in praying to a benevolent God?

Emilia was living in a household of devout Catholics when she first raised the question of heaven and hell. They not only read the writings of the pope, they believed them. Emilia was horrified. Praying before every meal she could endure, but daily mass was torture. The few boys who went concentrated on the service, not on her, and there was absolutely no one to flirt with. To make matters worse, she knew that the youngest boy in the household was madly in love with her and had once gone through her underwear. Emilia considered this behavior so depraved that she wanted to leave the country.

We wrote to each other every day, sometimes at great length, sometimes on a postcard with a single comment.

Twelve

Dear Magdalena, why are American fathers at home so much? I can never escape mine! He comes straight home from work and eats with us every night . . . !!! *Emilia*

Dear Emilia, so does mine! I have seen more of my American dad in four months than of my own father in as many years. I don't think our fathers would know what to do with themselves at home. Mine doesn't even sleep there very often! *Magdalena*

Dear Magdalena, have I told you that my family grows vegetables? We are all expected to put in an hour or two every day weeding and ruining our fingernails for the privilege of eating things we could just as easily buy in the supermarket. The other day our tomatoes were entered in a contest. The rules specified that in order to win, the tomatoes had to have a "conformity of appearance" (it means look the same) and "no blemishes." They were not tasted, only looked at. We did not win. Love, *Emilia*

Dear Emilia, are you sure you didn't participate in the Miss America contest by mistake? Ha, ha! I've just received a letter from your mother. Written by candlelight. She says the U.T.E. workers are on strike, and Montevideo is without electricity or telephones. I can't imagine that happening here, at least not because of a strike. I know that on the East Coast and in parts of

Canada, they had a massive blackout but that was because of a switch or something in Ontario. *Cariños, Magdalena*

⚜

Dear Magda, since leaving the airport I haven't stopped thinking of you. (I must add that I've tried.) Everything seems empty now that you're not with me. I spend my days in the air, perfecting my nagivational skills, or on my bike, going nowhere, trying to reach something that's far away.

Everything here reminds me of you. The songs we like, the sea, the sky, all make me feel terribly alone.

I love you in a way I've never loved anyone before, and when I think of you, I know that I'm alive.

I've just read what I've written so far. I wish I was a poet and able to express myself. Don't take this for a love letter; it is a poor representation of the feelings I can't put into words.

Everyone here is downcast and sad since you left. Except for Josefa, who says she knows you are well and happy. I asked her if she'd heard from you often (*I've* only had two letters from you) and she said she hears from you *every day.* Your American family must be very rich if they can afford to let you call Uruguay on a daily basis. Josefa looked at me strangely when I asked her if you had telephoned. Marco, who was with me at the time, laughed and explained that you are part witch. He said it's the Irish in you. What is the poor fool talking about? He and Josefa seemed to find it very amusing that I do not believe in telepathy or any such nonsense. Marco spends hours at the beach, swimming, and has turned so dark that I almost didn't recognize him. He continues his efforts to get arrested (he marched with the U.T.E. workers) and his father continues to rescue him. Such an idealist. I go back and forth between

thinking him the greatest fool I've ever met and a true aristo-
crat. A member of an order above the rest of us. As long as
there are Marco Aurelios in the world, the rest of us need not
worry, because we know that he will hold, true as steel. He will
embody the democratic ideals we all admire; he'll even die for
them, making the rest of us look good at no cost to ourselves.

Would you do me a favor? Find out the addresses for some
of the big airline companies. I want to write to them about getting work. I don't care if I start as a baggage handler, I know
that once I'm there, I'll find work as a pilot.

Thanks for the Charlie Brown cartoon—I really like
"Peanuts." Send me more.

Will you marry me as soon as you get home? I adore
you, *Jaime*

❧

Dear Marco, I hope you received my last letter, in which I told
you about my wonderful family. I think I also complained a lot
about the cold. Well, I don't have to worry about it so much
any more. After that first day, when I was so frozen after my
walk home from school, I have not had to walk again. My mom
arranged a ride for me to and from school and also bought me
boots and mittens. My feet and hands look ten times bigger
than they really are, but they don't freeze. I have played in the
snow and tried ice skating—I spent more time sitting on the
ice than skating on it!

Did you hear about the race riots in Los Angeles? Thirty-
five people died.

Have you seen the Beatles in *Help!*? It's good!!

I know your brothers love soccer. What are they saying
about those British players accused of fixing the matches?

Talking of sports—Michigan won the Rose Bowl! Do you
know what that is?

Please tell your mother that I will write to her soon.

Love, *Magdalena*

Dear Magdalena, I am so sad today that I don't know if I shall
finish this letter, let alone send it. If I do send it, you will forgive its rambling nature. I am so glad you've written to me. I
keep your letters by my bed and read them whenever I feel a
need to laugh. Your descriptions of your fellow students and
the new dances you are learning make me envious. Here, the
students are angry. But aren't they always? Sometimes I wonder
whether their anger is not as much of a diversion as hit records,
clothes, and hair are for your friends in the U.S. Don't be cross
with me, but I think that Janet's questions are actually quite
sound. Have we ever accomplished anything with our methods?
As you can see, I am in a low mood indeed when I start doubt-
ing the very actions that have kept me feeling connected and
purposeful since I was twelve years old. I brought this depression on myself when I was on leave for a few days and decided
to join the demonstrators outside one of the electrical stations.
It reminded me of that day two years ago, when you and Emilia
saved Cora's life. Yes, I know—you think I exaggerate, but I do
believe she might have died that day without you. (Cora agrees.)

Anyway, there I was, suddenly cut off on both sides by a
cordon of police. My first thought was, if they don't kill me,
my father will when he finds out I haven't given up the tactics
he finds so reprehensible. They came among us using small
rubber truncheons and American *piñas*, laughing as we tried to
escape their blows. A photographer from I don't know which
paper or what planet was snapping pictures. It was obviously
his first demonstration because the poor fellow was announcing

to all who would listen that he would make sure the actions of the police became public knowledge. They swarmed toward him, and by the time they scattered, he and and his camera were wrecked.

We were marched under cover of darkness to the tunnel by the Palacio de la Luz.

And here's where I learned one of the bitterest lessons of my life so far. As I was pushed into the tunnel I felt a hand on my arm. It was Pepe. I hadn't seen him for a year or so, not since he left our beat. Well, he recognized me and pulled me out of the line. He asked me what I was doing there, had there been a mistake? I said no, I was part of the demonstration. He shook his head and grabbed my arm again, pulling me toward a group of policemen. He told them who my father is, said he knew me, and they ordered me to go home. I said I didn't want to go, that I belonged in the tunnel with the others. And they laughed at me. I got angry and tried to hit one of them, but Pepe stepped in and took the blow himself. I tried to enter the tunnel, and they wouldn't let me.

Pepe stopped by our house the next day, and of course, my father rewarded him. After Pepe left, *papá* reached for his whip. I took it from him and threw it out the window. I am twenty-one years old, and he will never whip me again.

Don't laugh—Pibe thought the whip had been thrown for him to chase and ran off to play with it. He lost it, who knows where. He's getting old and doesn't bring things back like he used to!

My father seems to realize that something has changed between us. He said very little, only that I was not to disgrace his name. By his standards, I fear I shall do so often. Now I know that all these years he has been secretly protecting me. It hasn't been luck, as I sometimes thought, or cleverness, as I would have liked to believe. Only good old Uruguayan politics at work again. It isn't what you do that counts, only who you are or who you know.

I want to believe from your letters that you have forgiven me for my unwanted piece of advice about Jaime at your party. I care what happens to you, Little Lion.

I haven't seen *Help!* yet. Perhaps we can go together when you get home. And yes, I do know what the Rose Bowl is. A big baseball play-off, right?

Jaime doesn't seem to mind if we write to each other. So perhaps I will send this after all. My mother encloses her latest poems and says she misses you.

Cariños, Marco

Dear Marco, I can't imagine how you could ever disgrace your name. I am proud to know you. I think your feelings about the workers are wonderful. I have always thought so, ever since that day on the Cerro when I crowned you with daisies. You are my hero.

I am really sorry I got angry with you at my party. I am the one who needs to apologize, not you. I haven't spoken to you since then and writing seems very strange. I wish you were here to put things in perspective for me. I try not to be critical. After all, I am far from perfect myself, and we don't live in Utopia, do we? Perhaps you can help me understand why I find it offensive to walk into places where there are so many things for sale I couldn't even look at them all in a single day. Why do I care that we throw bags and bags of things away? Is it because of what you tried to explain to me that day on the Cerro when you talked to me of how waste dulls the senses? I just don't fit in very well. I suspect you wouldn't either. I am finding passion hard to come by. You are the most passionate person I've ever known, and I keep comparing people to you. Here they are very sentimental. They love stories about children who are dying or have terrible diseases.

The students don't seem to care much about the government. I'm not sure if they believe in it or simply ignore it. I hope they won't be disappointed. They think that because they have free elections they are a free people. They seem more sedated than free. It's difficult to think when one is assaulted on all sides with things to buy. Which takes me right back to the Cerro and how you talked about two kinds of sugar.

Emilia is in Missouri. Her family is very religious. Mine are very kind, as I've told you a million times. I love this house. They are always laughing.

Will you really come to see me when I get home? I'd love to see *Help!* again!

It occurred to me the other day that my childhood is over. School is over. I feel like I'm standing on the edge of a precipice, and there's no choice but to jump. *Mamasita* warned me I'd feel this way. When I return home, I want to go to medical school, but I doubt that my family will approve. Emilia wants to be a lawyer.

Saying good-bye to the Nortons will make me very sad.

My mother wrote recently to tell me that my father's business ventures have not gone well and he has sold more land. My cousins have both found work to help support the family.

How is Lilita? Have you seen her recently?

I was thinking just before your letter arrived that I should have apologized sooner for snapping so rudely at you about Jaime and that I couldn't live with the thought that you were no longer my friend. Now I know you've forgiven me because you know as well as I do that they don't play baseball at the Rose Bowl.

Love always, *Magdalena*

Thirteen

The year that followed my return to Uruguay was a bleak one. Brazilians were flooding into the country to escape the military dictatorship newly established there, and Jaime and I had our first serious quarrel.

Jaime had received no encouragement from any of the companies he had written to offering his services as a pilot, but he was determined to leave Uruguay anyway. The Brazilians brought warnings that what had happened there was an indication of a trend away from democracy, and Jaime wanted to leave Uruguay while he could.

"I think you should stay, Jaime. Marco needs you. There are too few of you in the armed forces speaking out against military intervention. You agree with Marco, I know."

"I do. I agree with every ideal he holds up for us. But I will not die for ideals, Magda."

"Why should you have to? If enough of you in the armed forces resist, the extremists can't win."

"Magda, the bad guys *always* win."

"Marco doesn't believe that."

"Of course he does. He knows it as well as I do, but it doesn't matter to the dumb bastard. Who wins is not the point with him. It's a question of moral superiority. Marco is a dangerous man, most of all to himself."

I was shocked at such cynicism and told Jaime so.

"Magda, I've been poor all my life. No government has ever cared about me, and no government, military or civilian, ever will. Uruguay is going the way of the rest of Latin America, and Marco and his small, very small, band of friends are suicidal fools for trying to stop it." He took my hands. "Listen, Magda, I have a plan. You and I will break up, just as your mother wants us to do. Then I'll make sure she keeps her promise and helps me to get a visa. Before I leave, we'll get married. As soon as I'm in the U. S. and have a job, I'll send for you."

I laughed. "Don't be silly. I'm under twenty-one; I can't get married without my parents' consent."

"I know a judge who'll do it. For a price."

"Seriously, Jaime. I can't go. I'm needed here."

"By whom? I thought you wanted to go to college. You said you'd give anything to be able to do that."

"I couldn't afford to. Do you know what it costs to go to college in the U. S.?"

"I'll be earning enough to send you to Harvard if that's where you want to go."

"What if you're not? What if I leave everything and can't even go to college?"

"Is that all that's important to you? Whether or not you can go to college? What about us?"

"I'm not ready to get married, Jaime. I really am not. And I don't want to leave Uruguay forever. To go to college and then come back here, perhaps, but you're talking of staying there."

"It's Marco, isn't it?"

I felt myself blushing. I could not allow myself to acknowledge any feelings for Marco, but my silence was answer enough.

"You won't leave Uruguay because of his stupid ideas about

saving Uruguay's democracy. What in God's name can you ever do about it? I can just see *you* joining the Tupamaros!"

"It's not only that," I said, turning away.

"Oh?"

"I . . . Marco and I . . ."

Jaime laughed suddenly and bitterly. "Oh, what a fool I've been. Marco and you. Of course. I should have known."

I started to speak but he stopped me. "I want my wings back."

He had been awarded gold wings as the best pilot in his class and presented them to me instead of the engagement ring he could not afford.

"Are we breaking up then?" I asked, my voice strangely detached.

"Don't be so stupid. You know we are. You have as good as told me you love someone else."

I went upstairs and took the velvety case out of my bedside table. I gave the golden wings one last look and closed the box with a snap, feeling oddly relieved.

Jaime had worn the wings so proudly on his dress uniform, I remembered, as I walked back downstairs and put the box in his hands. He walked away without another word, leaving me to wonder what I would do with this love for Marco I had almost admitted to.

I walked slowly back to my room after Jaime's departure and lay on the bed to cry. There were no handkerchiefs in my bedside table, so I got up and went to look for one in the wardrobe. I noticed a bag hidden behind some clothes. I opened it and was surprised to find a brand new overcoat with the tags still on it. I had bought it in Michigan for Gabriela. A wave of guilt swept over me as I realized that I had neglected

Gabriela ever since my return. Absorbed in my own concerns, I had not thought of her until now.

I found a box and wrapped the coat. It was Saturday, and buses to the Cerro were not as frequent as they were during the week. I stood for quite a while waiting at the stop before an ancient bus rattled into view. I climbed on for the long ride out of the city.

As I neared the hill, memories of my last visit there made me clench my teeth in an effort to keep back the tears as I thought of Marco and his crown of wild daisies. Such a fool he must have thought me. How could a man like Marco ever take me seriously, let alone love me?

A cold wind was blowing and I shivered as I climbed the hillside to Gabriela's hut. Smoke came from a hole in the roof, and I hurried toward its promise of warmth.

There was no door to knock on, only an old blanket nailed to the opening. I called Gabriela's name, and instantly the cover was pulled aside and she was hugging me.

"Magda! I thought it was you! I looked out the window, saw someone coming and I said to Gervasio, it is Magdalena! Come to see us at last! As nice as ever but—" her fingers rested lightly on my face—"sad! So sad! Gervasio, put the chair by the fire! Yes, that very one she herself gave us! Right by the fire!"

Gervasio was a big boy now, tall and handsome, the red in his hair tempered to a rich auburn. He did not smile as he arranged the chair for me, and I thought I saw reproach in his eyes as his mother sat on a stool near me. He parted the blanket and went outside.

"Now," Gabriela said, "tell me why you have been crying."

"Here," I gave her the box, avoiding her question. "I brought this for you from the United States."

Gabriela clasped her hands.

"Open it!"

She did, and was ecstatic. The coat fit her perfectly and suited her too. I had chosen a fawn color with a dark fur collar, and as she danced around the hut, I remembered how I had always thought she looked like a movie star. "Gabriela," I said, touching her cheek, "are these new?"

She smiled happily, flashing a new set of perfectly white teeth. "Courtesy of the military!"

"The *milicos* bought you false teeth?"

"Yes! Lieutenant Pereira arranged it." She clicked her teeth happily. "The children love them!"

"Where are the children?" I asked, noticing their absence for the first time.

"With their father. Once a month he takes them to the Parque Rodó."

"Gervasio did not go?"

Gabriela shook her head. "He does not approve of his father. For my sake."

"Because he hasn't married you?"

"Yes, and because Gervasio thinks he should buy us a house. But he can't. He has a wife and five other children to support. Now answer my question," she said, hugging the coat tightly around herself and resuming her place on the stool. "What is wrong?"

"I discovered that I love someone."

"I hope I know him."

"You do."

She nodded. "I'm glad. The two of you are meant for one another."

"Do you think he has ever thought of me?"

"Yes. But he has a mission, Magda. Such men are difficult to love."

"What do you think his mission is, Gabriela?"

"I am an ignorant woman, Magda. I never finished school or anything. So my opinion is not worth much. But I've been going to the rallies. Lieutenant Pereira is often there."

"You mean the union rallies?"

"There are others too. Small ones. Some of them in *ranchos* as humble as mine. Men and women talk and make even us welcome—us from the Cerro, I mean. They are well-educated people, but they treat us like equals. The lieutenant has been helping Gervasio with his school work. I have always made Gervasio and all the children go to school, you know. My own mother didn't insist upon it, and I wish she had. I would have liked to be better educated." She looked sadly at the fire for a moment. "But Gervasio reads well, and the lieutenant makes sure he keeps up with his studies. The people at these meetings talk of change. I don't understand it all, but I do know that the lieutenant is highly respected. When he speaks, others listen."

"Someone told me today that Marco is leading a dangerous life."

"Isn't it always dangerous to ask for justice? When Gervasio reads to me from his history books, it seems to me that people always die before things change."

"Do you believe that the bad ones always win?"

"Oh, no!" Gabriela was emphatic. "Oh, no! Always, always we move forward! Evil may appear to triumph, but good must always follow or there would be no hope for us." Gabriela had put a kettle on to boil over the fire, and steam was rising from its spout. She rose to make *mate.* "The lieutenant let me read his palm once," she said.

I looked at her with interest. "I didn't know you read palms, Gabriela."

"My mother was a *curandera;* my aunts all read palms and

cards too. Cards have never spoken to me, but people's palms do."

"What did Marco's palm tell you?"

"That I cannot reveal. But I will say that I saw something in his palm that I had never seen before. A piece of his lifeline was missing. It stopped very suddenly and then picked up again. I have no idea what that meant. His love line was the strongest I've ever seen, except for my own. I wanted children for him, but they were not there. And now I have said too much."

"Will you read my palm, Gabriela?"

But she was upset with herself for having revealed so much and would talk only of other things that day. We sat for several hours drinking *mate*, discussing the children's exploits and her hopes for Gervasio.

We talked of Marco, revisiting all our conversations, his gestures, and his looks. I showed Gabriela the little ivory elephant he had sent me while I was in Michigan. I wore it on a gold chain around my neck, and Gabriela asked me if I still went to the zoo every week to visit Tomasito.

"Yes. He is very big now."

"Are you still friends?"

"Yes. I thought he might have forgotten me after I was gone for so long. But he hadn't."

"None of us did, Magdalena."

"I haven't been a very constant friend."

"What makes you think so?"

"Look how long it took me to visit you."

Gabriela made a gesture of dismissal. "It is difficult being young. So much is expected. You have your future to consider."

"Gabriela, I have no idea what the future holds. That's why I wanted you to tell me."

She shook her head. "I can't. It isn't always good to know.

I wish I had never read Lieutenant Pereira's palm. Now I don't
do it for friends any more, only for strangers. Then if I don't
like what I see, I keep it quiet and tell them only good things.
They prefer it anyway."

❧

My mother was triumphant about my breakup with Jaime. She
wasted no time impressing on me the necessity of learning a
quick, respectable form of making a living. Secretarial work
was socially acceptable, and if I applied myself, I could master
the necessary typing and shorthand skills within two years. I
explained that I wanted to continue my education and go on to
medical school, but my mother did not want to cope with
Sofía and Carmen's complaints. If they had to work, so should
I, they said. I did not deserve to be treated differently just because I was younger than they.

The rooms of the secretarial school were dingy and win-
dowless. Rows of typewriters sat on plain wooden tables under
several bare bulbs hanging from the ceiling on low cords—the
flowering avenues and marble columns of the college of my
dreams now well beyond my reach.

Emilia and I took to walking for miles on the coldest days,
battling the despair that rose in us as we contemplated our future. We returned to the rocks we had climbed as children,
where we had dreamed of our careers, our brilliant marriages,
and our talented children, and somehow we saw each other
through that desolate winter. Lilita understood our despair. On
days when her own depression lifted, she prepared hot chocolate, baked cakes, and encouraged us to accept every social invitation that came our way.

Before we knew it, summer returned, drumming in the surf.

For three months I was free. I either slept until noon or rose at dawn to run barefoot the two blocks to the river to watch the sun rise. Emilia and I swam no matter what the weather and, thanks to Marco, led an active social life. He had many friends, and Emilia and I were included in the invitations he received. We went to dances at least once a week, picnicked, and met at the amusement park to crowd into the bumper cars and ride the Ferris wheel.

As the sun darkened our skin and lightened my hair, we felt revitalized, and I decided to complete secretarial school in an accelerated study program. Then I would find a job and go to the University at night. Others did. I could. Emilia and I swore a solemn oath that we would help each other keep our dreams alive. Emilia, too, would enroll in night school, and I would help take care of Lilita.

As autumn blew dusty leaves across the pavement under Emilia's window, I worked hard and leapt to the front of my typing and shorthand classes.

The poinsettia tree was ready to flower, and one day in early winter, the miracle of one perfect early blossom was repeated. Surely it was a good omen. The last time the tree had bloomed early, we had met Cora and started our journey together into young adulthood. This time, through the leaves of the poinsettia tree, we beheld a young man across the street leaning against *señora* Francisca's wall, looking up at Cora's window, his motorcycle parked at the curb. Emilia and I almost fell off the low branch that could now barely support our weight. Tyrone Power and Robert Taylor had caused our hearts to beat faster; this light-haired man almost led to cardiac arrest. Here, at last, was romance in the flesh!

Ramiro was six feet tall, with long, slender legs; broad shoulders; and strong, artistic fingers, at that moment curving round a slim cigar. His eyes, we would later learn, were dark blue, his features perfect, with a generous mouth and delicate nose.

As Emilia and I watched, we saw him look up at Cora's window. The look on his face implied that the seven wonders of the world had been revealed to him in all their splendor. His expression seemed to lighten and glow; his whole body strained upward. Cora appeared briefly as he ran across the street and jumped onto the sturdy low trunk of the jasmine, catching the paper that fluttered into his outstretched hands. He was tall and the window low, and their hands almost touched. He kissed his fingertips briefly as the curtains fluttered out in a wave of lace poised on the morning breeze.

Emilia and I watched him leap on his motorcycle and turn the corner in a flash. Then we ran to Cora's house and rang the bell. Cora opened the door herself, looking flushed and anxious.

"May we come in?" I asked.

Cora hesitated. "Just for a moment. I promised Mamma I would study."

Emilia and I hurried in and surrounded Cora on the sofa.

"Who is he?" Emilia asked.

Cora blushed. "You saw him?" she asked anxiously.

"Cora!" Emilia laughed. "It's broad daylight, and a man that *churro* and on a motorcycle is hardly inconspicuous!"

"His name is Ramiro," Cora sighed.

"Where did you meet him?" I wanted to know.

"At a political gathering."

"How long ago?"

"Three days ago."

"And it was love at first sight!" Emilia cried.

"Well, perhaps not at *first* sight, but soon afterwards."

Emilia clasped her hands. "Just like in the movies!"

"Not exactly. He isn't Jewish," Cora whispered, looking around her as if the house itself could condemn her for such a transgression.

"So what?" I asked.

"Don't be such a turnip," Emilia said. "What will you do, Cora?"

Cora's eyes filled with tears. "I don't know."

In the weeks that followed, Emilia and I watched Ramiro daily, arriving on his motorcycle, parking it across the street under the big shade tree outside *señora* Francisca's house, and waiting.

As long as he was not right outside their own door, Cora's mother could not protest or have him removed. He would lean against the tree, his long legs slim in their light, fawn-colored trousers, his arms crossed, and gaze up at the curtained window surrounded by the jasmine behind which Cora sat. He knew he had no more chance of being admitted to that house than a side of pork. Emilia and I agreed that had we been Cora, we would have thrown ourselves out the window at a moment's notice.

And then one day my mother told us that Cora was to be married.

"She's marrying Ramiro?" Emilia asked ecstatically.

"I don't know his name," my mother answered. "A Jewish boy, Mrs. Allenberg said, a lawyer."

"What!" I cried. "She's in love with Ramiro!"

"Who is Ramiro?" my mother asked.

We told her, and she shook her head and looked grave.

Emilia and I tried telephoning Cora but always received the same reply. She was not at home or she was in the tub or sleeping. We wrote her notes and got no answer.

Ramiro still came every day, only now the window was always closed, the fluttering curtain hung limp, untouched by the breezes, and the jasmines wilted on the vine. Ramiro lost weight, his beautiful eyes were shadowed, and he smoked one cigarette after another.

Then he disappeared.

Emilia and I wondered whether he had killed himself in a fit of jealousy or whether he stood now under some other unattainable young woman's window, his blue eyes piercing the curtains, his slender arms crossed and still empty.

Then one day the whole appearance of the house changed. Mr. Allenberg took an ax and chopped down the climbing jasmine, and Mrs. Allenberg replaced the billowing lace curtains with heavy, black velvet ones, closed all day.

Cora had eloped.

⊱✿⊰

Emilia and I were not particularly surprised by the elopement. Cora had never behaved as we expected her to from the moment we met her.

For days the neighbors talked of nothing else. Conjecture ran high, along with the certainty that she would soon be found, the marriage annulled, and the baby—everyone was sure there would soon be a baby—put up for adoption. Talk had even begun about the Allenbergs selling their house when interest in Cora was superseded by the news that Raquel was to marry a millionaire.

Everyone rejoiced that now *señora* Francisca would finally be able to rest her eyes from the fifteen hours of knitting she did each day in order to keep food on the table. Blessings were poured on Raquel's head, and the block rejoiced until Walter, her intended, explained that his parents were insisting on a marriage contract, one stating very clearly what his obligations were to Raquel and their future offspring and making it clear that were she to divorce him, she would get no part of the family fortune.

Señora Francisca was humiliated for her daughter's sake, but swallowed the bitter pill philosophically. There would be no divorce, and Raquel would find a way of helping them indirectly.

Raquel took Emilia and me to the apartment she would be moving into with her new husband, to show us the furniture, all expressly designed and handmade, along with embroidered sheets and imported rugs. Everything was a gift, from the family and friends of the groom. The small maid's room off the kitchen was comfortably appointed, with chintz bedspread and matching curtains at the little window opening onto the building's skylight. Copper pans gleamed on the pale pink kitchen walls, and thick white towels hung in the sparkling bathroom. The account opened for them by the groom's parents already contained enough money for the pair to honeymoon in Europe.

Was she happy? I wanted to know. Of course, Raquel said. Who would be giving her away? Emilia asked, knowing that her father had not been invited to the wedding. Her mother's oldest brother, Raquel told us.

The wedding day dawned sunny and still, a perfect winter day for a wedding. Excitement on the block ran high.

Raquel's family bustled in and out of the house all day, rushing back and forth from the hairdresser's and the dressmaker's, as last-minute gifts and telegrams were delivered and neighbors emerged from their houses to offer assistance and ongoing congratulations to *señora* Francisca. Raquel was nowhere to be seen, but that was hardly surprising. This,

mothers told their daughters, was the most important day of
her life and she was, no doubt, preparing herself suitably for it.
Emilia had seen her entering the church around the corner very
early that morning. Looking serious, Marco added. Good heav-
ens, Emilia and I exclaimed, what could he expect? She was
marrying a Díaz Varela! Millions were at stake. Who would approach such a marriage lightly?

The neighbors left for the cathedral together, dressed in
their finest, as befitted the occasion, and sat quietly in the
church awaiting the bride. She, as tradition dictated, would be
half an hour late. The groom, his girth disguised behind the
folds of a black tuxedo, emerged and stood by the altar. Per-
spiration gleamed on his high forehead. The chandeliers were
lit, and the farthest reaches of the cathedral revealed, awash in
flowers. The organist struck the chords of the "Ave Maria," the
choir burst into song, and Raquel entered, regal, veiled, splendid, and glittering in a gown embroidered in hundreds of
pearls. Uncharacteristically, her eyes were lowered, and Emilia
and I thought we saw a tear gleaming on her lashes as she
walked by.

"Oh, Raquel, beautiful Raquel, say no!" I prayed. "If you
don't love him, say no!" I had watched enough Hollywood
movies to believe such things possible.

The wedding mass proceeded at a solemn pace. The bride
and groom stood, their backs to the gathering of five hundred,
as the priest intoned the opening rites of the marriage ceremony. After what seemed like hours, he turned to Raquel and
asked if she would take Walter as her husband. Raquel appeared to tremble for a moment in the golden light. Then, in a
silence grown electrifying, she lifted her veil and turned toward
the groom. Her "No!" shook the rafters of the ancient cathedral and caused *señora* Francisca, who was standing by her, to

reach for support. Her brother's arm went swiftly round
her waist.

The priest stood, benign smile frozen, and then did something he would always regret. He asked her why, and Raquel
told him. She told Walter. She told the entire assembly.

The night before, on her final visit to the dressmaker's, she
had missed her bus and had to walk several blocks out of her
way. Her path took her by a house of assignation, where, in the
shadow of the porch, she saw Walter and—here Raquel turned
and pointed to the front row where his cousin Graciela sat,
turned to stone—his lover, emerging. They had kissed, passion-
ately, and then each gone their separate ways. Graciela's husband rose as if to protest and was hastily made to sit again by
his father.

Raquel threw her wedding bouquet to the ground, sent the
rings flying with one blow from their place on the velvet cushion before her, and cast the shreds of her marriage contract
into Walter's face. Then she turned and walked back alone the
way she had come.

To everyone's horror, Marco, Emilia, and I applauded her.

As we left the church, Lilita whispered to *señora* Marta that
it seemed altogether fitting to her that the bill for this fiasco
would go to Raquel's father.

Señora Marta was not amused. She had bought a new dress
and was planning to rub elbows that evening with high society,
getting new ideas for her next *radio novela*. Instead, she had a
story better than anything she could have invented and, out of
loyalty to the Arteagas, could not use it.

Fourteen

Marco loved his mother dearly, was proud of her writing and happy to bring home his many friends, at which time *señora* Marta would go into her tiny kitchen and prepare her famous pizza—a thick-doughed pizza, lavish with cheese and tomatoes. Then she would serve it and hold court, while the young men played their guitars and sang love songs. Jaime, I remembered, had thought the guitar playing and the songs frivolous, but he had enjoyed *señora* Marta's conversation and her library. She had announced her plans to write a book, a book that was eagerly awaited by her young friends, since she told us we would all make an appearance in it.

Since Raquel's aborted wedding, however, *señora* Marta had not been in her usual high spirits. Her youngest son, Orsino, was courting a girl he had met on a street corner in Rivera, a town located too close to the Brazilian border to meet with *señora* Marta's approval. People there spoke a bastardized mixture of Spanish and Portuguese that offended *señora* Marta's Castilian upbringing.

One day, the young woman arrived with her mother for a family meeting. Aloof and fur-coated, they moved into *señora* Marta's guest room for the weekend. The three did not see eye to eye. Adriana and her mother preferred soap operas to books, a happy coincidence that Orsino believed would endear Adriana to his mother. It did not. *Señora* Marta had written many soap operas, but she never listened to them and did not associate with anyone who did.

Emilia and I could not understand why Adriana was interested in marrying Orsino, to whom she did not seem particularly attracted. *Señora* Marta told us that Adriana had one goal in mind, to get out of Rivera and into the capital, but this assessment of her character seemed too cold and calculating to be true.

Orsino chose that weekend to announce his decision to join his brother in the military forces. He had had a long conversation with Jaime and decided that he, too, wanted to become a pilot. His father was extremely pleased. *Señora* Marta simply shrugged and, in a move that mystified the household, removed one third of the pizza sauce simmering on the stove. When I asked her what she was doing, she sighed and said, "Watch. There will be fewer of us for dinner."

Then she sat on the large Spanish sofa in her front room and waited.

Doors started slamming upstairs, and Orsino's angry voice drifted down. High heels sounded on the wooden stair treads, and soon Adriana and her mother stood in the doorway, pulling on their gloves. They apologized for leaving earlier than planned, thanked *señora* Marta for her hospitality, and called a taxi.

Señora Marta asked no questions. She simply watched them go and then burned some eucalyptus in a small copper bowl, taking in the pungent aroma as it filled the room and wafting some of it gently in my direction.

Soon Orsino appeared, his eyes red. "She's broken it off," he said.

"Do you want me to leave?" I asked.

He shook his head, and his mother put her arms around

him. He sat by her, his head on her shoulder, and let her wipe away his tears. I patted his back.

"I don't understand," he cried, "we were so happy together!"

"*Ya pasó, corazón,*" his mother murmured. "She was too fond of fur coats anyway and would have ended up looking like her mother. A Santa Claus without a beard."

Later, after Orsino had left to play soccer with his friends, I asked *señora* Marta what she thought had happened.

"That was an ambitious young woman. She was interested in Orsino as long as he spoke of being an engineer. When he announced he was joining the air force instead, she lost interest."

Orsino's broken heart mended, and at the end of the year, he invited Emilia and me to attend the Christmas ball at the air force base at which he was stationed. It was Jaime's base, and I had not seen him since our quarrel. Orsino assured me he would not be there. Jaime, Orsino said, was devastated by the recent death of his best friend, killed on maneuvers. Orsino hinted that the young man had been forced to fly in a plane known to be faulty and had fallen to his death in a stormy sea.

When I asked Orsino how such a thing could possibly happen, he told me about Captain Prego, an officer who treated his men with inconsiderate contempt and, worst of all in Orsino's estimation, was a coward. He shunned responsibility and passed the blame on to junior officers for his own mistakes. Engaged to a wealthy young lady in Montevideo, Prego had openly boasted of his virility and of fathering more than one child among the working women whose homes lay in the small town near the base. Jaime's friend had chosen to confront Prego about his behavior, and his punishment was to be assigned the faulty plane and foul weather maneuvers.

Emilia and I were flown out to the air force base with the other guests and sat close together on the seat, enjoying the short flight. When the plane landed, Orsino got out first to help Emilia, and I followed. A hand in a white glove reached up, and I took it, jumping to the ground. I looked up to thank the officer who had helped me and found myself staring into Jaime's green eyes. Unaware that we were detaining all the passengers waiting behind us, we stared at one another until Orsino put his arms around us both and gently pushed us aside.

Jaime removed his gloves and took my hands in his. His warmth suffused me. The intervening months had been lonely ones. I had immersed myself in my secretarial studies and finished first in my class. I had not missed Jaime's demands to marry him and leave my family, and I had basked in my mother's approval of my decision to break up with him, but Marco and I had come no nearer to declaring our feelings, and I was beginning to think we never would.

Jaime's eyes glowed as he offered me his arm and escorted me into the glittering hangar under the stars, decorated with multicolored parachutes hanging from the tall rafters. The orchestra was playing "One in a Million," the Platters' song we had danced together on our first date, and we laughed nervously at the coincidence, oblivious to the approach of Captain Prego.

He greeted Jaime, and there was no mistaking the look in the senior officer's eyes. Jaime had just risen in his estimation. He returned Jaime's salute and extended his hand, but his eyes were on me. "Please introduce us," he said. "Your good taste is to be commended."

Jaime remained at attention, ignoring the outstretched hand. "The *señorita*'s name is Magdalena Ortega."

Lieutenant Prego smiled at me and touched Jaime's arm, indicating his outstretched hand.

"I have saluted the rank you represent, Captain, but shaking hands with you is a personal gesture of friendship no one can force on me."

The captain was taken aback. His smile wavered. "Come, come, Jaime, what have I done to offend you? The day you chose Miss Ortega you must have known that any man worthy of the name would notice her. If you cannot handle having a beautiful woman on your arm, perhaps—"

"This has nothing to do with Miss Ortega."

"What is it then?"

"Jorge Blanes."

The captain's glove struck Jaime's face so fast I did not see it coming. "My seconds will call on you," he said. Then he turned to me and bowed. "May I have the pleasure of this dance, Miss Ortega?"

For a brief moment, it seemed to me that the entire ball hung, like Sleeping Beauty's castle, suspended in time. All eyes focused on me. But instead of being awakened from this illusion by a prince's kiss, I found myself in the captain's arms, being whirled round the floor as he greeted friends with a nod or a smile. His eyes flitted from place to place, and his hands held me firmly and lightly, with the grace with which he reportedly flew his planes.

At the end of the song, I escaped and found Jaime outside, lighting a cigarette with shaking hands. I took the match and held it for him, then kissed the cheek the captain had slapped. I knew by then that I was not in love with him. That I would not be a part of the life he so desperately wanted for himself. But I was determined to help him, and if he still planned to leave Uruguay, I would convince my mother to assist him. "Don't fight him, Jaime," I said.

He looked at me intently, almost as if seeing me for the first time. "You don't understand."

"I know the foolishness of dueling, and its dangers."

"I am finished in the air force."

"Why?"

Jaime sighed. "If I refuse to fight I will be shunned as a coward. If I accept, and win, Prego's pride will not allow me to remain in the air force. He will make sure I never receive a promotion again."

"Which leaves only losing, and you have not lost at anything more important than card games since you reached puberty, am I right?"

Jaime's eyes hardened. "What an interesting perception, coming from you, the greatest loss of my life."

"You'll let your pride be more important to you even than your future?"

"Without my pride, I have no future! Do you think I could let Prego draw first blood, shake his hand, and forget it? If not for me, then for Jorge, I shall kill him!"

I laughed. The feeling of disbelief would not leave me. "Jaime, are you listening to yourself? We are talking about dueling! You have complained to me a thousand times that you want to leave Uruguay because we live in the Dark Ages here, and now you are catering to one of its darkest traditions! What happened to your decision not to die for an ideal? We both know what a duel is about. It's not about killing each other; it's about pride! Prego doesn't want you dead; he wants his moment of glory, the headline in the evening papers. He wants to be reprimanded by his superior officers at the same time as they envy him the opportunity of living for a few moments their own silly dreams of chivalry. I can't believe you are falling for this!"

"Jorge Blanes was my friend, Magdalena. And Prego killed him."

I took him in my arms. It was all I could think of to do. I asked him to resign and forget the duel. To let me help him.

"If I do, will you marry me?" He sensed the withdrawal in me before I could voice a reply, and he put his fingers gently to my lips. "Never mind," he said.

A date for the duel was set, and as the days passed, the feeling of unreality surrounding the event only grew. Dueling was against the law, but since the civilian authorities would not enforce civilian law with military officers, both men were placed under military arrest.

My mother was horrified. Under no circumstances, not even in my wildest dreams, she told me, was I to consider attending. Reporters would be present, waiting anxiously for the duel to end to photograph the protagonists. Dueling courtesy demanded that they wait until then, and like restless vultures, they congregated on the outskirts of a duel until the very moment after the first shots were fired or the sabres drawn. The name Ortega Grey, my mother reminded me, was not to appear in the newspaper in any section but the social pages, and discreetly at that.

Jaime had chosen Marco to serve as his second, and he came every weekend to give me the latest news.

"What weapon did Jaime choose?" I asked.

"Pistols."

"Pistols? He has gold medals in fencing!"

Marco rested his head in his hands. "Dueling courtesy demands that he not appear to take advantage of his opponent in that way."

Marco and I seemed to be the only ones taking the situation at all seriously. Others said it was a mere cockfight, a flash

of male feathers among the pine needles and sand. A little gun-
powder, a little blood, and it would soon be over.

Marco and I knew Jaime better than that.

⚜

The night before the duel I went to bed as late as possible,
dreading the hours I would spend lying awake in the darkness
waiting to escape. I had brought the leftist newspaper *Marcha*
with me and tried to read an editorial on Santo Domingo. *Tía*
Aurora had been wearing black again. This time for the small
country whose president was being held prisoner in Puerto
Rico for, according to *Marcha*, challenging American imperial-
ism. I could not concentrate on the story. My bed faced the tall
windows at the end of the room, and as I stared through the
slits in the blinds I saw the moon disappear behind the clouds.
The wind rattled the garden gate below. Soon rain glistened on
the glass, and I was afraid that the distant thunder rumbling
over the river would wake my mother. I waited, heart pounding,
for her feet to hit the floor. On stormy nights, my mother
often got up to make sure that the doors were locked, as if the
storms were raucous thieves waiting to steal the silences she
prized.

I looked at the clock. Four-thirty. Soon, our painfully elabo-
rated plan would be put into action.

First, it was necessary for my mother to go downstairs to
answer the phone and stay there long enough for me to slip out
the front door. Marco would see to that with the contrived
telephone call, pretending he had reached a wrong number.
Then Emilia would take my place in the bed.

The telephone rang, making me jump in spite of myself. I
heard my mother's bed creak and her tongue click impatiently

as she ran down the stairs. Her constant worry over my father's reckless driving precluded her sleeping soundly when he was away, and she never ignored the telephone, no matter at what time it rang. Marco would distract her long enough for me to leave the house. Under the bedclothes, I was fully dressed, and pausing only to pick up my shoes and handbag, I ran silently down the stairs and out the front door. There was Emilia under the *estrella federal,* looking absurd in a light wig under her father's enormous black umbrella. I could not help laughing. "You look like Harpo Marx!"

Emilia hugged me. "Go!" she cried and ran up the steps and into the house. We knew that before settling herself once more, my mother would look into each of her sleeping daughters' rooms. "Just to make sure," she would say when teased about this habit, "that they're breathing quietly." Emilia would be there, in my stead, with only the tip of her coppery wig showing.

A light drizzle touched my face as I left the protection of the old tree, and I realized I had brought nothing for the rain. I was glad. I wanted the sharp, clean feel of it on my face. I ran past the street lamps with their warm, yellow light, to the taxi stand around the corner. Not a single car was there.

I panicked. The stand was one of the busiest in the city, and I had never seen it empty before. The duel was miles away, down the coast, and I had one hour to get there. I should have ordered a taxi the day before.

I ran to the river, dark that night and stormy, rollers lapping the shore in brown swirls. I knew I had to stop crying if I expected to run the two miles to the next taxi stand. I took a deep breath, removed my shoes, and started moving along the hard-packed sand by the shore, the waves catching at my feet. The pain in my side began as I spotted the steps leading from

the beach to the taxi stand, still half a mile away. The blood
pounded in my ears. My breath burned in my chest, and I
stumbled as I reached the steps, falling to my knees and half
crawling my way to the top.

There it was. A solitary taxi, the driver reading a magazine
and smoking. He saw me as I reached the top of the stairs, and
his expression made me think for the first time of my appearance. I stood there barefoot, my clothes clinging wetly to my
skin, knees bleeding and hair plastered to my head.

I gestured to the man to open the taxi door. He got out
quickly and put an arm around my waist. He was a small man,
shorter than I, with a round face like a worried baby's.

"Do you need a doctor?" he asked, as he tried to lower me
to the ground.

"No, no! I need you!" I gasped, climbing into the back seat.
"I need you to drive me to El Pinar."

"Of course, of course," he said, "a family emergency, eh?
Where in El Pinar?"

"The woods by the monument."

"The woods?"

"Yes, please hurry. Look," I said, pulling money from my
bag, "I can pay!"

The driver looked offended. "It was not the money I was
concerned about, *señorita*," he said. "I am a father, you know.
I have daughters your age. What do you want in the woods?"

The first hint of day lit the horizon as I told him
everything.

Without a word, he got behind the wheel and turned
the key in the ignition. His little black Mercedes shot from
the curb.

At times, I wondered if we were driving or flying. There
were no other cars on the road, and the driver took full

advantage of this, his face intent as he peered beyond the wind-shield wipers into the rain.

We screeched to a halt at the monument, and I jumped out by the dunes. As my feet hit the sand, two shots rang out.

There was a moment of silence, then voices shouting just over the rise. The driver and I raced together through the pines and stopped when we saw the group of men below.

Captain Prego was being led hurriedly toward us, his face ashen, blood pouring from a wound in his right arm. "He walked into my fire, I swear it!" he cried as he saw me. "I aimed for his shoulder! I know I did!"

Cameras were clicking around him as the reporters, free to take pictures now that the duel was over, came at him from every direction. He was rushed by me in a flurry of voices and a flash of military brass. At that moment, the reporters saw me and I saw Jaime. Quick to spot a drama unfolding, they converged on me as I walked toward the pile of blankets on the sand. I knelt by Jaime and uncovered his body. A jagged hole in his chest leered up at me. For a few more seconds, I was aware of my surroundings as a camera was torn from a reporter's hand by the taxi driver and sent flying into the wet sand.

"*Hijo de puta,* I'll have to pay for that!" the reporter screamed.

I saw Jaime's mouth, as sensitive in death as it had been in life, and I wanted to kiss it but thought he might not like that, not in front of the reporters. So I brushed the sand from his lashes instead and wiped the blood off the golden wings pinned to his uniform—the golden wings I had returned a lifetime ago. The feel and the sight of blood on my fingers jolted me back to the windy beach and I looked up. Marco had torn off his uniform jacket and urged his friends to do the same. Together they made a curtain around Jaime's body, the gallant little driver standing with them, his head barely reaching their shoulders. Marco's fists were flying, and more than one reporter backed away. As Jaime's friends protected his body, Marco wrapped his jacket around me and dragged me to the car. I fought him all the way.

The rain was falling fast and furious now, and he put a hand up to wipe his face as he pulled his wallet from his pocket.

Again the driver looked pained. "That is not necessary, *Teniente.*"

"Take her home!" Marco ordered, pushing me into the back seat as he gave the driver my address.

My mother and my cousins, aware since daybreak that I was gone, ran out as the car pulled up to the curb. The rain had stopped. I saw the curtain flutter at Emilia's bedroom window and wished I could run there instead, to the shelter of that little room. Shutters were discreetly opened as curious neighbors glanced out. My mother took one look at me and reached for the garden gate for support. She gestured to Sofía and Carmen. "Pay the driver," she gasped, "and come inside at once!"

The driver sighed and took my hands in his. "So much preoccupation with money!"

"You have been my friend today," I said, speaking for the first time since leaving Jaime on the sand.

He kissed my hands. *"Señorita—"*

"If you won't take money," I said quickly, afraid his kindness would release the flood of tears I was holding back, "how can I repay you?"

"Be happy. Love a good man, like the proud *teniente,* and have babies whose beauty will light up the dawn, like yours did for me today."

Fifteen

My mother's worst fears were realized. Both the dailies and the one evening paper had pictures of me on their front page, my clothes streaked with Jaime's blood, my face a mask, unfamiliar, somehow hard. It was *Mamasita* who took charge. She appeared early the morning after the duel, ordered Josefa to pack a few of my clothes, and announced that she was taking me to Caupolicán. I had not been to the *estancia* for several years. *Mamasita* ran it without help from my mother or any of my aunts, who had disliked "camp life" from the moment they could talk.

Mamasita took me by the arm and led me to the car, where Frederick, who doubled as butler and chauffeur, stood with his usual quiet dignity ready to open the door.

We rode in silence for a long time. The summer had been a rainy one, and the streets were full of puddles. The river was still brown and choppy, and the cries of the seagulls were muted by the wind and the closed windows.

Feeling safe for the first time since the duel, I let my breath out in one long sigh and *Mamasita* patted my knee. We stopped for lunch in La Paloma when the *cerros* came in view. Frederick announced that the sun would shine before evening, and he was right.

Just as we reached the rough dirt road that would take us into the low hills, the clouds vanished. The sun turned the rain sparkling on the hillsides into a thousand rainbows as *Mamasita* and I got out of the car at the top of the first hill. This was what Marco had talked of that distant day on the Cerro. His Eden, a place where the only sign of human influence on the landscape was the road, weaving its way up and down the hills. The *gavilanes* floated in the air high above my head just as he had described them, and the sheep still called to one another across the green divides.

Mamasita pointed. "See that hill over there? The one with the dead tree pointing at the sky? Just beyond that hill is Caupolicán."

I rode the rest of the way with my head out the window, *Mamasita's* hand stroking my back.

I had remembered the house as a low, white villa, with its arches covered in purple bougainvillea. I found it smaller than my memory of it, surrounded by groves of tall, whispering eucalyptus and feathery mimosa trees. Parrots screeched from their nests in the highest boughs of the eucalyptus trees. "All Caramba's relatives," *Mamasita* said.

The house was dark and cool, full of old Spanish furniture, ponderous and gleaming. Ornate wooden chairs stood on sheep skins and on cowhide carpets in shades of brown and white.

Mamasita took me to a room overlooking the hills at the back, and as I opened my window, a cluster of orange and yellow butterflies feeding on the encircling vine entered the room. They fluttered over the bed with its tall carved posts and landed on the lace covering the tall dresser. *Mamasita* shooed them away and opened the mirrored wardrobe doors. Hanging neatly side by side were racks of gaucho *bombachas*, brightly colored sashes, plain white blouses, and long woven ponchos.

"It has always been my dream," *Mamasita* said, "that one of my granddaughters would learn to ride."

Mamasita's dream came true. I took to horses just as *Mamasita* herself had done. Sometimes we were up before the sun, brewing *mate* and cutting bread to take with us into the fields as we walked amongst the herds of *criollos* that were *Mamasita's* pride and joy. Her horses won ribbons every year at the Prado exhibition, but that was the least of it. *Mamasita* was proud of them because of who she said they were. There were horses in her herds who had never been ridden, descendants of the wild herds of her great, great-grandmother's day, and others whose ancestors fought in the wars of independence. As the sun came up and the horses woke, shaking the dew from their coats, *Mamasita* and I would slip the halters from our shoulders and choose our mounts for the day.

We rode out on the hills, checking the sheep, and sometimes, *Mamasita* would take me through the *monte*, the junglelike thickets along the streams, and lead me to hidden pools where we could swim with the fish in the crystal clear, cool water.

We were sitting on the trunk of a tree growing out over a stream, dangling our feet in the water, when *Mamasita* first spoke of what had happened.

"I have a message from your father."

"Must I go home?"

Mamasita shook her head. "He wants you to know that if you want to go to college in America, he will pay for it."

Only bird song and rippling water broke the silence that followed this announcement.

I began to sob. My heart's dearest wish had come true, and my heart could not bear it.

Mamasita held me for a long time, rocking me gently while the fish lay suspended in the water at our feet.

Finally, when I could cry no more, *Mamasita* took a letter from her pocket. "I think this is from your friend Marco." She

climbed up the bank while I opened the envelope and took out
the letter in Marco's familiar hand. A smaller, folded piece of
paper fell out and almost fluttered into the stream before I
caught it.

Dear Magdalena, I found this in a box of Jaime's things his
mother asked me to go through. It was for you. He never gave
it to you because he said the poetry was so bad. I liked it. The
love shines through. I'm no judge of poetry anyway. I miss you.
We'll go walking by the river when you come home. *Marco*

I opened the folded paper I had saved from the stream.
It was the page of a lined notebook, and several words had
been scratched out and written over. What remained was a
short poem.

> I've walked miles
> on the roads of your thoughts
> and cleansed my hands
> in the life of your body.
> I've breathed a breath
> of myself on you
> simply to watch it journey
> through labyrinths of mist
> never to come back to me.
>
> I've held to things
> with willing hands
> and no old voices
> called me back.
> I've looked at sunsets
> without blindness or fear

become a mirror
and not its image
a deep, deep lake
and not its shimmer
and if I am allowed
to touch you yet again
let it be with open hands.

◦⋰⋱◦

From the moment I first walked on the *cerros,* I understood that
I belonged on that land my ancestors had chosen generations
before. *Mamasita* also felt a weight lift from her heart as she
watched me embrace the land as a part of myself. For years, she
told me, she had been battling despair. She had given birth to
four daughters and they to eight children of their own. Not
one of them saw in Caupolicán anything more than a source of
revenue, a place to take visiting foreigners curious to see gauchos, or a convenient location for hunting. When *Mamasita* forbade hunting, the attractions of Caupolicán grew fewer still.
While refusing to hand over the land to a family member who
did not revere it as she did, the only other alternative was to sell
it to strangers. The very thought brought on a feeling of loss so
profound she would stop what she was doing and soothe herself by opening the drawer in which she kept her most treasured possession. On the night she heard about the duel, she
had gone to the drawer and removed the blue star puzzle.

Holding the agates in her hand, *Mamasita* had known that
she should take me to Caupolicán to recover. We were sitting
by her bedroom window, the moon shining in on us, when she
told me about her feelings, unwrapped the agates, and put
them in my hand. They glinted in the moonlight, and my old

and profound love for *Mamasita* and now for Caupolicán itself
told me what I should do.

I returned to Montevideo to enroll at the University and
round out my education with economics and land management
courses, not medicine and psychiatry as I had first thought.
Mamasita and I agreed, almost without speaking, that this was
what she wanted, what she had been waiting for, and that my
future now lay with Caupolicán.

I let my parents know of my plans and of my determination to support myself by finding a job. My family did not take
me very seriously but saw no harm in what I proposed.
Contacts were made on my behalf by my mother and a secretarial position offered me with the United States Information
Service, where I discovered for the first time what a prized
commodity my complete fluency in two languages could be.

Enrolling at the University was left entirely to me, and on
the first day of my new land management curriculum, I arrived
half expecting not to be admitted. The paperwork had been
considerable, and I was sure that I had not done it correctly.

No one appeared to prevent me from entering, however,
and I was soon in my first class, where to my surprise I found
Ramiro sitting at the desk behind mine. He had dyed his hair a
dark brown and changed his name, but I knew him at once. We
had never spoken, and as far as I knew, Ramiro had no idea
who I was. I scribbled a quick note saying I was an old friend
wanting news of Cora, and he wrote back asking me to meet
him after class at the café across the street.

I chose a table in a corner and ordered coffee, feeling
strangely excited. Ramiro had lost none of his old air of romance and mystery, and as I saw him make his way toward the
table with the same heart-stopping, easy grace that had first
made Emilia and me feel like throwing ourselves out of the

estrella federal at his feet, I found myself wishing I had taken more care with my appearance that day. I took a long, slow sip of my coffee.

Ramiro pulled out the chair opposite mine and smiled at me. I had to make a concentrated effort to remember that I did not know this man. I was no longer a susceptible teenager, and I was meeting him only to get news of Cora. The appearance of the waiter gave me a few seconds to compose myself. Ramiro ordered mineral water and took out a pack of cigarettes, offering me one. I was about to accept when I realized that not only did I not know how to smoke but that my hands were shaking. I declined just in time to avoid making a complete fool of myself.

"How is Cora?" I asked.

"She's expecting a baby."

"May I see her?"

He exhaled a long puff of smoke. "I'll let her know you want to. We live with my parents."

"I've thought of her often. Will you tell her that?"

He nodded. "She talks about you a lot."

"Does she?"

"She says it's thanks to you she was able to leave her house."

I laughed. "Oh, no! Cora didn't need me to find her way out. She's one hundred times stronger and more independent than I'll ever be."

"So what are you doing at the University?"

I told him about Caupolicán and my grandmother's idea that I should equip myself to run the *estancia* by learning the basics of agronomy and land management.

"She's not just going to give it to you?"

"Not my grandmother. That place is her life. She'll hang onto it until she knows I'll run it just as she does. Or better,"

I grinned, finishing my coffee. "I have to go now. I'm starting a job soon, and I have to stop by and fill out some forms. Don't forget to send Cora my love and tell her I want to see her."

"Where are you going to work?" he asked.

"I've been offered a job at USIS." I was looking for my wallet and almost missed the expression of sudden interest that crossed Ramiro's face.

"I'm sure that Cora will want to see you very soon," he said.

Sixteen

Two days later, Ramiro invited me to his parents' home, telling me that it had been a long time since he had seen Cora as happy as when he announced that I had recognized him and asked to visit her.

I found Cora looking radiant. We hugged and cried in each other's arms until Ramiro said he was afraid that so much emotion would hurt the baby. Cora sat me by her side and looked at me closely.

"I read about Jaime in the newspaper. I'm so sorry, Magda."

I nodded. "My grandmother took me away. To Caupolicán. It helped to be there."

Cora took my hand. "Do you ever see my parents?"

"I see your father sometimes. Your mother doesn't go out much any more."

"I am hoping that when this is all over . . ."

"They will want to see their grandchild, certainly!"

"I meant when a new government is in place, then—"

"Magdalena doesn't know anything about that, Cora," Ramiro interrupted.

There was an awkward pause. Then Ramiro got up, saying he would get refreshments for us. I waited until he had left the room before asking Cora how it felt to be married.

"Oh, we're not married," Cora said. "We're waiting until the new government is in place so we can have a real celebration."

Her voice took on some of its old softness. "With all our friends."

"Tell me about this new government."

Cora hesitated.

"You don't trust me, Cora."

"Magda," Cora asked, "why did you go to hear Che speak?"

"I was curious. Idealistic. I liked what Che said when he asked us to feel in our souls any injustice done to anyone anywhere in the world."

"Do you know why a student was shot that day?" Ramiro asked as he returned. He poured Coca-Cola into three tall glasses.

"I was told it was done on purpose. To make sure that Che's visit didn't go peacefully."

"For years, the Russians and the Americans have been playing a very dangerous game with one another, with us as their pawns," Cora told me. "The arms merchants and the military of both countries have persuaded their governments that each is poised to annihilate the other."

"So the U.S. and Russia are bankrupting themselves buying weapons," Ramiro added. "Latin America is their playground. The place where they can test each other with relative safety."

"The Russians, Magda, want to prove that, given the opportunity, the people of Latin America would not choose American capitalism," Cora said.

"The Americans know the Russians are right and that their only hope of preventing the success of anticapitalism is to make sure its alternative—socialism—is never given a chance, because—"

"Because," Cora interrupted, "if socialism succeeds then they can no longer make money off us."

"How do they do that now?" I asked.

"They own our mines, our plantations, our land, our oil. But there are groups of us all over Latin America determined to fight back. Here, we are called the Tupamaros."

I caught my breath. "You two are Tupas?"

They nodded.

"Did you ever discuss this with Lilita or with *señora* Francisca?" I asked.

Cora smiled. "Often. It was *señora* Francisca who took me to the meeting where I met Ramiro."

And then she told me of the work she and Ramiro were doing. Of how they were educating and organizing people to form a new political party and vote it legally and officially into power. Of how much opposition there was to them because they wanted to eliminate the ways in which business and politics had always been conducted here—by a small group of powerful people who benefited from the system without sharing the wealth they accrued or any of its benefits.

I saw myself for the first time as a member of that group.

During the long bus-ride home after that conversation, I felt like a person marooned on a desert island, receiving, instead of sending, bottled messages. A whole underlayer of society, of people working to change the world, had been revealed to me. I felt that Gabriela, Lilita, *señora* Francisca, the students who helped me after Che's speech had been trying to tell me something and that it was time I listened. Everything I'd heard and seen until that moment started falling into place, even Jaime's death, and I didn't want to just absorb it any more. I wanted to act. I started to understand that if people like me stopped to think about why Gabriela lived as she did, about why a woman like *señora* Francisca hid guns in her house, about why Lilita's friend Juan was tortured, about why a group of students would be chased by policemen on horseback . . . if we only stopped long enough to think about such things, perhaps the world would change. I was young enough to think that I could change it, and I asked Ramiro and Cora what someone like me could contribute to the Tupamaros.

❧

The Tupamaros, I learned, were organized in small cells, groups of ten to twenty-five people, with a cell leader. Cell leaders reported to a contact, who in turn linked the cells to the central leadership, a small group of three or four men known, at least by first name, to every Tupamaro.

I joined Cora and Ramiro's cell and was instructed not to become involved in the increasingly violent student demonstrations, during which more and more students were being arrested. They were concerned with preserving the image I had of an upper-class young woman uninvolved in the student union or any of its activities. They encouraged me to talk little to other students and, when I did, to stick to superficial topics. My job at the USIS office made me too valuable to the Tupamaros for them to risk my arrest.

For me, it was a lonely choice. The student union dominated the University at every level and was strongly supported by the teachers, most of whom sympathized with the Tupamaros and many of whom were active in the leadership of the group. My only option was to present myself as a vacuous and flighty young woman, carrying out my grandmother's wishes until the day I could take over the *estancia*. This image was incompatible with the high grades I received in all my courses, but no one seemed to notice the incongruity or the fact that students inactive in the union did not usually do as well as I did in the exams graded by teachers sympathetic to the Tupamaro cause.

At cell meetings, a moment of silence was devoted to commemorating the dead. In Uruguay, two students died that year; in Mexico, almost one hundred. It was 1968 and democracies, Cora said, were falling with the regularity of clockwork in Latin America. The only hope for the survival of freedom on the southern continent lay with the election in Chile of Salvador Allende. Ramiro was the only one not elated when Allende was elected.

"He'll have his work cut out for him," he said. "The president of ITT has already offered one million dollars to whoever rids Chile of him."

I went to work learning the names of the men stationed with USIS and with the Agency for International Development, finding out which ones were not really part of either agency. Some, I found, were with the State Department, on special police missions, and some with the CIA, an organization I learned had been born the same year as I had, 1947, and whose activities in Latin America were connected with the downfall of at least six democracies.

My instructions were to observe the workings of the USIS office, which was closely linked to political and police activities, and to report on what I saw. My first report, that an Office of Information, financed by the U.S. Embassy, had been established at the Uruguayan Department of Intelligence Services, was no surprise to my cell members. Neither was the news that copies outlining the work of this office were regularly sent to the U. S. Embassy. Those involved were well aware that copying documents from Uruguayan Intelligence and distributing them to a foreign power was illegal.

Of greater interest was my discovery of a CIA plan to pressure the Uruguayan government into breaking off diplomatic
relations with Russia. Four Russian diplomats were to be set up
as having been the cause of the many strikes that had plagued
the country that year. While this particular plan was of interest
to my companions, the game itself was so familiar that I was
told not to bother to garner any more information about it, but
simply to concentrate on a man called Dan Mitrione, whose
name appeared in a "Who's Who" of the CIA. I discovered
that that was a mistake. Mitrione had been trained by the FBI,
served as a chief of police in Indiana, and been hired by the
State Department as a trainer for police overseas. His specialty
was torture, and many of Ramiro and Cora's friends had experienced his methods firsthand.

During my first year of working for USIS, I acquired a reputation for speed and accuracy in my translations and was frequently in demand to work after hours at a level of pay I found
hard to resist. Most of the work was of little interest to the
Tupamaros, but occasionally it yielded unexpected bonuses.

Mitrione himself asked for me one day and requested that I
come to his house in the suburb of Malvín. When his wife answered the door, I heard the sounds of several children running
up and down the stairs. Mrs. Mitrione told me that her husband
was busy with a guest but had left the papers needing transla-
tion in the room he used as an office. She showed me the room
and the papers, asked if I needed anything, and when I assured
her I had everything necessary to get on with the work, hurried
away. Every so often, I heard shouts and cries as the children
raced past the door and Mrs. Mitrione issued a reprimand, but
I was soon lost in my work, and by the time I took a break, she
and her children had left for the beach.

I went in search of a bathroom and, after opening several

doors, found one in a corner of the top floor. It was a bathroom with two entrances, and I was about to close the second one when the sound of voices reached me from the other side. One was Mitrione's, the other that of a man I did not recognize, who spoke English fluently, but with an accent.

"Interrogation, Manuel, is an art," Mitrione was saying.

I crept closer to the partly open door.

"First, you soften the prisoner up, humiliate him thoroughly."

"Make him feel helpless, I suppose," the man called Manuel said.

"Yes, helpless. You lock him up and then beat him, insult him."

"During the interrogation?"

"No, no. No questions at this stage. The stages are important. Isolation. Blows. Insults. Then only blows. In silence. This is hell. Pure hell. The subject is alone in a cell, and every few hours, he is beaten. Then you interrogate."

"The blows stop?"

"Yes. Only the chosen instrument should be used at this point. Precision is the key. A precise place, with the precise amount of pain."

"How do you determine the precise amount?"

"That is where the art lies, Manuel. If the subject loses hope, he dies. That is why assessing the state—physical and emotional—of each subject is crucial to the outcome."

I heard a controlled excitement in Mitrione's voice that helped me understand why his name was spoken in Tupamaro circles with a mixture of fascination and horror.

I wished I knew who Manuel was. Was he being trained? Mrs. Mitrione had referred to him as a guest, which implied some status above that of a mere torturer.

"I've heard," Manuel said, "that continuing the beatings is a good deterrent."

"If you're planning to let them go, yes. Is that often the case in your situation?"

"I don't have anyone with your skills working for me, Dan. My technicians either end up killing people or getting useless information."

"A preassessment of whether or not you have the luxury of letting the subject die is essential."

There was the sound of ice dropping into two glasses. "Same again?" Mitrione asked.

"Yes, please."

"You and I have the challenge, of course, of working with police who lack any kind of training. When I first arrived here, I had to change everything. The men had been taught to fire into the air, never at their subject, even if he was on the run. Can you believe it? I had to work with the politicians to issue a decree allowing the police to actually shoot at people!"

Manuel laughed. "It's a hard job."

"But necessary. This is a war to the death. These Tupas are clever. Very clever. All well-educated university men—and women! Can you believe it? No rabble here. Not like in . . . well, not like in other places."

"You can say it, Dan. I won't take offense. Cuba?"

"Well, that was a different situation, and there were educated men there too. But this place, Manuel, this is a real challenge! I have to combine the skills of a surgeon with the sensitivity of an artist. I can never lose my temper. I always have the feeling that I'm dealing with people who think they're better than I am. Sometimes I have to remind myself that they're the enemy. They're so convinced that they're fighting in a good cause."

There was a pause as they drank.

"I'd like to see the lab," Manuel said.

"We can, now that my wife and the kids are gone. It's in the cellar. There's only one way in, through the garage, and I have the only key."

"It's completely soundproof, I understand,"

"I once had one of the technicians fire a revolver down there while I was in the room upstairs. Nothing! Not a sound. I brought in the best people in the business to work on it."

"You offer courses there?"

"On anatomy, the nervous system. Important, basic stuff."

"And you do interrogations there?"

"Some. We've been experimenting with a couple of things—some drugs, some electricity. D'you have a strong stomach?"

"Would someone with a weak stomach survive in the CIA?"

They laughed.

I heard the sounds of a drawer opening. "I took pictures of some of our first subjects, *bichicomes*, street garbage. We had to experiment on someone, and the police were too gutless to use prisoners. This is one hell of a socialist country, d'you know that? Anyway, we picked up these four beggars and used them."

There were several moments of silence, and then Manuel asked some questions regarding voltage and the chemicals used in the drugs. Mitrione said he could answer the questions better downstairs, where the equipment was kept, and the two men left the room.

I hesitated for only a moment. Then I stepped into the room Mitrione had just vacated. Several black-and-white pictures lay on a low table. I picked them up and for several moments could not have moved if my life had depended on it.

The photos became a blur, but from somewhere beyond the

ringing in my ears, I remembered that Lilita had told me that one day I would have to make a choice.

I made myself take a deep, long breath, and gradually a feeling of icy calm flowed through me. With deliberate, careful movements I controlled my trembling and wiped the photos, moist with the sweat from my hands, replaced them on the table, and returned to the office. I took a piece of paper and a pen and, in an unwavering hand, wrote Mitrione a note saying I had been taken ill and had gone home. I put the completed work next to the typewriter, stacked it neatly, and left the house.

That evening, I went straight to Ramiro, and together we planned how we would kidnap Mitrione and use him in exchange for the Tupamaro prisoners being held by the government. Ramiro had been thinking of it for months. I told him how it could be done.

Seventeen

The best place to catch Mitrione, I told Ramiro, would be on one of the side streets his driver often took while chauffeuring Mitrione to work. It would be easy to cut off Mitrione's car, knock out the driver, and transfer Mitrione to another car. I could easily discover his route by chatting with any of the policemen who were assigned to drive him. One in particular, who loved American rock and roll, often asked me to translate the latest song he had heard and getting information from him would be easy.

On July 31, 1970, Dan Mitrione was kidnapped in exactly the way I had outlined and taken to a Tupamaro prison. He was there under sentence of death, but the Tupamaro leadership did not intend to kill him. Nor, to my silent fury, would they use any of his own interrogatory methods on him, in spite of the fact that 150 political prisoners were being held in Uruguay's jails and subjected, thanks to Mitrione's tutelage, to regular doses of electric shocks and beatings with wet paddles. A doctor was summoned to treat the bullet wound in his shoulder, and the young Tupamaro who had shot him while Mitrione lay on the floor of the truck transporting him to the Tupamaro jail was censured and made to apologize.

I had been having nightmares every night since I had stood in Mitrione's house holding the photos of his victims in my hands. It was not the first time I had heard of torture, but it was my first experience seeing the victims. At cell meetings, stories abounded about the *máquina.* I had learned that the term *máquina* was not necessarily applied to any particular device, but could be used to describe each individual's ordeal with whatever method of torture was experienced. I had heard Ramiro describe one man, a former gymnast, who had been made to stand for three days with a brick in each hand. On the third day, a log weighing twenty-five kilos was laid across his shoulders. These methods and the beatings that accompanied them were crude, Ramiro said, compared to the little electric rods designed to be inserted into every body orifice and activated. I had heard, too, of the *submarinos,* where electricity and water were combined or sometimes, if one was very lucky, water only, a test of the lungs by prolonged submersion.

The faces of those who told the stories, their quiet voices, averted eyes, and reluctance to speak came back to me after I saw the pictures in Mitrione's house. Along with the horror of what the victims had gone through had come a slow, creeping fear that I, too, might face the *máquina* some day.

I lost interest in food, and soon my clothes hung loosely on me. I cared only about seeing Mitrione suffer but kept all my feelings, especially that one, under tight control. To my family and friends, I appeared simply as a serious student pressured by upcoming final exams. Ramiro, mistaking my self-control for triumph at the success of our plan, allowed me to visit Mitrione.

I wore a hood and was instructed not to speak. I had no desire to. I just wanted to look at him, in his underground prison, being held by those he had called his enemies. I hoped that he was afraid. I wanted to believe that when one of the Tupamaro guards approached his cell, he felt a surge of panic, asking himself if the stages of terror he had so carefully orchestrated for others were about to begin for him.

The more I watched him pacing his cell, occasionally

massaging the wounded shoulder, which was healing rapidly under expert medical treatment, the angrier I became. What right had he to live when I had held the evidence of his work in my hands and had seen what he had done? Only Ramiro and Cora knew that among Mitrione's victims was one of the people I had most loved in the world.

For a long while, Gabriela had not come to our *barrio* on a daily basis; several of her children were old enough now to do it for her. Marco had seen to it that Gervasio enrolled at the University where he was studying law, and occasionally our paths crossed. I often recognized Marco's clothes, a little large, but a good enough fit so that Gervasio always appeared well dressed. Until my recent involvement with the Tupamaros, I had not allowed more than a few weeks to go by without visiting Gabriela, and when I saw what Mitrione had done to her, I blamed myself. I had neglected her again, and this time failed utterly to protect her. Perhaps if Mitrione and his thugs had seen me with her, they would not have chosen her for their experiments. Her only crime was poverty. She had cared for her children and her horse, loved flowers and Beatles' music, hung my childish art on her wall, and Mitrione had called her street garbage. The image of her naked body, covered in burns from the voltage tested on her, her head in a pool of vomit, would not leave my memory. I tried to recall the others in the photos in Mitrione's house, tried to mourn them, too, but only that one image of Gabriela had imprinted itself on my mind with indelible hatred toward the man before me now.

I hoped that the government would not deal. That they would refuse to release the imprisoned Tupamaros. I hoped that Ramiro would have to carry out his threat and kill Mitrione. I would ask for the privilege of being his executioner.

Ramiro had underestimated the fury of the military forces waiting in the wings for the perfect excuse to take control of the government. The arrests and tortures did not stop with Mitrione's capture, as the Tupamaros demanded, but only increased. One week later, Tupamaro leader Raúl Sendic was caught, along with thirty-eight of his companions. The Tupamaro leadership gave the government until midnight to release them, or Mitrione would die.

Anxious to establish a policy for dealing with the guerillas plaguing him on all sides in Latin America, Richard Nixon declared that the United States would not deal with rebels. No negotiations with the Tupamaros would take place.

I went to see Ramiro, stopping only briefly to look in on Cora and her little boy before finding Ramiro standing by the dining-room table, surrounded by newspapers containing the latest news of arrests and searches for Dan Mitrione.

"Well?" I asked him.

"Well what?"

"When will we execute him?"

"Are you joking?"

"Were you?"

"No," Ramiro said. "But it is not a decision that will be made lightly or announced like some *Carnaval* procession!"

"You think I'm not serious? Look at me, Ramiro."

He did, and took a step back.

"Dan Mitrione killed Gabriela. I am asking to be his executioner."

Ramiro ran a hand through his hair and shook his head in disbelief. "Sit down," he said. "Now listen to me. The decision about Mitrione hasn't been made yet. When it is, it will be carried out professionally. Not by anyone he has ever touched or who feels about him as you do."

"We have professional executioners? Since when?"

"Don't mock me!" Ramiro said, his fist crashing into the table. "We are at the most crucial and difficult point in our struggle, and I have no time to waste on little rich girls who think they can do men's work!"

I grabbed the table and tipped it into his lap, sending him sprawling on the floor. I landed on his chest, my fists pounding his face. "I loved Gabriela! Don't you dare tell me that I am just a rich nobody you can use and then insult! I can kill as well as any man, and you know it, you prick!"

"Magda! Magda!" I felt Cora's hands pulling me off Ramiro's body, and eventually her voice penetrated my rage. "For God's sake! What are you doing?"

"I want to kill Mitrione! Why won't anyone listen? I want to be the one! Let me! Let me!"

Cora was stronger than she looked. She held on until I let myself be held, then she stroked my back and hushed me. "There, there, my dear, dear friend. Hate him; hate him forever if you want, but you must not be the one to make these decisions or to carry them out. We need you. This is either the beginning or the end, and I can't face one or the other without you. You are all of my childhood that is left to me. You were my hope for freedom, my friend in hiding; you are my family now. Please, please let me tell you that finally, after all these years, I have been able to do something for you." She eased me into a chair and knelt before me, taking my hands firmly in hers. "With the help of a friend I have discovered where they disposed of Gabriela's body." She turned to Ramiro. "May I tell her who helped me?"

"No, you may not," Ramiro answered angrily as he righted the table.

Cora gave him a look of annoyance and then turned back to

me. "He is someone very dear to me, with connections to the
police. He was able to discover where they buried her. The
'technicians' working with Mitrione were in over their heads.
They were only too glad to tell someone where those poor
souls were buried. Perhaps now we can put her to rest as she
deserves. What do you think?"

I had no idea what I thought. All I knew was that I was
being offered a chance to bring some peace to that racked body,
to honor Gabriela and her death. For a moment at least,
Mitrione lost his hold on me, and when I could talk again, I
apologized to Ramiro. He was holding a handkerchief to his
bloody nose and his voice sounded muffled. "I am sorry for
what I said. I really am, Magda. But—"

Cora silenced him with a quick gesture. "Come. We'll have
some *mate* and then decide what to do."

⸙

When I asked *Mamasita* for permission to bury Gabriela at
Caupolicán, she prepared a place for her in the old family
cemetery and went with me to the Cerro to talk to her
children.

I had visited Gervasio very soon after seeing the photos of
his mother. I felt he had a right to know that Gabriela was
dead. Beyond that, I had no idea of what I would say to him,
how I would explain my knowledge of his mother's death, or
what I would answer if he asked where her body was. I was
spared the necessity of any explanation. Gervasio already knew.
"A friend" had told him.

In his new role as head of the family, Gervasio gave his
permission for his mother to be buried at Caupolicán. He

collected the things that had meant most to her. An old picture of the children at the Parque Rodó, a ring Gervasio himself had given her, her *mate* gourd, and the paper flowers and clay plates.

Gervasio's friend, the one who had told him of Gabriela's death, had arranged for a coffin and a place to safely keep it. It was then that I realized that this friend and Cora's were one and the same. Someone very well connected with the police, I thought. Only a trusted colleague would have been allowed access to those bodies, I commented to Cora.

She looked at me strangely. "Magdalena, don't you see? They think no one could possibly care. After all, who was Gabriela? Do we even know her full name? She was a beggar, with no influence and no connections. Even if someone did see her body, they would never believe that her wounds were the result of torture. Let alone who was responsible for it."

Mamasita brought her covered pickup from Caupolicán. It was the only vehicle large enough to hold the coffin. We drove to the *rancho* several miles out of town where the coffin was being kept and put the plain wooden box in the back. We covered it with *tacuara* cane and drove all night, the road a mire after the recent rains.

We arrived at Caupolicán at first light, turned off the road, and steered the pickup over the moors to the old cemetery.

Mamasita's Irish ancestors were buried there, surrounded by ancient *ombúes*, with their oddly shaped trunks and gigantic canopies. Jasmine grew rampant along the low wrought-iron fence surrounding the graves, and in the distance, a stream glinted in the early morning light.

Gervasio could not take his eyes off the herds of *criollos* in the pastures all around us. He told us that one of the earliest

memories he had of his mother was of her telling him how it is
against the law to kill a horse because of the part horses played
in the wars of independence. He was glad she would be buried
with so many *criollos* standing guard nearby.

Cora, Gervasio, and I used ropes to lower the coffin into the
newly dug grave. Then we put Gabriela's treasures on top, and
Mamasita, Cora, and I withdrew behind an *ombú* until Gervasio
had said his final good-byes.

It took us an hour to fill the grave. While we worked,
Gervasio and *Mamasita* spoke of how to conceal the site. It was
no longer legal to bury the dead in old family cemeteries, and
while it was unlikely that anyone would see or report Gabriela's
grave, Gervasio wanted to run no risks that his mother's body
would ever be disturbed.

We found a young *ombú* in the surrounding grove and trans-
planted it. To further conceal the freshly dug rectangle of
earth, we planted jasmine around the sapling. It was early
August and the plants were not in flower, but we knew how
sweet their scent would be when summer came again.

A cold wind was blowing, threatening more rain, but we
were warm from our work and stood for a long time by
Gabriela's grave before returning to the pickup.

A few days later, I got my wish.

In the early morning hours of August 10, 1970, Dan
Mitrione's body, shot twice through the head, was found in the
back of an old convertible.

I was surprised at how little I felt his death.

There had been a time when not only would I have felt
something but my feelings would have been evident to everyone

who came into contact with me. Friends told me that even when I did not say anything, I radiated emotions. Like beams from an extraterrestrial, Emilia had joked.

The last time I had allowed myself to feel anything had been that day at Ramiro's when I had wanted to kill Mitrione. I told myself this new numbness was because I had to pretend so much and so often. Whatever that transparent quality had been was dangerous for someone engaged in activities considered revolutionary at best, terrorist at worst.

There was no one familiar to turn to. Lilita was in the hospital for her depression, and Emilia, I feared, might never speak to me again if she knew of my involvement with the "subversives" she hated.

I had not seen Marco for weeks. Not that it would have done me any good, I thought. He would have been horrified to hear of my work with the Tupas. I heard of Marco mainly through *señora* Marta, who was proud of how quickly her son was advancing in the army. He rarely came home, and I feared our next encounter. In a way, we had become enemies, fighting on different sides. He, apparently content to work with the poor and do what he could for them through legal channels; I, now one of the terrorists the military forces incessantly cried out against.

So one late winter morning I knocked on *señora* Francisca's door. Raquel and her sister had already left for the University. *Señora* Francisca opened the door and did not appear surprised to see me standing there.

"May I talk to you, *señora* Francisca?"

"Of course. I've been expecting you for weeks. Would you like to go for a walk by the river?"

I nodded. *Señora* Francisca changed her shoes and put on a warm coat and gloves. She took my arm, asked me to stop

calling her *señora*, for we were *compañeras* now, and guided me to
the Rambla and down the steps onto the sand. The river was a
brilliant blue that day, the gulls a flurry of white at our feet.

We walked in silence for a while, and then I talked about
Dan Mitrione and my part in his capture. "I have come to believe that there are people whose ways are evil enough to justify
execution."

"But?"

"But could I have done it, Francisca? I told Ramiro I could."

"I don't think any of us knows the answer to that question
until the moment comes. We went too far in killing Mitrione.
Or perhaps not far enough."

"What do you mean?"

"According to the goals we set for ourselves in the beginning, violence was to play no part in our overthrow of the ex-
isting system."

"Yet you hid guns in your house."

"How did you know that?"

I told her of the day Emilia and I had crept up the stairs to
listen to her conversation with Lilita.

"Yes," Francisca said. "We were prepared to defend ourselves. It was never our intention to attack. Do you see the ab-
surdity of it? It is what I mean by too far and not far enough.
Either we should have been entirely peaceful, like Ghandi, or
entirely violent, like the IRA. It is this selective, halfhearted
killing that will destroy us. Because the Americans and the
Russians, you know, allow themselves the luxury of no such
scruples. George Bernard Shaw was right when he said that
those who make half revolutions dig their own graves."

"How can we hope to win?"

"That is not the point. The point is how the rest of the
world can allow the Americans and the Russians to get away

with putting the rest of us in constant danger. It comes back to what Che was always saying about individual responsibility. We may lose. We may be tortured. We may die. But there are some of us who cannot rest while injustice is being done to anyone, anywhere. And once we know ourselves to be one of that number, then we give up living according to any rules society can recognize."

"My question remains unanswered, Francisca."

"Would you have pulled the trigger on Dan Mitrione?" Francisca shrugged. "It doesn't matter. It was not the work you were called on to do. Someone else had to make that choice that day. Once you start along this path all you can hope for is to make one choice, one day at a time."

Eighteen

When Ramiro approached me with plans to kidnap the British ambassador, Geoffrey Jackson, I remembered Francisca's words: "One choice; one day at a time."

"What has Jackson done?" I asked.

"Directly, he's done nothing."

"So why are we kidnapping him?"

"So long as we hold someone the government doesn't want killed, we have a bargaining card."

"What do you need?"

"Information on Jackson's habits. You've heard of 'The Jesters,' of course?"

I nodded. Like British expatriates all over the world, Montevideo's Anglo community socialized, founded societies for the prevention of cruelty to animals, ran flower shows, and put on plays. Willing and not-so-willing volunteers were found to produce, act in, and provide props and furniture for an annual extravaganza at which a play was presented, along with Scottish reels, bagpipes, and a ball.

The play chosen that year was a British comedy, and Ramiro was certain I could get a part in it. I laughed outright and explained to him that many people auditioned for the roles and that I had never set foot on a stage before. The likelihood of my being cast was next to nil. Whether I got a part or not did not matter, Ramiro said. I could volunteer to help

backstage. What mattered was that Peter Wentworth, who
worked closely with Jackson, was to direct the production.

When Emilia heard that I was going to try out for a play,
she said she wanted to come along. I tried to dissuade her, but
Emilia only teased me about my being afraid that her English
was better than mine and that she would get a bigger part.

I could not prevent Emilia from accompanying me without
telling her the real reason for my own sudden interest in the
Jesters. The situation was not a dangerous one, I thought. I
would only be getting Peter Wentworth to talk about the ambassador and his habits.

My mother insisted on escorting us by bus to the auditions.
The Jesters' headquarters were in the only part of town the
group could afford—the red-light district, near the docks. My
mother had never allowed Sofía or Carmen to go near the
docks alone. After dropping Emilia and me off and arranging
a ride home for us with friends, my mother returned to the bus
stop, where she was approached by a man. Assuming that she
was being spoken to by one of Carmen or Sofía's many boyfriends, of whom she could never keep track, and not wishing
to appear rude, she chatted on as she waited for the bus, until
the question of price arose. My mother had had a sheltered upbringing, but something recalled to her that she was in that
part of town to protect Emilia and me from just such advances.
Her bus appeared at that moment, so she kicked her admirer in
the shins and made her escape.

Emilia and I had arrived at the run-down studio early and
were taking off our coats while avoiding the mousetraps at our
feet, when Mrs. Tillman tapped us on the shoulder. Mrs.
Tillman was president of the Jesters and appeared delighted to
welcome new members. She gestured to a tall young man

standing beside her. He was dressed in a suit of elegant English cut, which set off to perfection his athletic proportions.

"Girls, I'd like you to meet Peter Wentworth. He's new at the consulate and is assigned to work with the ambassador. He's also directing the play this year."

I held out my hand to Peter Wentworth, but he never noticed it. He and Emilia were staring at each other, and there among the mousetraps and the peeling paint, I knew that the Hollywood movies I had seen were true. Love at first sight did exist. People did get lost in each other's gaze. The world did stop turning when true lovers met. I heard no violins playing, but I knew that Peter and Emilia did. Their hands moved together as if in slow motion and once together they just stood, staring at one another until I felt it necessary to intervene.

Not surprisingly, Emilia and I were both cast in the play.

Night after night, the air was charged with the joy of Emilia and Peter's ecstasy over each other. They laughed and joked, their energy catching and pervasive. The play sparkled with a flamboyance the playwright never conceived or intended.

Emilia walked on air. "You know, Magda," she said one day, as we sat cross-legged on her narrow bed. "I've read about it, I've seen movies about it, I've dreamed of it happening, but I never, ever, had any idea of what it feels like to know that one has met the person for whom one is intended. To know that never, in my whole life again, will I ever feel this certainty."

"Has he spoken to your parents yet?" I asked.

Emilia frowned slightly. "Not yet. Perhaps it's not done in England. He may think it's old fashioned. But *papá* and *mamá* asked your mother to look into his background, and she found that he comes from a very good family. His father is a member of Parliament!"

"You will end up living in London, Emilia!"

"And it's thanks to you."

"Well, I'm glad I finally did something other than get you into trouble!" I laughed.

Emilia's parents were not quite sure how to deal with Peter Wentworth. Had he been an Uruguayan, he would by now have approached them, asking for permission to see their daughter and setting up a mutually agreeable schedule of visits. He was a foreigner, however, and clearly ignorant of how to behave. Emilia's parents were willing to forgive him for that, especially since he was a diplomat and obviously quite respectable.

For a variety of reasons, all plausible and involving his schedule at the embassy, he rarely came to the apartment, meeting Emilia downtown for dinner and dancing, a movie, or a night at the theater. If their date ended early, he sent her home in a taxi, the driver generously tipped to walk her to the door. If they were late, he drove her home himself in a borrowed embassy car. At those times, her parents were already in bed. They would lie awake until Emilia returned, and her mother would get up to warm milk and discuss the evening with her, but Peter was not expected to enter the apartment at that hour and had never done so.

I was truly happy for Emilia and wished only that she and Peter could have met under circumstances that did not involve me and my work with the Tupamaros. I often felt twinges of guilt when Emilia confided in me about Peter's work and the ambassador's busy schedule.

While in the flurry of acting in a play for the first time, trying to keep up with my courses at the University, and following Emilia's new love affair, I did not attend cell meetings for several weeks and was not surprised when Ramiro approached me at my bus stop near the University asking for a report.

With the information Ramiro received from me, he completed his plan for kidnapping the British ambassador, and on the morning of January 8, 1971, Geoffrey Jackson disappeared.

For several days, Emilia heard nothing from Peter. At first, she was terrified, convinced that Peter, too, had been taken. I tried to reassure her, knowing full well that Peter had been nowhere near the ambassador that day. Emilia, however, would not be comforted. She cursed the Tupamaros and their works, wished herself long gone from a country where such things could happen, and threatened to enter the British Embassy and demand to know where Peter Wentworth was. When Peter finally called, his voice tense and curt, it was to say that he could not talk for long but would call again in a few days.

Emilia meanwhile ate almost nothing. She sat by the telephone waiting for it to ring while Lilita and I tried to distract her by playing *conga.* When the call finally came, Emilia hung up the receiver with a look of pure joy.

"Well? What did he say?" I asked.

"He wants us to come to his house. For a very small, discreet gathering. He can't entertain while the ambassador is being held by the Tupas. He is sending a written invitation for *mamá* and *papá* and inviting you and a few of the people from the Jesters. The only thing he said was that the ambassador would want him to do the right thing and that it was time."

None of this made sense to me. "What does he mean?"

Lilita clapped her hands. "He is going to propose! What else could it mean?"

This sudden change in Peter's behavior appeared suspect to me, but I did not have the heart to voice my concern. Lilita, happier than I had seen her in years, announced that the time had come to open the silver box. She went to the dresser in her bedroom and from the back of a drawer extracted the box, overflowing with twenty-four years of savings. Emilia gasped when she saw it, and Lilita, in a moment of abandon, threw the bills into the air.

I left them, giggling together as they gathered money from under the sofa and chairs. I tried to contact Ramiro and Cora. I could not reach them and knew I should not continue to try. I could endanger everyone. Security measures were at an all-time high, and I was ordered not to attend cell meetings until I heard from Ramiro that it was safe.

The next day I accompanied Emilia and Lilita to Gigi's, Montevideo's most exclusive boutique, where Emilia bought a short, black dress discreetly trimmed in sequins. It made her look chic and youthful at the same time. I had not noticed until then how lovely Emilia had become. She still wore her dark brown hair long, only now it was highlighted in a color that set off her gold-flecked eyes. It was brought home to me once more that since Gabriela's death I had allowed myself to become increasingly detached from everyday events. Sometimes I caught myself functioning automatically, with no memory of what I had done the day before or intended doing the next day. I would change that, I told myself, trying to take an interest in Lilita's purchase at La Madrileña of a two-piece suit in bordeaux taffeta. Perhaps, I thought, it was time for me to take a break from Tupamaro affairs and focus entirely on my studies.

In the week that followed, I often stood at the bus stop Ramiro and I used as a meeting place, allowing bus after bus to go by, hoping he would appear. He did not, and I appealed to Francisca.

"You mean you haven't heard?" Francisca asked anxiously, drawing me into the kitchen and away from the living room where her daughters studied.

"No. What?"

"Ramiro has been arrested!"

"Cora too?"

"No. She's in hiding somewhere."

"Francisca, what shall I do? How can I help them?"

"We can do nothing. Ramiro has a powerful friend who won't desert him. The best thing you can do is to act as if you know nothing about any of it."

"I am tired of playing that part!" I said in sudden anger.

Francisca's hand rested lightly on my arm. "It is a part we each must play."

"But only I have to play it all the time and with everybody!"

"Not with everybody, *compañera*."

Only Francisca and Cora called me *compañera*. The Tupamaros used it as a term of solidarity and endearment between one another, and knowing the acceptance it implied helped to calm me.

But I was still afraid and told Francisca so.

"You would be a fool not to be afraid," Francisca said, giving me a quick hug. "I promise to tell you everything I hear about Ramiro and Cora. Meanwhile, keep up with your studies and invite me to that play you and Emilia are in."

"It's been canceled," I said. "Because of the kidnapping of the ambassador."

I told Francisca my worries about Peter Wentworth. He had not come to see Emilia or allowed her to meet him anywhere, claiming that security measures would not permit a meeting. Emilia and Lilita had not asked why these strict measures should be lifted for the upcoming party, and I could not bring myself to shatter their happiness by questioning Peter's motives.

Francisca advised caution. It was best for Lilita to be

focusing on Emilia's party and for me to appear unconcerned and not draw any attention to myself. I was relieved to follow Francisca's advice. It freed me from any sense of responsibility.

Two weeks after the ambassador's kidnapping, Lilita, Emilia, and I arrived outside Peter's house promptly at eight, escorted by *señor* Mario.

Emilia stopped for a moment when we reached the little house overlooking the Rambla to take my arm and whisper, "Look, Magda. It's perfect!"

I agreed that it was. A cottage, English in style, set in a small garden on a hill. Stepping-stones led up the front of the gentle rise, and the garden smelled of roses. A single light shone from beyond the flowered curtains, revealing a room decorated with taste and comfort. I was trying to envision Emilia making it her own when a cold breeze off the river made me shiver.

Peter met us at the door and ushered us in. He looked pale, and when Emilia commented on his appearance, he said that he had been working long hours. He did not touch her or notice her dress, but hurried us inside.

A waiter passed with a tray of food and drink as we joined the other guests in the small living room.

As the evening progressed, Peter grew more nervous and kept glancing at his watch. What or whom was he waiting for? I wondered.

Dinner was served, eaten, and cleared away with no sign of the anticipated proposal. Emilia looked concerned; her father wiped his brow repeatedly, and Lilita acquired a faraway expression. I was increasingly alert, my senses on edge.

As chocolates and cigars were handed round after dinner, I saw a large car pull up outside the house. I was surprised to see four men in military uniform descend, walk up the steps, and enter the house. The other guests, except for an embassy official named MacGregor to whom Peter seemed to defer, melted quietly away.

Once in the room, the officers bowed slightly. I noticed that Peter was wiping his hands on his handkerchief and looked ready to cry.

"Emilia Lanconi?" one of the men asked.

Emilia glanced at Peter. "I am Emilia Lanconi."

"You are under arrest for the kidnapping of Ambassador Jackson."

Emilia stepped back as if she had been struck. "What?"

"We have reason to believe that you gave information to the terrorists regarding the ambassador. Information that made it possible for them to kidnap him. We have just searched your apartment and found incriminating evidence."

Peter swayed slightly as if he were about to faint.

Lilita, who until that moment had stood frozen, let out a cry and threw herself at the men. "Assassins! Torturers! Leave my daughter alone! I am the one you want! Anything you found in the apartment was mine! Ask the neighbors! I am a Tupa! Not her! She is innocent!"

The same feeling of unreality that had overcome me years before at the air force ball threatened to immobilize me now. This time, however, I found my voice in time and shouted above Lilita's cries, "Don't believe her! I am the one. I gave information about the ambassador to the Tupamaros!"

No one appeared to be listening. Emilia's coat had been found, and she was being led away. *Señor* Mario was restraining Lilita with difficulty.

"Peter!" I said, clutching his sleeve. "Peter, stop them before you regret it! I swear by all I believe in, I am the guilty one. Emilia knew nothing. She did nothing. She adores you! You can't do this to her!"

"They're quite hysterical, Peter," the man called MacGregor said. "You did the right thing. It's over now, my boy."

Peter started to cry, and MacGregor coughed in embarrassment and looked away.

I took Peter's hands and shook him. "Peter! Listen to me!"

MacGregor stepped between us. "Peter has been through enough. Thanks to him, Miss Lanconi was not arrested weeks ago. Peter insisted on a thorough investigation. Leave now, Miss Ortega. If you wish to make a scene, for heaven's sake do so among your own people."

I ran out behind the four men. "Stop! *¡Paren! ¡Soy yo! ¡Yo soy la culpable!* I am the guilty one!"

One of the men turned toward me as Emilia was put in the car. *"Señorita,"* he said, *"por favor.* We understand your concern, but please—"

"Listen to me!" I said, forcing myself to act calmly. "I work for USIS. I am fluent in English. I was in the production Mr. Wentworth directed. Why would Emilia betray the ambassador? She is hoping to marry Mr. Wentworth! If you are looking for the person who gave the Tupas information about Mr. Jackson, take me!"

The man looked at me and laughed. *"Señorita,* if you work for USIS, the CIA has cleared you. Please, step aside."

"Magda!" Emilia called from the car, "what is happening to us?"

"They will let you go," I said, running alongside the car as it left the curb. "They must! You are innocent!"

"Tell Peter I did not betray him!"

A strand of Emilia's hair caught in the hastily closed car

window, and I could not tear my eyes off it until the car disappeared around a corner.

Señor Mario hurried up to me and asked me to take charge of Lilita. She was hysterical, running along the pavement, pleading with her husband to take her with him. He had called a taxi and was preparing to follow Emilia to the police station, where he assumed she was being taken. I did as he asked and took Lilita by the arm, leading her away, assuring her that it was best to let *señor* Mario follow Emilia on his own. I guided her down to the Rambla to look for a taxi there. Several drove by, all occupied. Lilita was shivering now, trying to escape me and threatening to throw herself in the river. Even if an empty cab did go by, the driver might see Lilita's condition and not stop.

I was feeling desperate when a taxi pulled up and a man jumped out of the backseat. The gold bands on his uniform shone under the street lights.

"Marco! I have never been so glad to see anyone in my whole life!" I cried.

He asked no questions. He simply picked Lilita up and put her in the cab. We were not far from home, and together, Marco and I got Lilita into her apartment. She had left her evening bag at Peter's, and Basco, the porter, had to be summoned for a spare key with which to let us in.

I called the doctor, and then Marco and I made coffee. Lilita lay sobbing on her bed and remained there until the doctor administered a drug to help her sleep. After he left, Marco and I sat staring at one another across the dining-room table.

I told him everything. He looked as shocked as I had expected. Unbuttoning his uniform jacket, he started pacing up and down the small room.

"*Bueno*," he kept saying, "*bueno.* . . . One thing at a time. One thing at a time. First, you are to keep quiet about everything you told me tonight. No!" he said, as I started to object. "Understand this once and for all! It will do no good for you to keep saying that you did it. They might believe you; they might not. Either way, your confession will not help Emilia. One thing they never do is admit they were wrong. She will be interrogated anyway."

"But, Marco, I know what that means! She will be sent to the *máquina*."

"Maybe. But she will be sent no matter what you say, do you understand that? You can be of more use to her here. Take care of Lilita. She will need you to stay alive. I will make sure Emilia hears that Lilita is being cared for."

"How?"

He dismissed my question with an angry gesture. "It doesn't matter how. Do you know where Jackson is being held?"

I shook my head.

"Good. That is good. Ramiro has some sense. Now listen carefully. You are to leave everything to me. Everything. Go to work as usual. Study as usual. And never again open your mouth in public about your connection with the Tupamaros."

"I don't like the way you're giving me orders, Marco. What does any of this have to do with you anyway?"

"You will do as I say, Magda. Because if they take you seriously and you are arrested, you will put Ramiro and Cora in even more danger than they are already!"

"Because I'd talk, you mean? Because you don't think I have the strength to keep quiet under torture?"

"Little Lion, you have no idea—"

"No, at firsthand, I have no idea! But I'm not as stupid or as weak as you and Ramiro think me!"

"I only wish you weren't involved in this ugly struggle," Marco said, resting his fingers gently on my lips.

I recoiled from him, ashamed. I thought he did not trust me or think much of me, and at that moment, I agreed with him. Emilia was in danger because of me; Ramiro had been arrested; Cora was in hiding; and from the moment he touched me, all I wanted was for him to kiss me.

Nineteen

Three days later, Emilia was home. I had not been able to sleep since her arrest. During the day, I took care of Lilita. The doctor came and administered sedatives. At night, I sat on the balcony and waited for a sign from Marco or from anyone about what I should do. And then one night, just before dawn, a car stopped at the corner, and I saw Emilia getting out. I wanted to shout her name and run to her, but when I saw how she looked, I could not do it. I was afraid she would never talk to me again.

It was worse than that. Emilia hated me. She cursed me and blamed me for ruining her life. She said she knew now that I had been involved with the Tupamaros all along and had used our friendship to arrange the ambassador's kidnapping.

She tried calling Peter's house and found that his number had been disconnected. She tried the embassy. Peter was not accepting calls. At first she could not understand why. They had released her, told her she was free to go. Surely now Peter would believe she was innocent. Then she found out, thanks to Marco, who Peter really was.

It was when Lilita confided in me about Marco's investigation into Peter Wentworth that I first suspected that Marco himself was more than he seemed. He had told Lilita that Peter had been aware that she held a high position with the Tupamaro leadership.

Lilita was furious when she learned this. She felt responsible for Peter's interest in Emilia, although as I pointed out to her, he could not have known who Emilia was when he first met her. Emilia's appearance at the auditions had been unplanned.

"Yes, but imagine his delight when he found out that the girl who loved him had a mother in the Tupamaros! What more could an ambitious young secret-service officer wish for? When Jackson was kidnapped, MacGregor, the man you met at the party, was sent from London to oversee the investigation into the ambassador's disappearance. Marco told me that MacGregor was sure that I knew where Jackson was being kept. MacGregor and Peter hoped that if they arrested Emilia, I would come forward and tell them everything."

"But Marco saw to it that you were kept so drugged that you didn't know what was happening until after Emilia was released."

"I'm not sure if I can forgive Marco for that, Magdalena."

"Lilita," I said, "Ramiro told me that there is a *milico*, a military officer friendly to the Tupamaros, who was negotiating with the British Secret Service for the ambassador's release. Is that officer Marco?"

"What makes you think that?"

"Marco seems to know a lot."

Lilita sighed and brought the subject back to Emilia. "She's angrier than ever at me now. She calls me a 'subversive.' She feels the Tupamaros stole her childhood from her, making me a crazy woman and a bad mother. I wanted to spare her, wanted her to live free. I thought that if I did all the fighting, Emilia would never have to, and she'd be happy. I thought that by now the struggle would be over. Now Emilia thinks I've robbed her of her future happiness and taken Peter from her forever. He has been transferred, you know. No one will tell us where."

"Lilita, I think it would be good for you to tell Emilia why you acted as you did. I think Emilia believes that somehow you don't think her good enough to join the fight. She doesn't understand that you only wanted to spare her."

Lilita nodded. "Perhaps the time has come. Will you be with me when I talk to her?"

"Emilia won't see me."

Lilita patted my arm. "I will arrange it."

❧

A few days later, at a time when *señor* Mario was at work, I sat with Emilia and Lilita at the dining-room table in their apartment.

"I don't know what you two feel you have to tell me," she said, "but the games you've been playing have cost me my happiness, not to mention three nights in jail and interrogations I want to describe to you, so you will have some idea of how innocent people pay for your actions."

Lilita put her hands out to her daughter in a gesture that asked her to hear her out first, but Emilia was not to be prevented from speaking. She took her mother's arms and pinned them fiercely to the table, her knuckles white with the force with which she held Lilita's frail wrists. "On the first night, I stood outside all night, next to a wall, only they wouldn't let me lean against it. They had stripped me first, so I was naked. Whenever one of the soldiers needed to go to the bathroom, he didn't use the toilet, he used me. Some put their cigarettes out on me." Emilia released her mother's arms and raised her shirt, revealing sores across her breasts and stomach.

Lilita's eyes filled with tears, but she never wavered. She

looked at Emilia's sores as I sat rigid, my hands clasped on the table, leaving a ring of sweat on its polished surface.

"The next day and the day after that they took me to the *máquina*. The other women in my cell told me that the *máquina* changes people. After such intimate contact with electricity and water, one's perceptions of other human beings are never the same, they said. They were right. I learned more from those women in three days than either of you have bothered to teach me in my whole lifetime." She looked intently at her mother, then at me. "Now I want to know why I wasn't good enough to be one of you. I want you to tell me what it was about me that made you exclude me from the fighting!"

"It's what I wanted to explain," Lilita said. "I wanted to be the one to take the blows, so you wouldn't have to. I am a fool, and you are right to hate me."

Emilia's eyes never flickered. She rested them on me and said with contempt, "And you? What excuse do you have?"

I felt at a loss for words. "I don't know, Emilia. I promised your mother that I would keep you safe, and I wanted to keep that promise to protect you. You were studying hard, almost ready to receive your degree. Your future seemed assured. I didn't want to spoil it for you. Especially once you met Peter. Then it became even more important not to involve you in anything that could threaten your happiness. Things didn't work out that way, but that is how I thought at the time."

"I want to hear it. Everything you and *mamá* have done."

We began slowly, with Lilita going first. She told Emilia of the early meetings, when Emilia was a baby, a time when there were so many factions Lilita had almost despaired of ever seeing one cohesive movement emerge. She told us about the later gathering of weapons and of information, the meetings in out-of-the-way *ranchos*, the eventual writing of the First Statutes that would guide the group that came to be known as the Tupamaros.

"I can still recite our goals," Lilita said, smiling nervously at Emilia. "'We aspire to be the organized vanguard of the exploited classes in their struggle against the regime. We represent a voluntary, fighting union of those conscious of their historic duty.'"

I in turn told of my chance meeting with Ramiro, of my feeling that I had somehow been sleepwalking through life, of the rage that swept over me when I saw the pictures of Gabriela's body, of my decision to serve as an informant to the Tupamaros. I talked of how I had felt when Mitrione was shot and of the doubts that assailed me still when events like Emilia's arrest brought me face-to-face with the consequences of my actions.

After I spoke, a long silence fell between us until I asked Emilia if she could forgive us.

"I don't know if I am capable of forgiveness yet," she said.

❦

In early September of 1971, Geoffrey Jackson was released, and a decree was issued relieving the police of their responsibility in the struggle against the Tupamaros. The armed forces would now take the lead in conducting what was deemed to be a state of internal warfare.

Marco was made a captain. He took me to dinner to celebrate, and I decided to ask him if he had been the negotiator for Jackson's release.

"Are you sure you want to know?"

"Marco, I am twenty-four years old. For as long as I can remember, you have been trying to protect me. I became involved anyway. You know the part I played in Jackson's kidnapping."

He nodded. "It is something Ramiro and I disagree on. The kidnappings, I mean. Mitrione I can understand. Jackson was a big mistake. At least they had the sense not to kill him."

"Were you the negotiator?"

"Yes." He paused while a waiter took our order. As soon as the man had gone, Marco spoke again. "MacGregor was sent from London expressly to negotiate with the Tupamaros. In secret. Publicly, the British government wanted to maintain the same position held by the United States. No negotiations with terrorists. But the British were very much aware that this policy cost Dan Mitrione his life, and they didn't want Jackson to meet the same fate. My superior officer knew that I had friends amongst the Tupas, and he recommended me as the intermediary negotiator between MacGregor, the Tupas, and the government. When Emilia was arrested, I went to MacGregor and told him he'd made a mistake. My contacts with the Tupamaros assured me that Lilita knew nothing about the whereabouts of Ambassador Jackson and not even holding her daughter could make her tell what she didn't know. I threatened him with a stop to all negotiations until Emilia was released. Things were at a delicate point, and MacGregor couldn't afford to risk making the Tupamaros angry. So he ordered the police to let Emilia go.

"In exchange for Jackson, the Tupas were demanding the release of Ramiro and the more than one hundred other Tupas being held in the jail in Punta Carretas, but the U.S., Britain, and Uruguay wanted to appear firm and inflexible. I sensed that perhaps the key element here was face-saving. I was right. All three governments were quite willing to find a scapegoat. It turned out to be the police, who were made to look like fools when 104 Tupas used an old tunnel into the city sewers and escaped from jail. Great Britain was delighted to have Jackson released; the U. S. had not been mentioned at all; and our government had not given an inch, publicly. I received a case of Scotch from the British, a case of bourbon from the Americans, and a promotion from our generals."

"You look very pleased with yourself. What else did you get?"

"Nothing!" he laughed. "Except the pleasure of a good laugh."

Our steaks arrived and again I had to wait, this time until Marco had tasted his.

"Well?" I said.

"It's fabulous!"

"What was the joke that gave you such a good laugh?"

"The joke was that I'd smuggled in the tools for digging that tunnel long before it was finished and used for this escape. I'd been getting prisoners out through parts of it for years! And now I could arrange the biggest jailbreak in Uruguayan history with the blessing of all concerned!"

I had to laugh at his delight. I raised my wineglass in a toast to him. "So when Jackson was released after the escape, everyone had already agreed to make it seem unconnected, coincidental?"

"Absolutely. Even the men who escaped didn't know it had all been prearranged. But MacGregor wasn't happy about the fact that no one was being prosecuted for Jackson's kidnapping. He told me he agreed to my terms only because he was under orders to do anything to get the ambassador safely out of the hands of the Tupas. I always felt he suspected me, though, that he saw under my uniform to the subversive underneath!"

"What's going to become of us, Marco?"

"That's an awfully serious question, Little Lion."

"It's beginning to seem more and more like some deadly game."

"The next few months are critical. I have tried to persuade both sides to give up their tactics. I believe that there are enough good men in the military to prevent a coup. I don't think we are inevitably headed toward a dictatorship. But the Tupas want it all now. They've gone too far to turn back. They'll succeed in bringing down the government, but it won't be replaced by anything better, and the country will be devastated."

Twenty

The day after my dinner with Marco, I received my first message from the Tupamaros since Cora had gone into hiding. My help was needed, and I was asked to go to the Rambla by the Casino and wait.

I could ignore the message, I thought, forget all that had happened, and get on with my life. If ever I was to leave the movement, this was the time.

"And will you?" Emilia asked when I discussed my doubts with her.

One choice; one day at a time. "I don't think I can, Emilia. Every time I want to, I remember Gabriela. Perhaps I can do this one last thing and then stop."

"I'll come with you."

I shook my head.

"You can't stop me, Magda. I'm in this now."

"Emilia—"

"Stop it. You've left me out long enough."

We took a bus and got off on the Rambla a few blocks before the Casino. As we walked along the promenade, the wind whipped our hair. We tried to keep warm by putting our coat collars up and sticking our hands in our pockets as we waited for a break in the speeding traffic. When it came, we ran across the wide avenue toward the Casino.

"Remember when the Tupas robbed the Casino?" Emilia

asked, looking up as we arrived at the balconies surrounding the stately old building.

"That money financed a lot of the work," I answered, noticing that the same, old, blue Renault had driven by us three times.

On the fourth round, the driver pulled up. "Who's this?" he asked, gesturing to Emilia.

"Emilia Lanconi. She was arrested for the kidnapping of Ambassador Jackson."

"They didn't tell me she'd be coming."

"She's an old friend of those we're going to see."

The driver argued with me until Emilia pulled up her sweater. The burns from the cigarettes put out on her during her nights of captivity had left evidence on her body familiar to any Tupamaro who had ever been caught.

"Get in," the driver said and sped onto the Rambla with his tires screeching.

Half an hour later we pulled up outside what looked like a vacant apartment building.

"Go to the basement. You'll see a door with a streak of green paint. Go in. In the back there's a chest. Move it aside. There's a loose panel. Remove it and follow your noses."

Emilia and I entered the abandoned building through tall double doors. Wallpaper hung in tatters from what had once been an elegant entrance hall. Birds nested over windows with no glass, and the stairs leading to the basement were littered with old newspapers, bottles, and rags.

We found the door with the green streak, opened it with difficulty, and walked across the creaking wooden floor to the back. The opening behind the dilapidated chest was narrow. The only way into it was on hands and knees.

Emilia hesitated. Ever since her three days in prison, she did not trust her reactions to the unknown. She hesitated before boarding elevators, was unable to open doors or turn corners.

"Do you want to wait for me here?" I asked.

Emilia shook her head, and I saw again the immovable determination that had become part of her character.

"Then I'll go first."

As soon as I stuck my head into the opening, I knew what the driver had meant when he told us to follow our noses. The tunnel smelled of urine, vomit, and unwashed bodies. I withdrew and took a handkerchief from my handbag. "You'll need one of these," I told Emilia.

Our journey was not a long one. The dark tunnel swerved sharply to the left, and not far ahead, we saw a square of light with a dark head in its center. It was Cora. She was very thin and her dark hair looked gray and unwashed. Her jeans were patched and her sweater worn at the elbows. She helped us out and embraced us.

"*Bienvenidas, compañeras.*"

The place we had come to held Ramiro and seven more of the escaped Tupamaros. It was in the cellar of the building adjacent to the one we had entered, and the door was sealed. The only way in and out was through the narrow tunnel we had traversed.

"We do the best we can," Cora said, "but we can't haul out the buckets and the refuse fast enough to keep the air clean."

Ramiro and his friends were happy for the diversion provided by two visitors. They asked if we had cigarettes or chocolate, and I found an old box of chiclets in my bag. I offered it to one of the men, and he held out his hand.

"Remember me?" he asked.

I looked at him closely in the dim light cast by the kerosene lamp. Several days growth of beard covered most of his face. "I'm sorry . . ."

"I once had the pleasure of lacing a pair of old sneakers on your feet."

I took his hand in both of mine. "Julio?"

He grinned.

"I have always hoped to see you again! To thank you again! Tell me, did Fernando become a doctor?"

Julio's smile faded. "Almost. He died last year. Just after being released from prison."

I thought I might cry, and Julio put his arms around me. "Come," he said, "we'll tell you all about our escape."

They had discovered a forty-five meter tunnel from one of the ground-floor cells into the city sewer system, and cleared and extended it, hiding the earth under their beds, he told us. The tunnel led to a house across the street from the prison.

"An empty house?" Emilia asked.

"No," Julio answered, "a house belonging to one of the bravest men in Uruguay. A *milico* who's on our side. I don't know how he managed it, but he made that house safe for us and arranged for our transfer from it. He gets visas for people. He finds hiding places, like this one. If ever they catch him. . . ."

The other men shook their heads. "Anything that's been done to us will be like nothing to what they have in store for him."

I started to shiver in the chill damp of that basement. I was perhaps the only person there who knew that for this particular escape, at least, Marco was in no danger. But I knew suddenly just how dangerous his attempt at helping both sides was. The words *if ever they catch him* went round and round inside my head, and I remembered what Gabriela had said about his odd lifeline, about seeing no children in his future.

"Cora," I said, reaching for her hand.

"What is it? Are you feeling ill? It's not unusual down here, the air's so bad—"

"No, no. Cora, was it Marco who found Gabriela?"

She and Ramiro took me aside, beyond the glow cast by the kerosene lamp.

"Please tell me. I know what he's been doing."

"Who told you?" Ramiro asked.

"He did."

"Yes, Magda," Cora said. "It was Marco."

"Cora, I am so afraid for him."

Cora sighed. "I've told him he's done enough. He should get out while he can. But he believes, Magda, that there are peaceful solutions. There aren't. Perhaps you can persuade him."

❧

Until Ramiro, Cora, Julio, and their companions were safe, I decided, I would help them by bringing supplies to the hideout. Emilia and I sewed large pockets into the linings of our coats, and there we stored the bread, cold cuts, cheese, chocolate, coffee, fruit, and *dulce de leche* the men devoured. We took it in turns to go to the abandoned building and often did so under cover of darkness. One by one, with Marco's help, Cora and the men were transferred to other places, their determination undaunted, their spirits lifted by Chile's success in reclaiming its iron, its banks, and its copper from foreign ownership. Chile's next plan was to nationalize the telephone system, paying ITT what its owners declared it to be worth on their Chilean tax returns.

I went to the shelter for the last time, making it ready for the next person who needed it by folding blankets and replenishing supplies of matches and bottled water. I was brushing some dirt from my coat as I walked to my bus stop when two men approached me. They flashed ID badges and asked for my identity card.

I remember clearly only the strange cold heaviness of the handcuffs on my wrists, the roughness of their hands pushing me into the car, and the terror of being blindfolded.

We traveled for at least an hour before I was pulled out of the car. I fell onto a rough surface, was pulled up, and lost track of time and of how many sets of steps I dragged myself up or stumbled down. I suspect some were the same ones over and over, because their surfaces eventually came to seem familiar.

Suddenly, my blindfold was pulled off. The dark was so profound that I had trouble focusing. A door was opened, and I was pushed into a cold, very small room. As my eyes grew accustomed to the dark, I could see cracks in the ceiling with a little light seeping through. I saw a basin, a bucket, a drain in the floor, and a bed with a pillow, but no blanket. I began to shiver, and in an effort to keep warm, I paced the little room and waited.

I discovered a lightbulb hanging in a corner. In the weeks to come, it would be turned on and off from its outside switch with no discernible pattern.

My turn had come, and I had no idea how I would behave. Everything Emilia had told me and everything I had heard from Ramiro and his friends, even Mitrione's own words, came back to me. I saw myself stripped naked, defecated on, burned, beaten, and strapped to the *máquina*. Of all things, I wanted most to prove that nothing would tear Marco's name from me. My greatest fear was that they would find a way to break me.

Hours passed like days, and days like weeks. No one came for me.

Every time I heard someone approaching, I expected to be taken away, to face the *máquina* and find out for myself the truth of what I had heard Ramiro and Julio say, that after a time what they came to hate was not the man manipulating the machine, but the bigger, societal machine that manipulated the man. I wondered if the electric shocks would make me, too, travel to that place where for the briefest of moments one could choose death. Or would my "technician" be one trained by Mitrione, thoroughly knowledgeable in how to keep hope sufficiently alive in me so I would choose to cling to life and face the *máquina* once more?

Every time my food arrived I took time to consider whether or not to eat it. How long did it take to starve oneself to death? Would starvation help or hinder my determination not to talk? I had heard that starving people sometimes hallucinated. Would I be able to hold out if I could not tell reality from unreality?

Sometimes they forgot to feed me. When that happened, I took hours washing and grew intimate with my toes, the skin on my knees, and every inch of belly and its unfamiliar sounds. When a meal came, it would last me a whole day, as I savored each bite and discovered the various textures of beef and bread.

The food was passed to me through a little door near the floor. I saw no one, spoke to no one, and slowly, in the profound isolation of that little room, I started to lose those feelings of detachment that had overcome me since Gabriela's death. There was nothing for me to do but think and dream, and so I did. I retold all of Josefa's stories to myself and imagined myself talking to her in the kitchen of our house. I sent mental messages to everyone I knew, with no thought that they might be received, simply as a means of keeping myself connected to everyone I knew on the outside. I held long conversations with *Mamasita* and promised her that if ever I got out of that room alive I would return to Caupolicán. Whenever I was cold, which was often, I imagined myself in Gabriela's hut by the fire, drinking *mate*, and one day, to my amazement, when I heard a sound outside the little food door and opened it, there was a *mate* gourd there, and a voice whispered, "From a friend."

Every few days I was told to empty the bucket by the drain, then a hose would be inserted for me to wash the floor and send my waste down the drain.

I kept rough track of time by setting aside a small balled up piece of bread each time I was fed.

About three months went by this way before the cell door opened.

The bright light from the corridor made me wince. My eyes were accustomed only to semidarkness, and the sharp electric light almost blinded me. It had finally come. My time. The moment for which I had been preparing since they first locked the door. The *máquina* was waiting.

The soldier standing in the doorway began unbuttoning his trousers.

I felt totally disoriented. For this I had not prepared myself. I stood up slowly, ready to fight, and the man suddenly laughed.

"Scared you, didn't I? But I'll have to wait, I'm sorry to say. I've been ordered to take you to a wedding."

I was so unaccustomed to conversation that I was certain I had not heard him accurately. It had been so long since I had spoken to anyone that my voice, when I tried to use it, came out as a croak.

"Calm down," the soldier said, thinking I was objecting to

the cloth he was tying around my eyes, "it's just a blindfold."

He led me out of the cell, and as we stepped outside, I gasped, lifting my face to the warmth of sunlight and air. I had forgotten how caressing a breeze can be, how scented, how full of sound. I wanted to linger and savor the outdoors, but the soldier pulled me along and soon the scent of flowers and the sound of birds was gone and we were inside once more. He removed my blindfold, and I found myself in a large room. It took me several minutes to adjust to the bright lights and to see that the room was full of people. Most of them were either in military or police uniforms, some in clothes as unkempt as my own.

In the center of the room stood Cora, Ramiro, and Julio. They smiled at me, and I cried out in surprise. Ramiro had no front teeth and his head had been shaved, revealing several stitches. The beauty that had made me feel like fainting when I first saw him was there only in the blue eyes looking lovingly at Cora standing by his side.

I was pushed toward them, and Cora quickly grasped my hand. "We're getting married!" she said.

"What? Here?" I asked.

"We can't wait for what may never come," Cora said sadly.

"And the child will have problems if he is not legitimate," Ramiro added, lisping slightly through the gaps in his mouth. "The military have a profound respect for convention. They think it very proper of us to want to legitimize our baby."

"It isn't quite what I had in mind when I told you that one day we would be married and our friends would be there." Cora smiled, wiping away my tears. "You mustn't cry. This is a fitting way for it to end after all. And you, my oldest friend and staunchest *compañera*, are here."

I felt Ramiro's arm around my waist. He held me to him

with surprising strength, considering his condition. "Remember, *compañera*. Remember this. Life is not worth living without a cause worth dying for."

A man approached us. "Is everything ready?" he asked.

Cora nodded. "These will be our witnesses," she said, gesturing to Julio and me.

The ceremony was quickly executed. As Julio and I signed the marriage certificate, I tried to ask him where we were, but Julio's hands were trembling so much he had to be assisted in holding the pen, and he could not answer. Immediately after he signed, he was led away, and the soldiers moved toward Cora and Ramiro.

Cora threw herself at her husband. *"Adiós, esposo, compañero, mi mejor amigo."*

"Good-bye, good-bye, my love, my dearest wife," Ramiro answered, clinging to her.

They held on to one another until soldiers were ordered to separate them. It took six men to pull them apart, and the last I saw of them, they were being dragged in opposite directions, their hands still reaching for one another like ragged branches against the gray walls.

I was blindfolded again and returned to my cell.

That night I heard the noises for the first time as I lay in that blurred state between waking and sleeping with which I had become so familiar. The sounds that had awakened me filled the room. Low moans, an occasional cry so piercing, so pure in its pain that my body would contract into as small a space as it could occupy, seeking to remove itself from all physical reality.

That night they made sure I knew whose cries I heard. Ramiro and Julio's names were spoken frequently in tones that cajoled, threatened, and punished by turns.

Occasionally, Ramiro and Julio pleaded with their tormentors for the love of God, for the memory of their mothers, but most of all, for mercy. I joined in, my voice a burning whisper against the sleeve I bit to keep myself quiet.

I was never to hear those voices again, but others took their place, and I learned their names as their cries and the voices of their torturers reverberated in the room above. I never uttered a sound in response, but the intensity with which I experienced their pain was such that I felt a part of myself leaving my body and penetrating the boards over my head.

Those boards, I soon discovered, leaked. Huddled on my bunk in the pitch dark, I had at first thought that I was under an outdoor roof and that what was dripping onto me was rain. I lifted my face to its touch, but when the light in the corner came on again and I could look at myself and at the floor, I realized that no such gift had fallen.

Sometimes, what fell from the ceiling was blood, dark and rich, staining the boards in surrealist brown shapes. Sometimes it was urine or liquid feces or vomit, lying in small pools, seeping into the floorboards.

At first, when the guard fed me the hose through the opening in the door, I was relieved to use it to wash away the nauseating smells. After a time, however, I came to revere the liquids that fell around me, regarding them somehow as holy—sacred remnants of an idealism I could feel dying within me with every drop that fell from that checkered ceiling. If I had had a single patch of earth at my disposal, I would have gathered the lifeblood of my country and buried it. Since no such healing was available to me, I saved whatever bits of toilet paper were given to me and used them to mop the pieces of humanity around me. Then I held them, conjuring faces for those disembodied voices, murmuring their names over and over, shredding the paper finely, slowly, one tiny scrap at a time, and washing it down the sink. I imagined those scraps being borne down to the river; water to water returned.

I wove an imaginary web around the ceiling and on it hung each name I heard uttered above me, along with its imagined face. On such occasions I lost track of time and felt myself floating, free as light, the cries no longer reaching me. Soon, the web covered all four walls, each and every portrait in place in my head.

It was only later that I discovered that several months had gone by before a guard came in, bucket and scrubbing brush in hand, acting as if his presence were a daily occurrence. He sang as he sent the blood of Uruguay into the sewers of Montevideo, and he ignored my pleas to stop. He had brought me back to reality, destroying the safety web of names and imagined faces I had woven to keep myself from falling into complete madness. The guard's presence, his voice, and his movements scattered and destroyed my web as completely as if it had been real.

I had believed that I could hold out, if only the web held. Now the web was gone and with it went my belief that I would not talk. Of all the horrors I fought in that room, the greatest was self-doubt. I had been certain that one day they would come for me. No one I had ever heard of had been left untouched. I wondered if the names, the places, the dates would pour from me in a shower of self-hatred. Or could I, like the voices I had heard in the room above, substitute chanting for the information the torturers wanted? I did not know, so I started repeating the same words every time a guard came to the door.

"Tell Captain Pereira I'm here."

Their silence remained unbroken.

Twenty-One

The sound of voices woke me from a shivering sleep. Loud footsteps, more voices, my door being opened, and Marco standing in the doorway to my cell. I could not believe he was really there. I sat on my cot, oblivious to everything except his voice as he sat down beside me.

"It's all right; it's all right," he said, putting his arm around me. "I'm here, Little Lion." He pointed to the bucket. "Remove that, Corporal, and return in five seconds!"

"¡Sí, Coronel!"

"Marco, you came," I said, looking at him incredulously.

"Of course I came."

The corporal returned and stood at attention, trembling slightly, by the door. It was he who had come to get me for Cora and Ramiro's marriage.

"Did he, or any of them, lay a hand on you?" Marco asked quietly.

I looked over at the corporal and saw fear personified. I could finish him with just one word, one little word, one murmured "Yes," and he was done for, and I on a par with those who had seen to it that blood rained from the ceiling.

I stared at the corporal and shook my head.

Marco's eyes softened. "It will be remembered, Corporal."

"Sir! May I be excused, sir?"

Marco laughed. "Go!" he said.

I had forgotten what a rich thing his laughter was. For the second time in my life, Marco removed his jacket on my behalf and lay it gently on my shoulders. I felt myself blushing painfully as I saw myself in his eyes. Hair unwashed, dried blood staining what remained of my clothes, and the pungent smell of my body suddenly filling my nostrils. In recent weeks, I realized, I had not washed much. I thought I might complete the nauseating picture by vomiting, so I made a joke instead. "You're a colonel now. This weighs at least ten kilos more than it did last time," I said, wrapping the jacket tightly around me.

"It's the damn gold braid. Sometimes I feel it pressing me into hell."

The door was open and light was pouring into the room, making it look so different from the room in which I had spent the last few months that I glanced at the ceiling. Had I been delirious? Under the light, the marks on the ceiling could have been damp stains, not blood at all. The floor had been scrubbed clean that day. The sodden paper had been entrusted to the river. Only my clothes bore evidence of what I had seen, but who would believe that the stains covering them were not of my own fouling? For the first time since Cora and Ramiro's marriage, I cried until my tears soaked Marco's immaculate shirtfront.

As we rode silently through the night, I kept glancing at Marco, his dark face lit by the occasional passing car. He looked tired and very sad, and I wanted more than anything to put my arms around him. That would disgust him, I was sure. With a chilling certainty I knew that we would never again dance the *candombe* in the streets, nor climb the Cerro to visit Gabriela, nor sit together under the *estrella federal*. Every sweet memory I had included him, and yet my future would be made of memories without him.

I loved him so intensely I thought he would surely feel it and turn toward me, but instead he took out his handkerchief and covered his mouth with it. I was sure that he was trying not to breathe my smell, pungent in the close confinement of the car, and I tried shrinking into myself as I had done in the cell. I did not know that he was just trying to wipe away the sweat that had broken out all over him as he contemplated his future.

He pulled up in front of my house and got out to open the door for me. If I had been clean, I would have thrown my arms around him and threatened never to let him go, to die if he left me. Instead I fixed my eyes on his face as he took my arm and led me to the house. I wanted to absorb him somehow, to ensure that no matter where I was he would be with me.

The door opened and Josefa stood there, still buttoning her dressing gown. She took one look at me and stifled a cry.

"Who is it at this hour, Josefa?" my mother's voice called irritably from the stairs.

"Magdalena!" Josefa cried. "I knew you were alive! I felt you sometimes, like a breeze in the kitchen when I was cooking!"

Soon I was surrounded by my mother, father, Sofía and Carmen, crying uncontrollably at the sight of me. My father was hugging Marco and pounding him on the back.

"Get her to a safe place tonight," Marco was saying. "They'll come looking soon."

Then he was gone.

Josefa ran a hot bath for me while my father got on the telephone.

The comfort of being warm again, cushioned by water, clean, and temporarily unafraid, was a feeling so intense and overpowering that only the insistent knocking on the bathroom door brought me back to the starkness of my situation.

"Magdalena! Magda!" Josefa said. "Your father says you are

to hurry! He is ready. I've laid out your clothes, the softest and most comfortable ones. Your bag is packed."

"I am coming, Josefa. Thank you."

The car was waiting outside. I embraced my cousins and Josefa and left my mother sobbing at the door.

"Where are you taking me?" I asked my father as he sped along the Rambla.

"To Caupolicán."

"Does *Mamasita* know?"

"It was her idea."

"Will I be safe there?"

My father sighed. "I hope so, Magda. I don't know where else to hide you."

"They will know about Caupolicán."

"They will also know about *Mamasita* and the Brigadier. She has already called and given him her word that you will not leave the *estancia*."

We drove through what was left of the night. The dirt road over the hills was full of holes, and the only light came from the moon. Even my father dared not speed on that road. Not a single vehicle was out on the moors that night, and a small sleepy town in the interior was barely stirring when we stopped for fuel. My father bought us coffee and croissants at a small café, where we sat in silence while we ate.

The owner of the café could not take his eyes off the pale gray-and-black Jaguar parked outside his door. Even in its mud-spattered condition, it spoke of a life beyond the man's imagining. He hovered by our table at my father's elbow until he was sent for more croissants.

"I am sorry to be the cause of this trouble," I said at last.

My father ate slowly, his manners impeccable as usual. "I must admit I was surprised," he said. "Had it been your cousins. . . . But you . . . I was surprised," he repeated. "We are deeply in Colonel Pereira's debt."

I nodded. I could not trust myself to speak of Marco.

As we approached Caupolicán, the early morning mist was lifting. A band of rheas ran across the road, and the horses in the fields shook themselves, sending dew drops sparkling in the first rays of the sun. *Mamasita* was waiting by the gate, her poncho draped across her mare's flank, her hat low over her eyes. She cantered ahead of us to the house and threw the reins to a waiting gaucho who touched his hat to my father as he led the mare away.

Mamasita touched me as if I were very fragile, kissing me lightly on the cheek.

My father said that he would not stay, and *Mamasita* gave him a quick embrace before he left. "I will take care of her," she said.

❧

That first night, as I paced away the hours in the walk beside the old house, Marco appeared as silently as a ghost. The moonlight filtered through the arching vines heavy with grapes, casting leafy shadows on the whiteness of his shirt.

It was the first time we had ever been alone together. We stared at one another for a long time. Thoughts flew in the air between us with the silent clarity of an old longing. Marco touched my hair and I kissed his hands, my breath returning in a ripple of warmth off his palms. He held me and I put my mouth to the soft place under his collar. I felt him sigh, and in a moment, we were kissing and the pleasure of it was so intense I could not have told how it was that his shirt came off and mine with it or how it happened that he was inside me and I possessed him utterly, lying afterwards with his head on my shoulder, stroking his hair.

I thought I had gone through the worst that hell could hold until Marco told me that he was returning to Montevideo. He was certain that this time the trail he had left in freeing me would lead them without a doubt to his door. I pleaded with him to escape with me, knowing even as I said the words that there was nowhere for us to go. Across our borders were Brazil and Argentina, with regimes more brutal even than the one being spawned in Uruguay. And Marco would not go out of easy reach of Uruguay. He had been too involved, had played too great a part in what was happening to walk away from it. He persisted in believing that he and the few military men like him would prevail over the others.

In the morning he was gone, and from then on I spent the days riding, avoiding the house and enclosed spaces. I slept outdoors, when I did sleep, and changed clothes several times a day. I cut my hair very short and bathed frequently. I could not bear the sight or the smell of meat. Loud noises startled me and bright lights hurt my eyes.

Then one day I stepped into *Mamasita's* room and told her I was ready to talk. I told her everything. About Lilita, Mitrione, and Gabriela's palm reading; about Peter Wentworth and the USIS office and Ramiro and Cora; about the hiding place under the ground; about the cell, and the rain from the ceiling; about my rituals; and finally, about Marco. *Mamasita* held me for three days and three nights while I sobbed and raged and sometimes threatened suicide.

"So Marco was the one Julio called one of the bravest men in Uruguay," *Mamasita* said when I told her about his work.

I nodded. "The prison escapes, the safe houses, the people smuggled out to Europe, all Marco's work. And by now, I am sure they have arrested him, and it's because of me."

"Perhaps, Magda. But they would have arrested him eventually anyway. He could not go on forever without getting caught. I shall see what I can do. But I am already more deeply in Brigadier General Paz's debt than I like to be."

"Because of me, *Mamasita?*"

Mamasita nodded.

"You are required to act as my guardian?"

"Yes. But this is nothing. It is what he did for me while you were in prison that I owe for."

"I should have known. Is it thanks to him that I wasn't touched?"

"I don't know how he accomplished it. Such restraint is unheard of."

"Will he exact payment?"

"Not in the way you're thinking of, no! He is too much of a gentleman for that. But he's always wanted to take back the piece of Caupolicán that once belonged to his family and that your great-grandfather won in a game of cards. That isn't much to ask considering what he did."

"He won't try to take it all?"

"Certainly not! I told you, he's a gentleman!"

"Can he find out if Marco's been arrested yet?"

"When I call to give him the deed to the property, I will ask."

Mamasita's inquiry revealed that Marco had indeed been arrested, but no one would say where he was being held. The ranks had closed. Brigadier General Paz was an air force officer, Marco was in the army, and the army had its own methods for dealing with those who betrayed them. The Brigadier could find out only that Marco was in solitary confinement.

"As you were, Magda," *Mamasita* said.

"Oh, no, *Mamasita*, not as I was. You can be sure that they are not leaving him alone. Ramiro told me once that they save

the worst for one of their own. I have to get him out before
they kill him."

"No one here will listen to a plea for Marco, Magda."

"Then what can I do?"

"You must go abroad. To Europe."

"To Europe?"

"There are many Latin Americans in exile there now. Many,
like you, who can expose what is happening. It is your only
hope. Nothing can be done here. It won't be long before the
military rule as openly in Uruguay as they now do in Chile,
Argentina, Brazil, Paraguay. The list goes on and on. Our only
hope is to tell the world what is going on and enlist help for
Marco from some human rights' group that can shame them
into releasing him."

"I can't leave Uruguay knowing that Marco is in prison!"

"What hope have you of saving him here? You might be arrested again. Then you'd be of no use to him at all."

"But to abandon him after what he did for me—"

"You will not be abandoning him. You will be working for
his release in the only way possible. And this will help pay your
way," *Mamasita* said, putting the old *Charrúa* puzzle into my
hands. "This is the only piece of its kind known to exist. An
old friend, an art dealer named Salazar, once offered me half a
million dollars for it. I can imagine no more fitting way for it
to find its way into the world than to assist Colonel Pereira."

"And what of you, *Mamasita?* You gave your word that you
would keep me here."

"I am an old woman. I can't watch you every second. You
will no doubt find a way to trick me and escape."

All that night, I paced under the grapevines, the agate
puzzle in my hand.

Everyone I knew who could be of any possible help to

Marco was in hiding, in exile, or in prison. I was the only one free and with the power to use my freedom. As the sun rose, I knew that *Mamasita*'s plan offered me my only hope of ever seeing Marco alive again.

I did not return to Montevideo. One of *Mamasita*'s friends picked me up in his private plane and flew me to Rio de Janeiro. It was months before I heard that Ramiro had been released and died shortly afterward. Cora had disappeared.

Epilogue

A sudden gust of wind shook the old poinsettia tree, and Emilia dropped the lace curtain, closing the two of us off from the outside world.

For seven years, Emilia and I had hoped for the day when we might sit down together and navigate our memories toward a point of healing, even of forgetting. Now there was one more story to tell. I turned to Emilia.

"I have news of Peter."

Emilia sat on the bed and nodded. "Tell me."

"I saw him, only a year or so ago, crossing a London street," I said. "He looked the same. I followed him and realized he was heading back the way I had just come, from the home of a friend of my grandmother's, an art dealer. Peter was admitted to his house, and after he'd gone in, I followed him and asked the butler to show me into one of the private sitting rooms. I waited there until Peter left and then I found out why he was there. He was being considered for the post of director of the South American branch of Mr. Salazar's business. I asked for nothing, but I told Mr. Salazar how I'd met Peter. He thanked me."

"And—?" Emilia asked.

"He allowed me to overhear his telephone call to Peter the next day."

"What did he say?"

"He asked Peter for his version of what had happened here. At first, Peter pretended not to know what Mr. Salazar was referring to. He kept trying to focus the conversation on the ambassador's ordeal—Sir Geoffrey Jackson's book was out by then and Peter wanted to know if Mr. Salazar had read it. Mr. Salazar told him that he wasn't condoning the ambassador's kidnapping, only questioning Peter's role in investigating it." I paused. "The conversation was painful. It evoked the past in ways that brought only anguish, and I could hear it in Peter's voice as he tried to explain that he had been young, ambitious, misguided. And in love."

"He said that? He said he'd been in love with me?"

I nodded. "He had to choose."

"And he chose his career," Emilia said. "It's what I've always suspected."

"He and Mr. Salazar talked for a while about the methods used by secret-service agencies, about how such agencies couldn't exist without everyone involved agreeing to suspend their ethical standards and obey orders."

"Did he get the job?"

"No."

I took Emilia's hand. "We have made the journey to the end."

"Yes," Emilia nodded. "Will you see him now? He's waited a long time."

There it was at last. The question we had avoided until this moment. Inexorable as time itself, the moment had come.

"How can I face him, Emilia?"

"Oh, Magda, he doesn't love you any the less."

"He was tortured because of me, Emilia!"

Emilia put her arms around me. "Magda, you know as well

as I do that he would have been caught and tortured anyway. *He knows it.*"

"He could have left Uruguay. Others did."

"Marco? This is his only life. Just as you are his only love. It's time, Magda."

"How do I look?"

Emilia turned me to face the mirror on the wardrobe door.

I looked at myself and started to laugh. My mascara had run, I had not brushed my hair since leaving the plane, and my clothes were rumpled. But for the first time in many years, the face staring back at me had a familiar, younger glow. Under the pale skin and the lines around my mouth, there was a hint of expectant hope.

I licked my fingers and rubbed away the mascara while Emilia went to the telephone. When she returned, she released my hair from its confining pins and brushed it until the curls lay softly round my face.

So absorbed was I in preparing myself to see him that the soft tap on the window made me jump. Emilia reached across the bed and moved aside the curtain.

Marco stood there, handsomer than ever in his civilian clothes, a touch of gray lighting his temples, a smile of wonder on his face. His hand reached through the iron grating and rested on the glass. I had conjured his image in my imagination so often over the past seven years that only the sudden weakness in my knees assured me that this time, he really was there.

Emilia hurried to let him in, and I reached out to touch the windowpane on my side. We stood and looked at one another until Emilia appeared by him.

I was determined not to cry, but as I saw him take her arm and walk slowly into the building, my determination failed me.

He looked immeasurably frail, and the horror of what he had
suffered hit me with the same intensity that used to prevent my
sleeping at night whenever I imagined what he was going
through. I wanted to greet him at the door, but I was incapable
of movement. I stood rooted in Emilia's bedroom, listening to
the sound of his cane on the wooden floor as he made his way
toward me.

There was nothing between us now. He stood in the doorway with a smile on his face and his arms open.

The force of my embrace made him gasp.

"I'm sorry. I'm so sorry!"

He dried my tears with kisses. "Little Lion," he murmured.
"Little Lion . . ."

"You're so thin!" I wailed.

"So are you," he laughed and offered me his handkerchief.

I wiped my eyes and blew my nose as Emilia came out of
the kitchen carrying a tray.

"*¡Masitas!*" I said, trying to smile.

"Let us start getting fat immediately!" Marco suggested,
taking my hand and leading me to the table. "Look, Magda,
your favorites — *milhojas.*"

The pastries lay golden, rich, and overflowing with *dulce
de leche.*

Marco pulled out a chair, disengaged his fingers gently from
mine, and made me sit. "They don't have *dulce de leche* in Europe,
do they?" he asked.

"The closest thing is condensed milk. Oh, how I've missed
these!" I said. "Can we start?"

We ate even the crumbs, licking our fingers and picking up
the flakes of pastry left like sugary leaves on the plate. Then
Emilia cleared the table, leaving Marco and me to wipe each
others' fingers and mouths, exploring new scars and lines, and

old familiar places time had left unchanged. Marco reached under my collar and touched the little ivory elephant.

"I have worn it always," I told him.

He nodded. "I had something of yours too. Do you remember that letter you wrote me from Michigan?"

"Yes."

Marco stood up slowly and walked to the window. "I carried it with me from the day I received it. I was never parted from it. Not even all those years later when they finally arrested me. I never understood why they let me keep that one personal item for such a long time," he said. "I suppose it was so that it would hurt the more when they took it from me. It was the only thing I was allowed to read for five years."

I thought I had imagined all the possibilities, suffered every torture in my mind with him, but as Marco stood by the window and spoke, I realized that what I had imagined had been physical torture. I had not allowed myself to think what else he had gone through, what subtle and infinitely painful torments his captors had thought to inflict upon him.

Seven years had not been enough to prepare me for this moment, and I wanted to be released from any obligation to listen to Marco's story. I wanted to believe that if we could leave that room we could leave behind what had happened, pretend that it had never been. I would nurse him back to health, hidden away at Caupolicán, and we would never think of these things again.

Marco's voice prevented my escape.

"One day a new man took over the solitary confinement cells. He took my letter from me. It was in pieces by then, but precious to me. At first I thought I could not go on without the letter to hold. I considered not eating or drinking and simply letting myself die in that hole. I was thinking about how that would feel when I realized that I had lost the letter, but not its contents. I had read it so many times over the years that each word was engraved in my memory, and I could call the words back as often as I wanted to." He closed his eyes and leaned his forehead on the windowpane. *"I can't imagine how you could ever disgrace your name. I am proud to know you. I think your feelings about the workers are wonderful. I have always thought so, ever since that day on the Cerro when I crowned you with daisies. You are my hero."*

Marco's shoulders began to shake, and I put my arms around him.

Emilia joined us, and the three of us stood together until Marco spoke again.

"The sun is going down," he said. "I haven't missed a sunset over the river since I was set free." He wiped his eyes and offered me his arm.

"Will you come, Emilia?" I asked.

"No. I will wait for you here." She stood at her door watching us stroll arm in arm down the street.

We stopped for a few moments to look at all that remained of the jasmine that had once grown up the wall to Cora's window. Cora's father had taken an ax to it in a fury of grief one day and had stood sobbing among the starlike flowers at his feet. Not even their sweet scent could banish the bitterness he felt toward the man who had used the jasmine as a means of climbing into his daughter's heart.

"Will we ever find Cora, do you think?" I asked.

"Hope is all that is left to us, Magda."

"I want to believe that one day we'll find her. That I'll see her making lace behind new jasmine or walking down the street or waving to us from this window."

Marco nodded, and his hand, warm and strong, closed over mine.

"I hear you've left the military," I said.

"The doors of hell don't yawn so wide at night."

"And you've been visiting the Cerro?"

"Yes. To see Gervasio. I promised him that when you returned, we would take him to Caupolicán to visit his mother's grave."

Our eyes met, and we both looked away, unsure of what to say next. We had reached the Rambla.

There was no air as sweet, I thought, as the air that blew off my river. I filled my lungs with it and felt it reach old wounds.

It would take time, but the river would heal me, as I had known it would throughout those lonely years of exile.

We walked down the wide steps to the sand, still warm from the sun. Gulls were feeding along the shore, and the river murmured quietly on the sand.

Marco stopped and turned to face me. "I want to know what Emilia has told you."

"About what?"

"About me."

"Nothing."

"What did you do in Europe for seven years?" he said, disconcerting me with his sudden change of subject. "Apart from what you did for me, I mean."

"I worked. I wrote articles."

"Did you fall in love?"

"I was in love when I left here. Seven years didn't change that. But, Marco, I would understand if for you that were different. I had the opportunity. I met many people. I was free to choose. You weren't. If you were to tell me that you need time or even that your feelings have changed, I would not for a moment blame you."

Marco looked at the river for a long time before answering.

"Little Lion," he said at last, "I don't know exactly what parts of me survived my imprisonment. But I do know that one thing and one thing only remained constant through it and that was the knowledge that for one night out of the thousands of nights of my life I was a part of you and you of me, and nothing ever felt so right. I was made to love you always. I only wish that always were not for me so short a time."

And then I knew why they had let him go. My efforts on his behalf had had nothing to do with their decision. They always released the dying.

"How long do we have?" I asked.

He shrugged. "A few months perhaps."

His arms as he soothed me felt so firm, his heart so strong beating in my ear that I believed I could heal him. Whatever was wrong, my love would make it right. I would take him to Caupolicán where Mamasita waited and not leave him for a moment. Somehow I would will my own life into him and spend my days making up for every breath we had not breathed together.

A large black dog emerged from the river, chasing the waves, ignoring the sticks his owner threw for him. He came bounding out in front of us and shook himself. Marco and I backed up to escape him. The man came hurrying toward us, his limp preventing him from moving very fast. He apologized profusely as he tried to catch the dog, who thought the chase another merry game and crouched on his front paws, his wet tail arcing happily back and forth in the air behind him.

"He keeps me young," the man smiled and turned suddenly to surprise the dog. His movement was too abrupt, and it sent him sprawling in the sand. The dog leapt forward and reached him before Marco or I could. The three of us helped him up.

He laughed and brushed the sand from his clothes. Then he slapped his leg.

"A legacy from Punta Arenas."

I froze, my hand still on the man's arm. He saw me turn white and steadied me with both hands. "You were in Punta Arenas?" I asked.

He nodded cautiously, afraid he had said something to offend me.

"So was I."

"When?"

I told him and his face brightened.

"Ah! The year of the light."

"What?"

"Oh, nothing. Some of us who were tortured there that year were subject to hallucinations. You know how that is. There was a room, a room with a wooden floor."

"Yes?"

"And sometimes, those of us who were tortured there could see a light floating through the floorboards." He smiled. "We were a little crazy, you understand. But it helped. Whenever we saw the light, it was as if. . . ." He hesitated.

"Please tell me."

He studied my face for a moment. "It was as if someone loved us," he said quietly.

The dog jumped up and licked his face. "Like this." The man laughed. "The kind of love that heals." He called to the dog, waved good-bye to us, and limped away.

The river was green that evening, translucent and pale, as beautiful almost as Marco's smile.

Gratitudes

For years after leaving Uruguay, I carried stacks of notes and stories with me on my travels. I began writing as a means of combating loneliness and homesickness, but until the day I decided to submit a story to the Loft—the nationally known literary center in Minneapolis—for consideration, I had had no serious thought of showing my writing to anyone.

When my submission was among those chosen for inclusion in the Loft's Mentor Series, I began an appreciation that has grown each year for the many contributions to the rich life of the Twin Cities made by this organization devoted to promoting writers and their work. It was at the Loft that I met Carolyn Holbrook, who has since gone on to establish her own writer's organization, S.A.S.E., The Write Place. Carolyn was the first person to call me a writer. She encouraged me to apply for other Loft programs and thanks to her I met my friend and mentor, author Sandra Benítez. It is because of Sandra Benítez that this book was finished and read by Emilie Buchwald at Milkweed Editions. I also owe the Loft a debt of gratitude for the opportunity of working with Kim Stafford, whose insights into this book helped shape its final form, and whose selection of writers for his workshop allowed me to continue working with the extraordinary talents of Joan Oliver Goldsmith, Greg Stark, and Marcella Taylor.

During the writing of *The Tree of Red Stars*, I was privileged to have the friendship and encouragement of my compatriots, Beatriz Cabrera, who made her library of Uruguayan books available to me, and of Estela Villagrán Manancero, who came to my first reading, her support a force that has never waned. At this first reading I made a new friend of journal keeper and teacher Eloise Klein, who has stood by me as I wrote, rewrote, and struggled with the issues in this book.

Deep appreciation also goes to María Alicia Arabbo, Anne Welsbacher, Amy Ward, Valorie Gifford, Catherine Born, Mary Rockcastle, and Graciela Cuadrado. A very special thanks to Joan Lisi, who has been at every public reading of this book and whose rejoicing is a constant gift.

Diego Arabbo and Sergio Manancero deserve particular mention for seeing me through the shock of computer initiation.

In Uruguay, my thanks to my brother, Dion, and to his wife, Marcela, for their assistance with my research; to Rosario Cibils at the Public Library of Montevideo, who allowed me access to documents and papers not on public display; and to my dear friends, Anita Ransom and Raúl Rodríguez.

I owe a debt of gratitude to A. J. Langguth, for his courageous book, *Hidden Terrors*; to Eleuterio Fernández Huidobro, for his *Historia de los Tupamaros*; to Ernesto González Bermejo, for *Las manos en el fuego*; and to Sir Geoffrey Jackson for his memoir, *People's Prison*.

My thanks also to my parents-in-law, Maxine and Kenneth Lebsock, whose enjoyment of my stories about my parrot and my aunts led me to write about Caramba and the *tías*.

Appreciation and love to my sisters, Gloria and Carole, consummate storytellers who will no doubt recognize where and how liberally I have borrowed from the tales they have shared.

It has been my good fortune to have Emilie Buchwald as my

editor and Milkweed Editions as my publisher. This book could not have been in better hands.

My thanks to Scott Edelstein, whose knowledge of publishing and book contracts was invaluable.

I learned in the United States to "keep the best to last." So at the end I thank my daughters, Ana and Kate, the unexpected and most joyous gifts in my life. And my husband, Randy, whose insights into life in Uruguay and with Uruguayans reminded me of what I took for granted. He made me laugh, sometimes at myself, and his joy over this book has been the greatest reward of writing it.

Tessa Bridal has published numerous articles in journals and magazines, including *Colors,* which published "Retazos" in 1993. Her work has been anthologized in *Do You Know Me Now?* and *Speaking in Tongues.* In her capacity as Director of Public Programs at the Science Museum of Minnesota, she has served as a guest editor of the *Journal of Museum Education* and *Science on Stage Anthology.* She is the chair of the Museum Theater Professional Interest Council and an innovator of the "museum theater" education technique. She has often been the on-site educational theater consultant for museums and zoos in the United States and Canada. Prior to her work at the Science Museum, Bridal spent three years as the Artistic Director of the Minnesota Theater Institute of the Deaf.

Bridal spent the first half of her life in Uruguay and Brazil. She has also lived in Washington, D.C., and in London, England. She has now settled in Albertville, Minnesota, and has dual citizenship in Uruguay and the U.S. She and her husband have two daughters and share their home with a dog, a cat, two rabbits, and seventeen birds.

Interior design by Wendy Holdman
Typeset in Centaur
by Stanton Publication Services, Inc.
Printed on acid-free 55# Sebago Antique Cream paper
by Maple-Vail Book Manufacturing

Winners of the Milkweed National Fiction Prize:

Tivolem
Victor Rangel-Ribeiro
(1998)

The Tree of Red Stars
Tessa Bridal
(1997)

The Empress of One
Faith Sullivan
(1996)

Confidence of the Heart
David Schweidel
(1995)

Montana 1948
Larry Watson
(1993)

Larabi's Ox
Tony Ardizzone
(1992)

Aquaboogie
Susan Straight
(1990)

Blue Taxis
Eileen Drew
(1989)

Ganado Red
Susan Lowell
(1988)

More fiction from Milkweed Editions:

Agassiz
Sandra Birdsell

What We Save for Last
Corinne Demas Bliss

Backbone
Carol Bly

The Clay That Breathes
Catherine Browder

Street Games
Rosellen Brown

A Keeper of Sheep
William Carpenter

Winter Roads, Summer Fields
Marjorie Dorner

Kingfishers Catch Fire
Rumer Godden

Live at Five
David Haynes

Somebody Else's Mama
David Haynes

The Children Bob Moses Led
William Heath

The Importance of High Places
Joanna Higgins

Circe's Mountain
Marie Luise Kaschnitz